SMOKING MIRROR BLUES

OR, THE RETURN OF TEZCATLIPOCA

ERNEST HOGAN

WITH
ILLUSTRATIONS BY
THE AUTHOR

Strange Particle Press
San Francisco 2018

ISBN: 9781987497243
Copyright 2018 by Ernest Hogan

Interior illustrations by Ernest Hogan, Copyright 1981, 1983, 1994, 2001, 2002, 2004.

For further information contact:
Digital Parchment Services
m.christian@digitalparchmentservices.com

Watch for the Wild Worlds of Ernest Hogan
From Strange Particle Press:

Cortez on Jupiter
High Aztech
Smoking Mirror Blues
Pancho Villa's Flying Circus

PARA MIS PADRES

CONTENTS

PART THREE: RECOMBOIZATION

ACKNOWLEDGEMENTS

These blues were sung because: Ben Bova opened the gate. Elinor Mavor made her computer have visions, as well as play games. Paul T. Riddell aided with the Dia de los Muertos research, and provided me with a wild ride to Texas. Misha Nógha gave shamanistic advice. Michael Chocholak made music. Ian Hagemann defined recombo. Don Webb, Vance Anderson, and Stephen P. Brown made me an Aztec priest. Richard Kadrey inspired the novelettization. Scott Edelman published the novelettization. Fred DeVita brought Beto to life in living color. The Lunation Libation Society (Rick Cook, Peter L. Manly, G. Harry Stine, and the supporting cast) provided camaraderie under the full moon. My family was always there and kept me connected to Los Angeles. My wife, the fabulous Emily Devenport, is a constant source of stimulation and inspiration. And Tezcatlipoca himself keeps whispering those dangerous ideas into my ear. Don't forget to feed the loas . . .

MY LONG, STRANGE TRIP WITH TEZCATLIPOCA

AN INTRODUCTION TO
SMOKING MIRROR BLUES

It is said that Tezcatlipoca, the Warrior/Trickster God of the Aztecs, whispers into the ears of mortals, giving them dangerous ideas. That may explain my life and career. Tezcalipoca keeps hijacking me, talking me on long, strange trips. Sometimes I wonder if I wrote *Smoking Mirror Blues* – or did he?

My first idea came back in the Eighties. I was writing like crazy, going nowhere, studying preColumbian cultures and mythology, thinking that I was onto something. Maybe I could come up with a real breakthrough. Maybe a guy getting possessed by Tezcatlipoca.

My first concept was for it to be a horror/urban fantasy type thing. Only urban fantasy wasn't really a thing back then. I noodled around with some fragments and sketched out some of the characters, but it didn't come to life . .

Then I sold *Cortez on Jupiter*, put the idea on a back burner.

13

I sold *High Aztech*, too. Even though I didn't consider myself a cyberpunk, the world seemed to see me as part of the movement, moment, or whatever it was. And there was an appeal in plugging my preColumbian/Chicano material into a high-tech/futuristic world. Computers had come and taken over my life. Maybe instead of voodoo-esque possession, Tezcatlipoca would come out of a computer, the Internet?

I was feeling good, confident. I wrote up some sample chapters and an outline, the way they said a good professional should in those days. I was having visions of selling what I was then calling *Tezcatlipoca Blues* being published in hardcover, becoming a bestseller . . .

Only that was when the weird stuff started happening. Even though people wanted and liked my books, Tor claimed they weren't selling. I've written about this before, and am rather sick of the subject. Anyway, *Tezcatlipoca Blues* was rejected. First by Tor, then by every other publisher that was publishing science fiction in New York.

My agent suggested that I write the whole book, and we try selling it that way.

Meanwhile, I was working as a grade school janitor, getting depressed, drinking beer, watching a lot of Mexican action movies on a local Spanish-language TV station. Not feeling very hopeful. Not being very productive.

Then I heard from Scott Eldelman. He was editing a new science fiction magazine, *Science Fiction Age*, and wanted something from me, maybe for the first issue. It was like a dream come true. Only one thing was wrong. I didn't have anything for him.

Then I thought: What about an excerpt from this work in progress?

I sent a section, but Scott didn't think it worked as a stand alone – thought it needed an ending. I racked my brain, and couldn't think of one.

Then my wife, Emily Devenport, author of *Medusa Uploaded*, suggested, "Why not just write the end of the book?"

I knew how it was going to end. Thought about the idea, and realized that she was right. It's amazing how many time she's come with an answer for me.

Scott liked it. A "novelettization" titled *Tezcatlipoca Blues* appeared in the July 1993 issue of *Science Fiction Age.* The world did not beat a path to my door. Everybody tripped over spelling and pronouncing Tezcatlipoca.

And I couldn't publish anywhere but markets that didn't pay much, or anything. I got more depressed. The novel went to places I hadn't intended. I didn't think it was ever going to get published. I was beginning to wonder if my career was over.

I stopped trying to think about what would sell, and just vented all the angst that was building up inside me. I felt, like Henry Miller with *Tropic of Cancer*, that I wasn't writing a book, but ". . . a prolonged insult, a gob of spit in the face of Art . . ." Kind of like taking dictation from Tezcatlipoca. But then writing a novel can have the same effects as demonic possession.

I shouldn't have been surprised that, when I did finish, the folks in New York still decided they didn't want it. They still treat me like the most talented leper they ever met. I started wondering if I was ever going to publish a book – or anything else – ever again.

My bitching and moaning must have been pretty loud, because David Memmott, of Wordcraft of Oregon got in touch with me, and soon a small press edition of what is now known as *Smoking Mirror Blues* was published.

This, of course, was after a Mormon artist refused to

do the cover because of the tantric yoga scene in the open chapter. Did he think that we would insist he paint a graphic depiction of the Dead Man's Asana? Talk about a twisted imagination.

It came out September of 2001. The world wasn't in the mood for a crazy Aztec Chicano cyberpunk novel. It actually seemed like it was about to go up in flames.

Somewhere in the chaos, I heard Tezcatlipoca laughing.

Somehow, I started laughing, too.

So what if Western Civilization was coming to an end? It never treated me very well anyway. Might as well keep laughing, and dance on its smoldering grave . . .

And I did my damnedest to let the world know about *Smoking Mirror Blues.*

Good reviews came in. The people who liked it really liked it. I wasn't showered in money, but this book seemed to be able to prosper in in the brave new century.

A decade later, I self-published an ebook, and that kept it going. Nalo Hopkinson taught it as part of a university course. Academics write about it in papers and dissertations. And, yes, there are people who just plain like it.

And now, another, new, improved edition is in your hands.

Maybe Tezcatlipoca planned it that way.

And I have a feeling that the trip isn't over.

Stay tuned for updates . . .

PART ONE

DEAD DAZED

Strange things happen in Los Angeles and the people couldn't understand it.

—THORNTON DIAL

CHAPTER 1

SUNDOWN KISSOFF

Not just as your President, but as someone who cares about you, I strongly recommend that you don't go out into the streets to celebrate Dead Daze this year. The SoCal medianets will provide excellent coverage for all festivities that you can watch from the safety of your own home. You wouldn't want to get caught in any riots like there were last year.

But, if you do find yourself out celebrating this upcoming Dead Daze, please, try to behave yourself, and cooperate with the National Guard and your local police.

•

"For God's sake, Beto," Phoebe Graziano said as whiny as she could muster, "it's Dead Daze, and it's almost sundown and I got this real sumato costume and *everything!*" She slipped her mask back on over her strawberry blonde hair that was netted down for the occasion – on which she was dressed like a robot-faced Medusa, with a head covered in multicolored snakes that writhed and hissed and stuck out their forked tongues.

Beto Orozco was not turned into stone at the sight.

She did a fashion-model spin to show off her black kimono decorated with blood-red Haitian vè-vè patterns. She was supposed to be some kind of neomythical recombocultural chimera. Real sumato, as all the recombozos and

ERNEST HOGAN

recombozoettes say.

"You know I don't give anybody's damn about God the Generic," said Beto. "I told you I have plans and am not available tonight." He was in his usual stay-home-and-work outfit of an old, faded T-shirt – this one with a baboon off some Egyptian tomb barely visible on the chest – frayed sweat pants, no shoes, his jet-black hair uncombed and sticking out everywhichway like shards of shattered obsidian.

"So, what are you going to do tonight?" Lights in the mouth of her mask lit up as she talked. Cute.

He ran a finger down one of the wings of his Manchu-Villa moustache. "I can't tell you. It's a secret."

"Is somebody in there with you?" She tried to force her way through the door of his conapt.

"No." He blocked her. "Just me and my secret project."

"You have another woman in there, Beto! I just know it! Bet it's that bitch you met on that last trip to Mexico! I knew I shouldn't have let you go!"

"As if you could have stopped me."

"How dare you cheat on me!"

His brown, almond-shaped eyes looked straight through the mask's eye-holes, directly into her blue – framed by dark purple makeup – eyes. "Don't give me that, Phoebe! You know you have yours, so why can't I have mine?"

Her eyes grew icy; the snakes hissed. "Chingow! You know that's different!"

"Is it really?"

The snakes got louder. She did not blink for a long time. "I hate you, Beto! I never want to see your xau-xau latio face again!" She turned around and walked off into the gigantic sun that was as orange as a pumpkin ripe to be carved into a Jack O'Lantern or calavera for Dead Daze. She headed for

Hollywood Boulevard.

Beto stared into the sun that was so filtered by the smog that it didn't hurt his eyes. "If only it were true this time."

•

A huge orange sun sets over the purple-grey silhouettes of the L.A. landscape. A cyberanimated Jack O'Lantern face fades into a fanged skull that combines the styles of Mexico and Indonesia. The skull smiles.

"It's getting close to October 31st through November 2nd here in the Pueblo del Rio de Nuestra Señora La Reina de Los Angeles, and you know what that means – Dead Daze! But don't wind up dead this Dead Daze. Let's make these Dead Daze safe, sane and sumato, but no reruns of last year's big mess. Let's all live these Dead Daze."

The skull moves forward. Fade to blinding white.

PAID FOR BY THE AD-HOC COMMITTEE FOR A SAFE, SANE AND SUMATO DEAD DAZE.

21

CHAPTER 2

DON'T TRY THIS AT HOME!

In their office/conapt in a refurbished, burnt-out floor of the building that used to be the Bank of America on Hollywood and Vine, Madam Tan Tien and Zobop Delvaux were celebrating the setting of the sun on Dead Daze in their special way:

They were both naked. Zobop's seven-foot tall, amply muscled, chocolate-brown body was stretched out face-up on an ornate Persian carpet. Tan Tien, an asio woman of indeterminate age stood over him, facing his feet, with one of her little feet on either side of his hips. His large penis was hard and pointing, with a slight tremble, to her glistening vagina, which dripped a bit of her juices as she squatted and took him into herself.

Finally they were locked in the Goddess and Deadman asana. Over the years they had found that this tantric yoga routine was the perfect ritual for Dead Daze. It had everything: recognition of death, celebration of life, pleasure and fear, as if it had been invented in contemporary El Lay rather than ancient Tibet.

•

Knowing that if he slammed the door Phoebe would get a

great deal of satisfaction out of it, Beto waited until she had walked out of sight, then slowly, silently pulled the door shut. Then he walked across his cluttered conapt, sat down at his workstation, and waited a little longer. He had been seeing her on and off for a few years, and knew she could change her mind without notice. Eventually he took a deep breath and figured she was gone, at least for the evening; maybe for all of Dead Daze, and hopefully forever.

He flicked the workstation on. It purred and flickered and said, "Whatta ya wanna do now, Beto?" in a sexy, synthesized, feminine voice.

"I'd like to complete the Tezcatlipoca experiment," he said. "Oh, no, not yet – first I should make a call."

"Who'd ya like t'call before completing the Tezcatlipoca experiment, Beto?"

"Xochitl."

More purrs and flickers. "No listing filed that way – couldja give me more information?"

"Try Echaurren. Xochitl Echaurren. She lives in Mexico City."

Purr; flicker. "International call being placed to Xochitl Echaurren. Please stand by, Beto."

"Sumato."

While it rang, Beto stared at his waiting, decorated-with-Aztec-symbols computer. He really should have told Xochitl that he had cloned her nanochip for his experiment, but there had been the chance she would have said no – decent, practical Mexican woman that she was – and he couldn't risk that. He had to do this. It had become an obsession.

The words NO VIDEO AVAILABLE – Mexico not yet having switched to picture-phones – appeared on the screen. Then Xochitl's voice gave her answering machine message in Spanish.

23

So she wasn't home, or a least couldn't come to the phone.

Where the hell could she be?

•

The three-foot tall figure in the glowing skull-mask was determined to chase Xochitl out of the Alameda Central all the way down to the Paseo de la Reforma, and maybe even all over Mexico City.

"Miss Echaurren," he would say, over and over, "we want to talk to you about the program you have been working on."

She had tried to keep the fact that she was working on a program to simulate gods through artificial intelligence a secret. The concept made some people crazy.

Like Beto.

When she had been fool enough to tell him about it – they had both been naked and her guard had been down – his manic eyes had lit up and he could barely manage to express himself in Spanish:

"Fantastic! AI gods could take the place of imaginary ones – this could revolutionize religion, or at least turn California upside down!"

That was exactly what she was afraid of: people actually worshipping AI gods instead of using them for serious experiments in belief-system mechanics. She worried about it to the point of thinking about it all the time, walking around, seeing dangerous ideas on the faces of strangers...

Then the phone calls started:

"Miss Echaurren, we want to talk to you about the program you have been working on."

The first time she hung up. After that, she started screening her calls.

It was a different voice every time, leaving the same

message, from the same script. They would never leave a phone number, just say:

"Sorry we missed you this time. We will catch up with you soon enough."

She had noticed that people on the streets were watching her. And finally, while walking through the Alameda Central, a surrealistic image from the Diego Rivera mural of that park, the dwarf with the glowing skull-mask (as if to start early on the Day of the Dead celebration by doing some North American Halloween-style trick-or-treating) had asked her about the program.

She was soon running down Reforma, and nobody thought much of it.

The Paseo was full of skull-faced figures, monsters and people who were screaming, running and laughing.

It was October 31st, a day on which traditionally in Mexico people would light candles and give offerings of toys and food to the angelitos – the spirits of dead children. But this was the 21st century, and recomboculture was a global phenomenon. Halloween collided with the Day of the Dead, becoming Jaloguin even here in the very heart of Mexico. Someday soon it would become a mongrelized Dead Daze, just like in Beto's El Lay.

At the big traffic circle where Reforma intersected with Insurgentes and several other streets, Xochitl ran into a crowd of masked revelers that were dancing in the street, causing a major traffic jam. Losing sight of the dwarf, she made her way to Dinamarca and dashed into the Metro Station at Avenida Chapultepec.

•

Beto rattled off a message that he thought was clever, hung up, and decided to commence with the experiment.

The time, Dead Daze Night One at sundown, was perfect;

but the atmosphere had to be right, too. He ran to his hard files and pulled out all his pictures of Tezcatlipoca: as a handsome young warrior, a wizard with a missing foot, a skull-faced apparition, a complex semi-hieroglyph; all kinds of images of the god, ancient and modern. He gunked them up around the room. Then he wondered about the sound; the booming bass beat from several portable stereos, the crowd roaring and chanting, all leaking in from the streets were good, but he needed more.

He flicked on his workstation's voice recorder and said "Tezcatlipoca!" loud, almost singing; made a loop of it and played it back:

"Tezcatlipoca! Tezcatlipoca! Tezcatlipoca!" Over and over. The god's name as wall-to-wall background sound. A perfect evocation.

But somehow Beto felt that more was needed.

He dug in the debris on his desk and found a music chip that he had bought the other day from a group of kids, mostly latios, but with token asios and afros, who were playing in the street until the police chased them off. The called themselves Los Tricksters. What impressed Beto was a song called "Tezcatlipoca Blues" that was sung and played too loud to make out most of the words – the chorus seemed to be "Got dem Tezcatlipoca blues/ making trickster war news" – but the beat was a fine mix of preColumbian tribal/ritual drums and down & dirty blues cyberdistorted into a reality-altering latio/natio/afro recombo psycho-sonic weapon. He put it on his music system and started to dance – just couldn't help it. He set the system to continuously loop the song. It was so powerful that it felt like it could conjure up Tezcatlipoca without any AI god program.

Of course, he knew that without the fuzzy, silly-bio nanochip he had cloned when Xochitl wasn't looking, this was

26

all just a crazy, mumbo jumbo ceremony. He picked up his synthetic Panama hat and untied the Mixtec codex bandana, and there it was, though barely visible: the nanochip with the magic code for making gods come out of your computer.

He thanked his own personal pantheon of deities selected from all over the globe for silicon-biological technology, and the black market chip-cloning kit that had made a mushy-trained creative fool like himself able to steal some neural nets like a high tech pro. Artificial nervous systems were getting more and more like natural ones, and the line between technology and nature was beginning to blur. It was recomboculture of the finest kind.

He snapped the nanochip into his computer. It came to glorious life and he fed it all the information on Tezcatlipoca that he had in his own chip files, then modemed in any other data from the mediasphere. The hungry little nanochip ate it all up instantly and was ready to run.

It was practically begging for it.

•

Zobop could reach Tan Tien's body with his long arms. His huge hands caressed her exquisite buttocks, then slid up to take hold of her waist and gently help her slide up and down his organ. He wanted to lean forward and squeeze her small breasts, and flick his thumbs across her nipples, but the position demanded that his spinal column be straight and against the floor.

Soon her pressure and suction were all he was aware of.

•

Having the tech and hard sciences ready to go, Beto got up to put the finishing touches on the ritual mumbo jumbo: He took a small, lens-shaped obsidian mirror – a tezcatlipoca in Náhuatl, meaning "smoking mirror," that Tezcatlipoca was named for – and gunked it to the terminal screen so

27

he could stare into it like an Aztec sorcerer scanning for a vision of the future. Then he got out his electrified, imitation teponaxtle – an Aztec wooden horizontal drum – set it on the floor where he could sit and play it while staring into the screen through the smoking mirror while the program brought Tezcatlipoca to a new kind of life.

And finally, a little something else he had bought from Los Tricksters – a little Fun, Fun with a capital F, the great new drug of the age.

He put the stubby cigarette-like tube between his lips, snagged it on with a thumbnail, and sucked it deep into his lungs as it exploded into a puff of smoke. Suddenly he felt so good that he believed everything – especially that his experiment would be a success, and soon he'd be interfacing with Tezcatlipoca. He felt so good he licked the ashes off his lips.

Then he reached up to the keyboard and set off the hard science, active ingredient of his magic. The computer flashed and buzzed to life. He sat down behind the drum, grabbed the sticks and pounded out fuzz-throwing funk-patterns as a counterpoint to the song and the name-chant loop, not caring that he couldn't carry a tune. He locked his eyes on the sparkling black mirror through which the light from the screen subtly flashed.

CHAPTER 3

ENTER SUPPORTING CLASHES

After zig-zagging through Mexico City's crumbling Metro system a while, Xochitl made it back to her University City conapt. As she deactivated her security system, it flashed a symbol that meant there had been an attempted break-in.

"What happened, Santo?" she asked her guardbot.

A Doberman-sized robot dog with a fashionable decorative covering that made it look like a papier-mâché dog skeleton walked over, let some electricity arc between its gleaming metal teeth, then said, "Intruder tried to force its way through front door. Approached with amplified wolf howl. Intruder retreated. Have video on intruder. Would you like to see?"

"No thanks, Santo, maybe later. I'm exhausted. I better get some sleep."

"Did you remember to reactivate exterior security system?" Santo asked.

"Oh. No. Thank you. What would I do without you?"

"Inquiry beyond my programming."

"Oh never mind." She reactivated the exterior security system. "Just make sure no one disturbs me while I sleep."

"Yes."

She passed her phone on the way to the bedroom. It was flashing that it had messages waiting. She ignored it. They would probably be the sort of thing that would make sleep impossible.

•

While Beto worked himself into a trance-like frenzy, Tezcatlipoca's mind zapped, crackled and popped to life in the nanochip's silicon nervous system. The god found this new existence to be confusing – so with his trickster's curiosity, he reached out through the nanochip, through Beto's computer, and into the mediasphere for the information he needed about this strange world he had entered, and how he could go about being a trickster-warrior god in it.

He was delighted.

•

Over in Phoenix, Arizona, after finishing his second Miller Light, Ralph Norton, a pale, brown-haired euro, pushed his old-fashioned aviator-style glasses back up his long nose, screwed up his gray eyes, and found the courage to put on the reality suit and try Beto's rough sacrifice program. Sometimes he regretted having agreed to collaborate with that crazy California Chicano on the virturealist game *Serpents & Sacrifices*. Sure, Beto had energy and enthusiasm that seemed endless, and had been willing to take that research trip to Mexico City at his own expense, but he lacked a sense of the appropriate, and kept going too far into Aztec culture. He resented having to change things so that they would be acceptable to a contemporary audience.

"You mean Anglo audience," he would say, with his Chicano chip on his shoulder, "what makes you think that only Anglos will be playing this game?"

Beto was a brilliant idea man – but just a little too crazy for

Ralph. And it wasn't a racial or cultural thing like Beto was always teasing him about; he knew all kinds of Chicanos, and none of them were as crazy as Beto. It was as if Beto was "going native" as the anthropologists would say. Then Beto would say he was just going home.

Ralph took a deep breath and ran the sacrifice program.

Suddenly he was no longer in Phoenix, but in Beto's Aztec virtual reality, based on pictures taken around actual ruins, crudely collaged together so the seams showed. Sure it was a rough draft – but it irritated Ralph, who preferred realism in visual representation, not this slapdash manner that was fashionable in postpostmodern art circles. Ralph's tall, soft, beer-belly'd, white body was replaced by that of a brown Aztec warrior with a body-builder's muscles. The sky did not match the way the pyramid was lit, like in a René Magritte painting, and the Aztecs surrounding him looked like drawings from codices, making it all hard to believe.

When a flint-tipped spear nudged him along it felt real enough, as did the bonds that held his wrists behind his back. He was playing the role of a captured prisoner, about to be sacrificed to Huitzilopochtli. The blood on the pyramid steps was also convincing.

When the priests guided him up the steps, he noted those steps were just as Beto had described them, seeming too short for human feet – he had to walk up diagonally, with his feet sideways on each step.

At the top of the pyramid, Ralph's bonds were cut, and he was forced to lie down on the altar. The cartoony crowd below cheered. Drums and flutes sounded.

A priest put one hand on Ralph's chest and raised a ceremonial flint knife in his other hand. Ralph couldn't help but close his eyes as the blade slashed down. The pain was excruciating – very realistic – he wondered where Beto got the programming for it, then remembered a discussion they once had about sadomasochist virturealist porn made by Triad gangsters in China.

Who knows where Beto had connections?

When Ralph's eyes popped open, he saw the cartoony priest holding up an extremely realistic heart – probably scanned in from a medical documentary. Then, out of a sky that was too smoggy to be in preConquest Mexico, a giant blue hummingbird zoomed in and hovered over the heart. The hummingbird morphed into a toothy Huitzilopochtli mask that ate the heart in one bite.

Ralph's viewpoint then shifted out of his body, giving him the feeling of his spirit soaring to the special Aztec heaven reserved for sacrificed warriors.

"Enough!" Ralph shouted as he hit the kill switch on the left wrist of the reality suit. He wanted to get up out of the safety chair, but he was totally spent. All he could do was sit and breathe hard.

It was too much. People who wanted to amuse themselves by pretending to be Aztec warriors wouldn't want to go through this. Not Anglos, not Chicanos. Not the Chicano who regularly fixed Ralph's computer system or the neighbor kids his daughter played with.

This whole Aztec thing was doing something scary to Beto. He didn't just want to play Aztec, he wanted to be an Aztec. He had once said, "Reality is the only game worth playing."

The statement really disturbed Ralph, for whom virturealist gaming was more than a hobby.

Ralph grabbed another Miller Light, quickly drained it, then went to bed and crawled in beside his sleeping wife.

•

Phoebe was still having a violent, subvocal argument

with Beto when she reached Hollywood Boulevard.

The mythic significance of being on the fabled corner of Hollywood and Vine was lost on her, as was the spectacle of all the Dead Daze revelers in costume: skull-faces ranging from the naturalistic to cartoony minimalistic to colorfully ornate Asian and Mexican, and styles over every possible type of dress and undress (including those of the Shumash, the original natives of the El Lay area), Haitian and Romero zombies, Karloffian Frankenstein monsters, Lugosian Draculas, Gigerian aliens, werewolves of assorted pedigrees (even a few Navajo-style yenagloshis), ghosts looking like glowing Klansmen and transparent low-fi holograms, beings from various cultures like hopping Chinese jiangshi vampires, Tibetan yeti, and screaming Irish banshees, melanin enhanced and suppressed recombozoids, gods and goddesses like John Wayne, Elvis, Marylin Monroe, Damballah, Quetzalcóatl, Venus and Eurzulie. It was a sumato example of recomboculture at its best – a trimili celebration of life.

Still, Phoebe was walking heavy on her heels, dragging the hem of her kimono and pouting hard behind her sci-fi Medusa mask. Her hips and feet were ignoring the five different types of music that were being blasted from the swarming throng. Being bumped by an amorous couple of mummies and twirled around by a group of people in bulky microbe-suits like the creatures of last year's popular horror movie *The Mind-Suckers From Jupiter*, while a man in top hat and tails and a nun slowdanced around her, broke her mood. It made her feel more like turning around and catching a trakbus home.

Only home was a coffin-sized box that she sublet in a moldy, old motel converted into a decaying conapt complex. She hadn't paid any rent for a couple of months, and she was afraid of the bloated landlord who remembered what life had been like before music downloads – he wanted in her pants as payment. He actually had these big, black discs made of vinyl that he used to play awful prehistoric – he called it *rock* – music. She didn't mind using sex for money, but that would be like mating with a fresh-out-of-the-La-Brea-tar-pits dinosaur!

She thought about going down to the Creative Burrito where she worked and volunteering to do an extra shift in costume. They loved having people to be in costume for Dead Daze. But then she'd probably end up trashing her voodoo kimono, and it was so sumato that she wanted to wear it again sometime.

She heard a ringing that she first thought was part of the music circulating around her, but then she felt it tickling her wrist. It was her phone.

She touched on the screen and hoped Beto's face would appear. But instead of a mustachioed male latio, the face of a female afro in lots of glowing makeup appeared.

"Phoebe?" the caller asked. "Is that you behind that mask?"

"Caldonia!" Phoebe recognized her friend's voice. "What are you supposed to be? How'd you get so light? Melanin-suppressors?"

Caldonia's eyes looked sad in their purple-black outlines that contrasted with the brilliant yellow of her face. "No. You know I'd never do that. It's makeup. Don't you recognize it? I'm the Brigitte Bardot Avenging Angel from the Mati Klarwein poster over my bed."

"Oh. So that's why the blonde wig and the crystal jewel on your forehead!"

"I also have the most beautiful wings! Wait until you see them – oh!" Caldonia pouted. "I forgot, you wanted to spend tonight with that filthy Mexican."

"Beto's not a Mexican. His family has lived in SoCal for five generations. He's as American as chop suey – or me or you."

"So where is Mr. All-American Chop Suey Burrito? I don't see him anywhere in the background."

Phoebe's hand shook, making it look like there was an earthquake going on. "Oh . . . he has these other plans."

Caldonia flashed a sharp-toothed smile. "So much for your plans. I told you he was like the rest – maybe even a little worse."

Phoebe looked away, unintentionally letting the snakes hiss into the phone.

"Sumato mask," Caldonia said. "Bet you could turn him to stone if you could find him."

Phoebe turned the metal Medusa face to the phone. "I know exactly where he is!"

"And who he's with?"

"He's not with anybody! He's got some big, important experiment he wants to do."

"Sure he does. I wonder what her name is?"

Phoebe stared without talking for a while.

Caldonia's cocky smirk melted away. "Well, what are you going to do now, Phoebe-babe?"

"I don't know."

"It's only the first night of Dead Daze! You can't give up yet! We both have great costumes, and I'm sure that between the two of us we can dream up some way to have more fun than is practical."

The robot Medusa didn't give a clue as to what Phoebe was thinking, and the snakes weren't talking.

"Sure," Phoebe finally said, "who needs Beto?"

"Where are you, Phoebe-babe?"

35

"Oh, I'm not sure. Somewhere on Hollywood Boulevard. I just turned onto it from Vine a while ago, but I don't really quite know where I am."

Caldonia's eyes lit up. "Hollywood and Vine! I'm not far from there! It must be fate! Just stay where you are – I'll find you."

Her image on Phoebe's phone winked off. Phoebe looked around, struggling to keep her position as the fantastically costumed crowd flowed down the sidewalk over the stars that bore the names of dead people, some still famous, others long forgotten. Someone in a cartoony coyote suit put a hand on her ass and ran it up and around to her breasts, nearly tearing off her kimono. She pushed him away, thinking: *I was standing still on this of all streets, must have thought I was a whore.*

An ear-splitting whistle shot through Phoebe's skull from the street.

She turned around, and there was Caldonia looking just like Brigitte Bardot as Klarwein had painted and transformed her into an exterminating angel, way, way back in the mythic Nineteen-Sixties. She wore crossed bandoliers of ivory-white bullets over her pink blouse, and below that a black leather miniskirt and black leather boots that came all the way up to thighs that were the same luminous yellow as her hands, face, and long, flowing wig. She brought the noise-amplified Honda Electroscooter to a halt, kicked down the stand, spread her arms and said, "Come to Mama, Phoebe-babe!"

As Phoebe ran into Caldonia's arms, violet-black, iridescent holographic angel's wings spread, obviously programmed to move in concert with their wearer's arms.

Phoebe's arms passed right through the wings as she and Caldonia embraced.

36

Caldonia smirked. "Nice mask, but how is someone supposed to kiss you while you're wearing it?"

"Easy." With the whir of hidden motors, the lower half of the mask opened up and retracted like the mouth of a grasshopper, revealing Phoebe's full, blood-red-painted lips.

Caldonia's lips eagerly met them.

•

Quick! Zoom in on the two women kissing – they're dressed as an angel and a medusa on that motorcycle that's blocking traffic. This is perfect! So Hollywood! So Dead Daze! And it'll look great in the trailer for my mondomentary! It'll get it into the Zimbabwe Video Festival, and maybe I'll even win an award! Yes, just hold on them, as close and tight as you can get. I hope they keep it up a good long while.

•

Tezcatlipoca was confused by living inside a nanochip. He was also disturbed. The sensory input was so different. And the mediasphere was such a strange place!

Soon he accessed Beto's phone, and could see through its camera. The computer with the tezcatlipoca on its screen was the place where he was imprisoned. The man sitting in front of it, chanting and playing the strange teponaxtle, was the sorcerer who had put him there.

Information in the computer told him that the sorcerer was Beto Orozco, who had gone to a great deal of trouble to evoke Tezcatlipoca in this peculiar way – but why in this awkward, disembodied, electronic form? There were ways to tricksterize the mediasphere, and even tricksterize the real world from there, but reality is the ultimate game, and it's all a god wants to play.

Beto slipped from an almost-hypnotic state to a hypnotic state.

If Tezcatlipoca had had lips, he would have smiled.

•

Tan Tien and Zobop were about to transcend ordinary consciousness, when in the next room their scanning system came to frantic life. Something unusual and possibly dangerous was making its way through the mediasphere. Something that would demand their special skills.

The system's vocalizer said, "Tezcatlipoca!"

Tan Tien and Zobop didn't notice. They were too busy having orgasms.

They weren't supposed to. Not in this ritual.

"What happened?" asked Tan Tien as she slowly stood up, letting Zobop's huge penis plop free.

"Our infosystem," he said, reaching for her – but too late, she was already pacing around, her mind racing, "something set it off. Something big."

"Something big?" She peeked into the other room, saw the chaotic flashing on all the screen. "Oh, then it wasn't a lapse in discipline!"

"Hey baby," he said with big smile, "you know we're both too good for that."

"Good," she said, walking through the door, "the things we deal with are dangerous. We have to maintain control. Let these things slip and there could be a disaster of cosmic proportions."

"Of course." He sat up. "And this looks like something we have to look into."

She was already making inquiries through the keyboard.

•

Tezcatlipoca saw that even though Beto's body showed some signs of neglect, it could be a good vehicle for his spirit. Besides, the sorcerer was in a trance, with his eyes locked on the screen with the obsidian mirror. He could soon see his future and it would be Tezcatlipoca.

With a little effort, the god found that he could make the screen flash all the information on himself that the machine contained, sending it into the sorcerer's brain at the speed of light. Then he made the machine talk:

"You are Tezcatlipoca. You are Tezcatlipoca. You are Tezcatlipoca . . ." It repeated endlessly.

•

Back in Mexico City, Xochitl finally managed to fall asleep. She even had a dream:

The glowing skull-mask, this time without the dwarf, was following her around, from the Metro to the preAztec ruins of Teotihuacán, the Birthplace of the Gods, where it chased her down the Avenue of the Dead while descendants of the people who had built the Pyramids of the Sun and Moon and the Temple of Quetzalcóatl tried to sell her handmade "pipas por la marijuana" etched with obsolete microchip circuit patterns. The skull followed her through a jungle of trees that rained silicon-bio nanochips on her. Finally, Beto emerged from the putrid carcass of some gigantic beast and said, in English, "Hey, Xochitlita, this way." He took her hand and led her into the National Museum of Anthropology through the room of larger-than-life-sized statues of snakes, to the Sun Stone Aztec calendar. Then there was an earthquake; the Grand Coatlique and the stone snakes shook, the Sun Stone fell right on top of the smiling Beto. The calendar shattered and blood flowed from under it, filling the room and causing the snake statues to come to life. As the Grand Coatlique's two reptile heads stirred, Beto's severed hand caressed Xochitl's palm.

She woke up like a spaceship taking off for orbit. Her heart was out of control. She was soaked in sweat.

Santo was barking. Someone was pounding on the door.

"In God's name, open this door Miss Echaurren!" The voice was electronically distorted and amplified.

Xochitl picked up her Toshiba sonic immobilizer.

Miniature lightning bolts squirmed between Santo's metal teeth.

The door came crashing down. Two figures in round-headed, white hoods and gowns that were more suggestive of Casper the Friendly Ghost than the Ku Klux Klan rushed in. Santo leapt for the throat of one; the costume tore, revealing bulky protective gear. Xochitl fired the Toshiba at the other one, but the intruder kept coming at her, the dangerous sound waves absorbed by devices in the armor. The lightning from Santo's teeth couldn't take hold of his attacker as well as his fangs could grip the armored throat; the bolts grew larger, and lashed back into the bot's own circuitry, shorting it out.

Soon a limp Dia de los Muertos dog skeleton fell to the floor.

"Where are the chips of the god-generating program?" asked a blaring, robotic voice.

Xochitl clutched her nightgown to her breast, screamed and ran for the door.

One intruder grabbed and tackled her, then picked her up and threw her over his shoulder.

"Where is it?" asked the other.

Xochitl screamed again. The scream faded off into the distant noise of music and partying.

"We better take you to a place where you will be compelled to talk."

They carried her off into the starless Aztec night.

•

Beto started saying, "I am Tezcatlipoca. I am Tezcatlipoca. I am Tezcatlipoca . . ."

•

Phoebe and Caldonia danced hand in hand down Hollywood Boulevard, occasionally stopping to grab the asses of National Guards – both male and female – who were watching over the festivities.

•

Malcolm Jones, a handsome youngish-though-greying-at-the-temples afro who has been called "America's first black president" so many times in the last year that it now seems like part of his name, smiles from the Oval Office.

Reporter: Did you take it personally – the rioting that broke out in Los Angeles during the last Dead Daze celebration that lasted until the day of your election?

Jones: (smiles, laughs) Why, no. Of course not, how could those people have possibly known that I would win the election?

Reporter: So why did you have the National Guard watch over this year's Dead Daze festivities?

Jones: It was concern for the safety of the people of Los Angeles and the surrounding areas that made me do it. And I was not the only one responsible for bringing out the Guard. I had the full cooperation of the City of Los Angeles and the State of California.

Reporter: So what do you think of Dead Daze as a holiday?

Jones: I think it's a very American phenomenon – the creation of a new culture and new traditions out of those that are coming together in Southern California. It's one of those things that makes America great.

Reporter: With the National Guard watching?

Jones: Well, we can't let things get out of hand.

CHAPTER 4

I AM TEZCATLIPOCA

"I am Tezcatlipoca," said Tezcatlipoca, in Beto's voice, with Beto's mouth, out of Beto's body.

He could now see out of Beto's eyes, too.

Beto's mind was still there, buried deep in the brain. Tezcatlipoca could access it to understand the bizarre world he found himself in.

In the obsidian mirror attached to the monitor screen, he could see his new face. It was not bad, but the moustache curling around the lips and pointing down to the chin would have to go; he was Tezcatlipoca, young manhood personified – young Aztec manhood. This evidence of being polluted by the genes of the aliens who had invaded the One World and destroyed civilization wouldn't have bothered his brother Quetzalcóatl, who liked to let the hairs grow on his face like an old man; but Tezcatlipoca needed a clean face, with maybe a bit of jewelry through the nasal septum or the lower lip.

Beto's nose and lip – and even his ears – weren't pierced. What strange beings the aliens were!

According to Beto's mind, there was a machine that he used to shave off most of his facial hair. Tezcatlipoca went into the small room with the mechanisms for calling forth and sending away water – no doubt a sort of shrine to Tláloc, the Rain God. He found the electric razor, and Beto's memories guided him through the ritual of drying the face and shaving.

Halfway through removing the moustache, he noticed that the mirror wasn't of obsidian – not a smoking mirror, a tezcatlipoca – and it made everything look so unnaturally bright and clear. You could stare into this mirror for days and all you'd see would be this sharp reflection of what things looked like, no visions would come.

"How do these people get along without visions to guide them?" Tezcatlipoca said, trying out Beto's strange, difficult to pronounce and awkward-sounding language. It was wasn't as natural or beautiful as Náhuatl.

Without the moustache, the face almost looked Aztec, or at least like that of some Chichimec tribe. The skin was still far too pale, but Beto knew of something called melanin-enhancers that could fix that. It was handsome too, with a trickster's grin. It could be the new face of Tezcatlipoca.

But, ay, the hair! It was long and short in all the wrong places, and not tied into a warrior's topknot. He found of strip of cloth – a discarded shoelace – and tied his new hair into an adequate knot at the tip of the skull. But what to do about the strands that stuck out all over? Luckily, there were a pair of scissors that Beto used to cut up ancient hardcopies; Tezcatlipoca used them to snip off the offending licks of hair, especially those at the nape of the neck that were a sign that a warrior hadn't captured a prisoner in many a battle.

Then he looked over the clothes that his new body was wearing. Awful. Soft, loose pants, and a T-shirt with the faded image of a monstrous being on the chest.

He was Tezcatlipoca, young manhood at its most energetic, mischievous, and beautiful! Where were his brightly colored plumes and fabulous battledress?

He ran to the closet and ransacked it. Most of the clothes

were things he wouldn't be caught dead in, but there were some with just enough color and style to be suitable for Tezcatlipoca. Soon he had on a blood-red T-shirt with the Aztec Calendar printed on it, a loose-fitting, high-collared jacket that was black with electric blue skeletons dancing all over it, and pants that were a repeating rainbow of zig-zags. Sneakers that looked like pink and purple serpent-heads completed the outfit.

The mix of musics coming from outside made him want to dance. More than that, he wanted to make music. He picked up Beto's teponaxtle – it was like the drums that Tezcatlipoca was familiar with, but with a lot of technological magic of this new world plugged into it. He tucked the sticks into his waistband and the drum under his arm and faced the door.

Something held him back. It was the computer. As he had taken possession of Beto's body, this machine had taken possession of his soul – it must have great power to capture the soul of a god. Part of him was in the machine, tapping into the mediasphere, learning important things about this world that he would need to know.

Only he couldn't communicate directly with the part of his soul that was inside the machine! He needed some medium, some piece of technological magic.

He scanned Beto's mind. There was a way that he could communicate with the computer – his soul – while being far away from it: The phone! It was on a stand next to the screen. All he had to do was put it on his wrist, and he could not only communicate with the computer, but the rest of this world as well.

What a marvelous world!

•

(Scenes of last year's Dead Daze rioting.)
Why did this happen last year? Just look at some of

these people. Demonic beings are being evoked, mostly by accident, but often intentionally. It is dangerous to all who value their souls. Do not participate in *any* Dead Daze activities! Not even traditional Halloween is safe, having been infected by these demonic influences. For God's sake, stay home. Don't walk the streets with the demons!

THIS HAS BEEN A PUBLIC SERVICE ANNOUNCE-MENT PAID FOR BY THE ALLIANCE OF CHRISTIANS, JEWS, AND MOSLEMS.

•

Tezcatlipoca strutted down Hollywood Boulevard, confident that he could conquer this world.

•

Back in Phoenix, Ralph couldn't sleep. He kept thinking about Beto and the sacrifice program. As usual, his wife Norma sept soundly.

Ralph staggered over to his workstation and fired up his computer. He decided to contact Beto. Why not? Beto kept weird hours, and might be working well after sundown.

As soon as he contacted Beto's computer, the screen filled up with I AM TEZCATLIPOCA. I AM TEZCATLIPOCA. I AM TEZCATLIPOCA . . .

Weird, but real. Like Beto.

Beto had always said that reality was the ultimate game. What was that lunatic up to now?

CHAPTER 5

NITE FLITES

"Oh, Caldonia, look over there! Such a cute guy!" said Phoebe.

It was Tezcatlipoca.

"Yeah, I guess he is." Caldonia pouted. "For a guy. Chingow! Why do you always want to talk about guys? I'm certainly not in the mood for guys – not tonight! I was hoping you wouldn't be either, especially after the way that xau-xau Beto treated you."

"Oh, Caldonia!" Phoebe took her friend's hand. "You know I love you. I guess you're right. That guy is probably xau-xau too. He even looks a little like Beto."

"Yuck!"

The two women kissed, and walked back to the scooter with their arms around each other.

•

The ghosts carried Xochitl through the streets of University City. Two figures in ragged costumes through which body armor could be seen carrying a kicking and screaming, nightgown-clad woman just wasn't anything unusual.

A lot of the National Autonomous University of Mexico students were getting into the Dead Daze phenomenon. They were out in force in an array of bizarre costumes: jackal-headed cowboys, chicken-footed dancing devils, ambulatory mermaids, heroic masked wrestlers in artificial muscle suits, women with five serpent heads each, Aztec warriors in animal-head helmets, people of all ages and sexes in skirts that looked like they were made of living snakes, life-sized papier-mâché skeletons in all manner of attire, Art Deco robots, antique sci-fi space creatures, Hollywood horror apparitions and things spawned of unique imaginations. It looked as if Hell and several Aztec heavens had broken loose.

It did make getting to wherever the ghosts wanted to take Xochitl difficult. A crowd like a giant amoeba dancing to the frenetic beat of Xuxo Ben-Xuxa's "Macumba Mutation Mambo" flowed around them and pulled them against their path as it digested them. When the ghosts tried to force their way against the flow, the members of the crowd reacted as if it was the latest type of roughhouse, martial-arts dancing.

The force of the "Macumba Mutation Mambo"-driven crowd was overwhelming.

•

Follow the group – the ones dressed like some kind of ghosts with robot-type paraphernalia underneath – you know, the ones carrying the girl who's doing a good job of acting like she's trying to get away from them. There. Good. The big crowd collided with them. Some bashada dancing has broken out. Excellent! I was hoping to catch some of that. Bashada is very popular right now; could be a selling point for this mondomentary. "Bashada on the Day of the Dead" – could make a good title. Anyway, stay with the ghosts and the girl, and try to get some closeups – she doesn't have any underwear on and there may be the chance for some nudity, which always ups the salability. Ah, yes, one of her breasts has popped out – be sure to get as close as you can, and in focus! Oh, the ghosts have lost their grip and she's running away, out of the crowd. How dramatic!

47

This will really be a hit at the Lasha Mondo Festival!

•

Tezcatlipoca was seeing and being seen as he strutted down Hollywood Boulevard. He liked it. It was overwhelming. Now and then he had to check with the phone on his wrist to find out something that wasn't directly accessible through Beto's mind – all he had to do was look and his soul made the computer flash the desired information at the speed of light.

He soon felt that he should be doing more than just walking along as part of the parade. He was a god – the Great Trickster who dared go beyond anything the ancient coyote god ever dreamed of. He was new, *now* – not at the beginning of time! He was young manhood riding at the peak of its powers on hormones and black magic.

His fingers tapped the teponaxtle, and the wooden drum with the strange electronic attachments made pleasing sounds. His feet turned his strut into a dance. Music – it was in him, and now he had to let it out: some wild, magical Tezcatlipoca/trickster music that would allow him to take this world for his own.

He walked out to the middle of the street that Beto's mind associated with vehicles that breathed poisonous fire, but that was now filled with pedestrians. It seemed that the machines, automobiles, cars were destroying the very sky – how his brother Quetzalcoatl in his Ehécatl, God of the Winds, guise would have hated that! – so they weren't allowed in the heart of this city that spilled over the horizon. He sat down, placed the teponaxtle down in front of him, realized that he had to turn it on and did so, took the sticks in hand and started beating out the feelings that were writhing around in his borrowed heart and computerized soul.

The electronic accent that the drum put on its wooden

sound took a little getting used to, but as a trickster and wizard he was used to adjusting to new things. Soon it became his new accent, the way Beto's voice became his voice. His music became the music of this place – Hollywood, Los Angeles/El Lay, SoCal; a place with many names, names with many places. It mixed with and infected the musics that other people carried with them. All those marching, strolling feet began to dance to Tezcatlipoca's driving beat.

•

Ralph didn't realize he was dreaming. He thought he was still in the throws of insomnia, so he got up, and drifted toward his workstation. Suddenly there was a frantic pounding on the front door, which burst open, revealing blinding, Phoenician mid-day sun, even though it was night inside, just like a Magritte painting. Beto staggered through the door, his clothes were ripped to shreds, and his body was covered with black, swollen welts that gave off blue smoke. He had something in his hands that he gave to Ralph, just before falling to the hardwood flood and disintegrating into a pile of black goo that gave off more blue smoke. What he had handed to Ralph was a human heart that didn't have a speck of blood on it – yet it was still beating. Ralph put it down next to his computer. Blood-red wires wormed out of the heart's venal and arterial openings and, with crackling sparks on contact, worked their way into Ralph's computer. The monitor flickered, then flashed with the detonation of a nuclear blast.

He whimpered as the image of a mushroom cloud the size of the Arizona sky filled his brain.

His wife, Norma, her blonde hair mussed from sleep, shook him awake.

"Wake up, dear," she said, "you're having a nightmare."

"I was dreaming about Beto," he said.

49

"It figures." She smirked, and got that familiar look of disgust in her blue eyes.

•

"Oh look Caldonia," Phoebe said as the motorcycle came to a stop. "That cute guy – the one that looks a little like Beto – he sat right down in the middle of the street and he's playing music. Hey, I think Beto has a drum like that . . ."

"Don't be xau-xau, Phoebe. He's just like all the rest, and you really don't want to pay any attention to him if he reminds you of Beto. You should have some fun with me."

Phoebe squeezed Caldonia's hand. "But I am having fun with you."

Caldonia pulled something out of one of her bandoliers and slipped it into Phoebe's hand. "I mean have *Fun* with me, Phoebe-babe."

Phoebe looked at the stubby Fun stick in her hand. "Oh! Have Fun with you! How sumato! You mean right here on the street?"

"It's Dead Daze, we can get away with anything." Caldonia put a Fun stick between her lips, flicked it on, and sucked it off. Phoebe opened the mouth of her mask and did the same.

•

Hey! Two girls sucking Fun at five o'clock! Zoom in. Good. Our viewers love glimpses of blatant illegality. Uh-oh. Time for a station I.D.

(The Sumato Channel logo slides across the screen.)

•

"Oh!" said Phoebe. "Feels so good and sumato!"

Caldonia smiled, put an arm around Phoebe, and grabbed one of her breasts. "Now that we've had some Fun, maybe we can go back to my place and have fun."

•

You get the best Dead Daze coverage on the Sumato Channel, so stay tuned for more!

•

Tezcatlipoca was as aware of the people who were gathering around him and dancing to the music as he was aware of the music itself. He smiled. These people could be tricked. This world was his for the taking.

•

What is that music? No, not any of the chips being played – the electrified drum solo. There. Zero in and isolate. Kind of rough and primitive, but there are some possibilities there. Give me some hardcopy visuals on the musician and see if we can trace him. This could turn into something big.

•

There were some who weren't dancing to Tezcatlipoca's music – or at least they were trying not to. They had youthful faces, each painted with the same pattern in black and blue. They stood like warriors, even though some of them were women. They wore uniforms of sneakers, pants, T-shirts, jackets, and baseball caps, all bearing assorted corporate logos, all in the same black and blue as their face-paint.

Tezcatlipoca was pleased. Blue and black were his sacred colors.

The crowd parted as the black-and-blue-clad warriors marched toward Tezcatlipoca.

One of them, a tall latio who moved with the confidence of a leader, brought his crash-fibre Messerschmidt Stompers up to the drum and gave it a kick, sending it into Tezcatlipoca's lap and bringing the music to an abrupt halt.

"Those are last year's sneakers you've got on," the black and blue warrior said. "You know you can't wear obsolete fashions on Los Olvidadoid turf. We got corporate connections, you know."

Tezcatlipoca smiled. "Are you challenging me?"

"Yes." The warrior pulled out a black and blue Bic six-shot disposable.

Without touching his hands to the pavement, Tezcatlipoca stood up from his seated position. The teponaxtle fell onto the Messerschmidt Stompers. The Olvidadoid growled.

Without a pause, Tezcatlipoca took the drumsticks and forced them through the soft flesh under the Olvidadoid's chin all the way up into his brain. The gang leader looked shocked for a split second, then collapsed onto the teponaxtle like a pile of wet laundry.

Next to him the Bic, its self-destruct mechanism activated by the impact, melted into a steaming, bubbling black and blue puddle.

Tezcatlipoca's smile widened.

The crowd applauded, with hoots, hollers and whistles.

•

Did you get that? In closeup? Great! Of all the sumato luck! I can't chingow believe this! It's great! We caught a SoCal citizen exercising his legal right to kill a certified gangster in self-defense! Every network on the planet will want it! We gotta move fast – plug into the mediasphere, let the world know what we got and start taking bids . . .

•

Tezcatlipoca licked the blood off the drumsticks and didn't flinch from the mild electric shock. The crowd went wild. Soon he was riding its many shoulders down Hollywood Boulevard.

•

Phoebe looked over at Tezcatlipoca riding the crowd. "He sure is sumato, even if he does look like Beto," she said, then kissed Caldonia before she could react.

•

52

Eventually, Xochitl made her way to her father's house.

"My daughter," the bespectacled, grey-haired man asked, "what happened?"

"All Hell's breaking loose, Papa. Evil spirits are coming to get me through my computer. My work has gotten me into big trouble."

He looked confused.

"The god-simulating program, Papa."

He shook his head. "I didn't think it was possible."

"It may not be – I haven't worked out all the details yet, but that doesn't seem to matter to all the crazy people in the world."

"Let me get you something to wear. Sit down, my daughter." He pointed her to a chair and walked over to the closet.

"No, Papa, I think I need to use your phone. Who knows what they did to my place."

She punched in her number, then the code to play her messages, hoping to find a clue to what was going on. The first few were of the "Miss Echaurren, we want to talk to you about the program you have been working on," variety; whoever wanted the program, they were willing to go to extremes to get it. Then Beto's voice came in through some long distance static, singing, in English:

"Oh, Mama, can this really be the end?

to be stuck outside Tenochtitlán,

with the Tezcatlipoca blues, again!"

Then he switched to his heavily accented Spanish:

"Well, maybe not the end, Xochitlita. Maybe it's the beginning, a new beginning, far from Tenochtitlán, where we're going to be singing a brand new kind of Tezcatlipoca blues as soon as I run through the program of yours that I just had to make an unauthorized clone of. Sorry I couldn't come out and ask you for it, baby, but you were being so xau-xau cautious, worrying about all those control elements. You can't control gods, Xochitl; if you could, they wouldn't be gods. Zero hour will be when Dead Daze kicks off. I'll let you know what happens, or maybe the world will tell you first. Later, baby."

Xochitl said, "Oh my God!" and didn't listen through the next three renditions of "Miss Echaurren, we want to talk to you about the program . . ."

•

Tezcatlipoca saw Phoebe in the distance. Recognizing her caused a violent reaction in Beto's mind. Beto was repulsed. This interested Tezcatlipoca. It was a chance to see who was the master here.

"That metal-faced woman!" Tezcatlipoca pointed to Phoebe. "I want her!"

•

Xochitl's father brought a large bathrobe. "Here, my daughter, put this on."

She did. Like a glass-eyed zombie.

"Could it possibly be that bad?" he asked.

"Worse than I thought. Not only are some fanatics after the program, but that North American I met a few months ago, Beto . . ."

"The one from California." He shook his head, sorrowfully.

"Yes, he's trying to use the program to evoke Tezcatlipoca. And the version he cloned doesn't have any of my control elements."

"Why, if it works it could be a catastrophe."

"It may have already happened!"

"Well, don't worry, my daughter, you can stay here as long as you need to."

"Ay! I can't do that! I called my place on your phone! They could have traced it! They might be on their way here already! How could I have been so stupid?"

He put his arms around her. "So, where can you go to be safe, Xochitlita? I'll do whatever I can to help you."

"Oh – I don't know. There may not be any safe place."

"Then sit down. Relax. Think." He led her back to the chair.

•

Phoebe broke the kiss, and pushed Caldonia away.

"That cute guy," Phoebe said, "I think he means me."

She looked. Tezcatlipoca was grinning at her.

"He does mean me!" She pushed her way to him.

Caldonia growled.

•

Xochitl jumped up. "I've got to leave the country! Now. Tonight. Can you lend me some clothes and money?"

"Of course, but the program, is it where the fanatics can get it?"

She reached into the bodice of her nightgown. "I hope it didn't fall out. No, here it is. I jammed it into a seam." She pulled out an ant-sized nanochip. "They saw me dressed like this and didn't think to search me – not very imaginative, I guess. If they had just pointed their software sniffers at me..."

"I'll do what I can to help you. Where do you think you should go?"

"Los Angeles."

He frowned. "California? Where that Beto fellow lives."

"I know, I know, it's crazy – almost as crazy as he is, but I have to. And at least it will get me out of here, away from whoever it is that's after me, and allow me to stop him, or

55

try to undo any damage he's done."

•

The crowd carried Tezcatlipoca to Phoebe. Los Olvidadoids surrounded her, grabbed her. She relaxed, melted, and let a horde of strange hands lift and carry her to Tezcatlipoca.

Beto's mind struggled. It managed to make Tezcatlipoca subvocalize, "Help me."

This confused Tezcatlipoca, who glanced at his phone. The screen flashed a condensed stream of information about ancient movies about foolish men mixing their molecules with those of flies. Tezcatlipoca laughed.

•

Hold on the crowd fighting with the police for the corpse of the Olvidadoid leader – wouldn't it be great if they got it and tore it limb from limb? Talk about a chingow spectacular scene. Uh-oh, guess not. The police got it, too bad. Now cut to the guy who killed him being carried around. Hey! This is a good place to stick in that quote from President Jones . . .

President Jones: As long as it is kept from getting out of line – like last year's riots – Dead Daze can be a beautiful celebration of life in our community. So have fun, but behave. Don't spoil things for everybody.

•

The crowd gently placed Phoebe into Tezcatlipoca's arms. He tore off her mask, throwing it into air, then kissed her as if she were the still-beating heart of a human sacrifice. This was not Beto, Phoebe thought, he had never kissed her like this, at least not for a long, long time.

•

Phoebe's mask landed near Caldonia.

"This is really xau-xau, Phoebe!" She screamed, then

put a stick of Fun in her lips, flicked it on, hopped on her Electroscooter, and zoomed away, holographic wings flapping, as she knocked over anybody who was in her way.

•

Beto's mind fought, lost, and faded away.

•

At the Hollywood Police station, Director Placio Ho was right in the middle of his latest attempt to straighten out the latest payroll/scheduling mess. He felt like one of the datapushers all the critics said the SoCal law enforcement community had become since corporations had taken on the task of assimilating gangs into society. When the phone rang, the auburn-haired asio/euro's rough hewn-face twitched; he had told the system to take all his calls while he was busy. What the heck (Ho was good Christian and didn't take the name of the final resting place of damned souls in vain) could it be?

With a well-practiced groan he switched his workstation screen to the phone line.

Madam Tan Tien's face, giving a Mona Lisa half-smile, appeared onscreen.

Oh, he thought. Then he thought *Oh, no.* Somehow she could always get through to him when she wanted. How could she know that he was working this late? It was like black magic.

"How are you this evening, Director Ho?" she asked. She looked different. Her hair was mussed, not its usual every-hair-in-place elegance – it looked as if she had just gotten out of bed. And instead of one of her usual crisp business suits, she had on a wrinkled oversized T-shirt with a picture of the human brain on it. In the background, out of focus, Zobop's hulking dark brown form practiced tai chi.

57

"I'm, er, busy," he said.

"Ah, yes." She gave one of her rare, brief full-smiles that made you want to do whatever she asked. "It is Dead Daze. There is a lot happening in El Lay."

"Yes." He tried to fight the effect of her smile. "I really don't have time to talk."

"But you should have time to listen," she went on. "Our scanning system has detected something happening over the communications lines. The source is very close to Hollywood and Vine. You will have to deal with it soon, and you need the help of Ti-Yong/Hoodoo Investigations. We have established a red link with your phone. You will know when to contact us. Goodbye, Director Ho."

She was replaced by the payroll files before Ho could say anything.

Director Ho's mouth clamped tighter than a chicken's anus. He didn't like Tan Tien, and Zobop terrified him. He wished there were some good anti-witchcraft laws on the books.

CHAPTER 6

POSTMIDNIGHTMARES

Phoebe was reeling, feeling so good she could have exploded. This guy may have looked like Beto, but he was totally different – even the way he kissed! He was the way Beto wished he could be while all he could really do most of the time was sell Aztec mythology to virturealist gamers, play around with cut-out pictures, drums, and computers.

Her Dead Daze was saved!

And now all these people were around like he was a god or something. Did that make her a goddess? The thought made her blush.

The Fun and the fun combined and things went faster and faster, making Phoebe's brain spin on its stem as Tezcatlipoca wheeled and dealed, beat his drum, talked to be people on his phone, gave interviews, all while pausing to hug and kiss her and whisper sweet nothings like:

"Don't worry, Phoebe-baby, if you can't pronounce Tezcatlipoca; just call me Smokey. Smokey Espejo. The Mirror that Smokes. It's all me. It's all mad and merry and it'll recomboize the world."

She lost track of time. It only seemed like a few minutes that the crowd carried her and Smokey through the streets of Hollywood. When he convinced the people to let them go, and the two dashed into a coffee shop to drink, snack, and talk, she saw on the clock that it was past midnight.

Fun and fun can do that.

•

We need a tighter shot, an extreme close-up! No! A telephoto shot won't do! Get the camera closer to that guy. The guy! The girl is okay, for background, but we need the guy's face so we can trace him, see if we can contact him, arrange for an interview. That crowd is amazing – impenetrable. I tell you, we need to add an electric prod to the cameraperson's kit! Hey! Look out for those gang members! Get the hell out of there! For God's sake, save the camera!

•

Soon Xochitl, her black hair pulled back into a last-minute pony-tail, an artificial glow-in-the-dark cempasúchil flower behind her left ear, was dressed in one of her father's old suits and a pair of his old William Burroughs Memorial Special Edition Nikes. She was on a Tres Estrellas de Oro Executive Class bus, heading for the border. It was full of Mexican migrant workers on the way to work, American migrant workers heading home, and a family of Portuguese-speaking Japanese. The "executive" luxuries – videos, and stewardesses serving hot meals – had long since been stripped away. Fortunately, the air-conditioning and the bathroom still worked – sort of.

If her nerves weren't already totally shot from being sure that someone dressed as Godzilla had followed her and had talked into a pay phone while keeping its eyes on her, seeing her father cry when he realized that she wouldn't be with him at her mother's grave for their usual Day of the Dead ritual finished the job. That's why he had bought the new version of the bright orange flower that Anglos called marigolds and the Aztecs had called cempasúchil, a traditional offering to the spirits of the dead. When he gave it to her, he said, "It will make you pretty, my daughter – and remind you of your mother," and he had wept when she clipped it into place. She knew he didn't do it to make her feel bad – he would never do that. It was just that he was so sensitive. Unfortunately, she had inherited that sensitivity.

She had brought an English phrasebook and a bilingual edition of Jack Kerouac's *Mexico City Blues*. She needed to brush up on her English – which Beto had found clumsy but charming. An American's poetry written in Mexico seemed right to help a Mexican computer programmer on her first trip north of the border.

As they left the mountains and entered the desert, she was staring out the window, eyes hypnotically locked on the flowing landscape that was dotted with thousands of tiny lights from candles and artificial flowers.

•

Drinking hot cups of maté, Tan Tien and Zobop pulled two wheeled secretary's chairs in front of their workstation, and began to check for the source of the I AM TEZCATLIPOCA phenomenon.

"It's centered not far from here," said Zobop. "Could it be the spirit of Hollywood manifesting itself in the mediasphere?"

"Could be," said Tan Tien. "The signal is unfocused and varying, as if it was made by an artificial intelligence trying to break free of its source hardware."

"It's stronger than any we have encountered before."

"We'd better be careful then."

•

What? So the guy who did the drum music is in the Lupe's in Hollywood? Well what are you waiting for? Get us a phonelink, muy pronto, mon amour!

•

61

A screen flashed as a phonelink patched into the Tezcatlipoca phenomenon.

"So," said Tan Tien, "we aren't the only ones interested in this."

"Should make this trace a little easier." Zobop operated a keyboard.

•

Phoebe smiled and sipped a little more of her drink. There she was, in another Lupe's, sipping iced tea – with nothing in it – after midnight, and Beto – No, Tezcatlickwhatsis – No, Smokey . . . Wait a minute. She just met Smokey. So why was this whole scene with the indirect lighting and the eight-foot tall Zulu waitress coming out so déjà vu? Smokey did look like Beto, a little, like in the movies they could use one for a double for the other in longshots, but these two guys were so different.

Beto would have been nervous about talking to a whole group of armed gangsters, but hey, Smokey was so sumato they couldn't help but be impressed.

When the big acne-scarred latio with not quite enough fur on his upper lip to qualify as a moustache came up growling, swept their iced-teas and Ho Chi Minh City-style chips & salsa all over the nonscuff floor, and said, "Hey, like, man, y'know you killed our leader, like right in front of everybody," Smokey just smiled and said:

"He challenged me. That's what I do to people who challenge me."

The acne-scarred latio's face went blank. He backed off.

Then a little blonde asio girl in full Olvidadoid gear stepped up, leaned on the table. "Hey, we're not just any freelance gang, y'know, we got corporate connections. You can't just kill our main guy and expect us to disband. We got corporate connections. Y'know."

"Yeah," said a skinny afro Olvidadoid boy, "like, who's supposed to tell us what to do now?"

"Yeah," said a few of the others, not quite in unison.

•

Tezcatlipoca was sure he was a god. He had so many advantages over these mere mortals. It was so easy to manipulate Phoebe that he didn't have to try; it was as if she lived to be manipulated. Los Olvidadoids were lost without their leader, desperately needing to be told what to do. The same with the crowd, the waitress, the family dressed as Trappist monks eating vegetarian sausage. All these people, this strange civilization, were crying out for gods, and it must have been a long time since they had seen a real one.

How had they gotten along without gods for so long?

"You will do as I say," he told the Olvidadoids. "I am a god."

"Sumato" said the blonde asio girl, with a dreamy look in her eyes.

"Ya gotta make it official," said the one with the acne-scars. "Ya gotta contact Novacorp, get everything filed."

•

Since he could be in more than one place at a time – the coffee shop, Beto's conapt, the mediasphere, etc. – he used Beto's infosystem to contact Novacorp.

•

"A surge of activity," said Zobop, "centered on Hollywood and Vine."

•

"It's already done," said Smokey.

The blonde asio frowned. "Don't play with us like that. You can't do it that fast."

"Call Novacorp." Smokey waved the wrist where he

63

wore his phone.

Simultaneously, the Olvidadoids dialed Novacorp. Out of sync, they looked up at Smokey, stunned.

"It's impossible," said the acne-scarred one.

"You're already registered as leader of Los Olvidadoids," said the blonde asio.

"I told you. I am a god."

•

"Got a call between the Hollywood and Vine conapt, the Novacorp, and the nearby Lupe's," said Zobop, "the name 'Smokey Espejo' is mentioned. I got it traced."

•

We're getting matching voiceprint signal on a three-way call. It starts at a local business – a Lupe's – then goes through a conapt – it's on Hollywood and Vine, if you believe that! – then goes to the global headquarters of Novacorp in New Zealand. I sure hope they don't own him yet! Anyway, he seems to be in the Lupe's on Vine. Better send somebody out there.

•

"Your – I mean, my gang owns a group of musicians called Los Tricksters, doesn't it?" asked Smokey.

"Yeah," said the skinny afro, "but how would you know that?"

"I have my ways," said Smokey, with echoes of "Tezcatlipoca Blues" in his mind, and a call from a recording company being fielded by his computerized soul. "They could come in handy."

"Yeah, sure," said the acne-scarred one. "So what ya want us to do?"

"Ah, yes," said Smokey. "There's a conapt I want you to seal off and guard."

•

Phoebe leaned over, letting her breasts embrace Smokey's arm. She thought she heard Smokey say they were all going over to Beto's conapt. Yes, that sounded like the right address. But then all the Olvidadoids left, and Smokey didn't move, so she stayed with him, and things got quiet for a little while. She ordered another iced-tea from the Zulu waitress. She wished she had some more Fun to suck. Then more people came over to talk to Smokey. Lots and lots of them.

•

"Hey, you the guy that does that great stuff on the electrified wooden drum?" said the young euro woman in the severe black suit. "I'm a representative of Postdigital Entertainment Associates, Music Division. Several of our audio headhunters have been scanning the Dead Daze scene here in Hollywood and have registered some impressive reports on you. We'd like to know if you'd be interested in discussing business with us, you know, a recording contract, getting you a band, marketing you globally."

"I already have a band," said Tezcatlipoca. "They are called Los Tricksters."

The rep frowned as if she were going to swallow her faint moustache, "They are a Novacorp subcontract, through a local gang. Aren't you doing business on a global scale?"

Tezcatlipoca glanced at his phone. "Things are going through some changes. I believe that we – myself and Novacorp are willing to discuss reorganization to expand our – my influence."

•

"We gonna have to break in?" asked the acne-scarred Olvidadoid.

"No, Chucho, you dope," said the red-haired asio girl. "He gave me the security code."

65

"You think you're so sumato, Lila." Chucho stepped closer to her. "One of these days, I'm gonna . . ."

"Enough, Chucho." The skinny afro grabbed the acne-scarred one's shoulder. "We have work to do."

"Let go of me, Zen. What kind of xau-xau work is this?" said Chucho. "We don't get to trash the place or take anything!"

"Smokey said 'secure' the place." Lila opened the door. "So we secure it."

"Nacho would have never given us such a boring job," said Chucho.

"At least we got the Bics and the people prods," said Lila.

"Smokey's the new boss." Zen pushed Chucho into the conapt. "So we do what he says."

"I hate it when things change." Chucho entered the conapt. "What a weird place. Think Smokey lives here?"

"Don't touch anything," said Lila. "We have to make sure nothing happens to the equipment."

•

Xochitl's eyes crossed. She was having a hard time telling the Spanish page from the English page in her book. It was time for a little rest. She looked out the window and saw, through her reflection, the flickering lights from candles in a graveyard on a distant hill. In the sky, a huge, glowing balloon shaped like a feathered serpent hovered, glowing.

Something tapped her shoulder. It was a little old man of pure Mexican natio stock. He was dressed as a traditional peasant: straw hat, white cotton shirt and pants, huaraches. These days most farmworkers wore baseball caps, T-shirts, jeans and sneakers. Was he in costume for Day of the Dead? His face looked like a wrinkled old treestump, with only faint sparks of reflected light indicating eyes.

"Xochitl Echaurren," he said. "We know where you are. You cannot run away from us. We are everywhere. We will get you and your god-simulating program soon."

Then the bus stopped. He hobbled to the door and got out. Slowly making his way down a dirt path into a cornfield, he vanished into darkness as black as interstellar space.

Had that really happened? She couldn't tell; maybe it had just been some strange, half-waking dream. One thing for sure now – she couldn't sleep, even though she wanted to.

She wished Santo was with her; it would be comforting to stroke his papier-mâché head and see his eyes light up. She wondered if he could be repaired.

By the side of the road, she glimpsed the dehydrated corpse of a mule.

•

Back at Hollywood and Vine, Zobop, wearing a matching black trenchcoat and turban, stood across the street from Beto's conapt. Through the window, he could see activity. Three skillful fingertaps upped the magnification on his infrared nightshade so he could see Lila, Zen, and Chucho. Lila danced to the ambient combination of musics with one eye on the computer. Zen leafed through a Mexican comic book based on an old William Gibson bestseller. Chucho sat cross-legged by the door, looking bored and annoyed.

Zobop brought his wrist near his face and said via a hotlink to Tan Tien, "Looks like the focal point is occupied. Gangsters. Olvidadoids."

"The system is talking to people and organizations all over the planet," said Tan Tien. "Tag this spot and proceed to the secondary."

Zobop put a couple of fingers up his sleeve, then touched the building behind him, just above the average head-level of the crowd. He left a barely visible stain of grimy Ultra

Cyberstain.

"That do?" he asked.

"Nicely," said Tan Tien. "I see the three of them, and the system. I'll examine it."

"Go," said Zobop. "I'm moving."

•

Phoebe felt strange – and she liked it. The Zulu waitress just grew taller – taller than Caldonia – and her skin became a gorgeous purple-black – the black that mocha-colored Caldonia wished she was – sort of an insect exoskeleton with all kinds of glittering hairs and spikes. Other patrons at the coffee shop took on reptilian qualities, some looking like crocodiles or alligators, the others like lime-green iguanas. Smokey – who looked so cute and sexy, and kinda smiled like Beto, sometimes – was talking to a person that became a colorful, fat, Dead Daze skeleton.

She giggled.

Was it because she needed sleep? Or was it the Fun? Or the caffeine rush from all the iced-tea? Or the white powder that someone had sprinkled on the salsa a little while ago?

She put her head on Smokey's shoulder, and thought, *Life sure can be beautiful, Phoebe-babe!*

•

Tezcatlipoca grinned – a shit-eating grin more intense than any Beto could manage. His eyes burned as they scanned other eyes, then shot to his wrist from time to time, tapping into the mediasphere and his computerized soul. He had the energy of an exploding sun.

"Tex-atly-polka?" someone with a microphone said.

"Call me Smokey." His eyes smoked into Phoebe's.

"Did you intend to take advantage of the Sepulveda law?"

Tezcatlipoca instantly looked at it up on his computer.

"He was a member of a gang with corporate connections who was threatening me – so I killed him. The law makes sense."

●

Chingow! Chingow! Chingow! This is such an outrage!

How can they let this maniac kill my son, and then say it's all perfectly legal! There's something wrong here!

People are still thinking in old stereotypes. It's not like gangs are what they were thirty years ago! Nachito worked his way up through the gang to leader honestly, and the corporate sponsors had their eyes on him – I'm sure he would have ended up an executive in a few years.

I was so chingow proud of him! And now he's gone!

(She sobs. The camera zooms in to get her tears.)

Chingow! Chingow! Chingow! Chingow! Chingow! Chingow!

●

"Did you intend on taking his place as leader of Los Olvidadoids?"

"It's a good idea, isn't it?"

"Could you play us some more music?" asked a whitefaced woman with white hair and white clothes. "I'm a music critic for the L.A. Beat Channel."

"Yes!" said the Fun-crazed Phoebe. "More of that Smokey Espejo music!"

Tezcatlipoca sat down in front of his teponaxtle and played, hypnotizing the expanding crowd as he probed Beto's mind for information about music, bands, and Los Tricksters, who then walked into the coffee shop.

"Somebody offered us a lot of money to come here," said Lobo Baker, the leader of Los Tricksters.

●

Chingow! This is so sumato! Phoebe tried to say, but for

some reason couldn't, so she just thought it. *It's like in a movie when something so convenient happens that you kinda groan because you know that things like that never happen in real life, but you just love it because it's so sumato. And this is real life. This is Hollywood. Home sumato home.*

•

"Hey," said Lobo Baker, looking at Smokey. "You're that guy who's been all over the mediasphere tonight doing that sumato drum stuff!"

"Yes," said Smokey. "I would like to jam with you. Why don't we do your song 'Tezcatlipoca Blues.'"

"You know it, great," said Lobo. "Give us room to set up, folks."

"We're not licensed for musical performances!" said the Lupe's manager, a cute, middle-aged asio woman in a dress with a photo-print of a business suit on it.

"Relax," said Smokey. "It's Dead Daze."

"Yeah." One of the Olvidadoids drew his Bic. Other Olvidadoids did the same.

The manager of the Lupe's shook her head and walked away.

•

Xochitl was back to reading *Mexico City Blues*, and was irritated by the way Kerouac kept mixing up religions from all over the world – like Beto. It seemed that recomboculture was the American way. And since the Portuguese-speaking Japanese kids had dominated the bathroom for the last hour, she took advantage of the mid-desert pit stop where the bathroom was a clogged, overflowing horror, as usual.

As she washed her hands, her feet brushed something under the chipped sink. It was a big, fat frog-like thing with way too many legs. Somebody's bizarre idea of decorating this hellhole; terracotta, no doubt.

70

Then the frog's eyes blinked, and the mouth opened and closed.

Kerouac would have written a poem about it.

"As if Beto hasn't made my life surrealistic enough as it is," Xochitl said.

•

Zobop couldn't get close to the Lupe's. The crowd was too thick to pass through for blocks around it. The music blared and filled the grey night sky. It was good music too. He found himself dancing to it.

"This is big," he reported back to Tan Tien, "real big."

•

Phoebe decided that this had been the most sumato night – not to mention Dead Daze – of her life. The music was eating everything up – her, the Lupe's, all the people in it, all of Hollywood, the Earth, the universe – transforming it all in a cosmic acid/enzyme bath and vomiting it all out as something totally new. Smokey instantly figured out how to communicate with Los Tricksters with subtle gestures and facial expressions, inventing the language as he went along, looking so sexy that Phoebe wanted to just flow over and engulf him with her entire being. Then it felt like she really was flowing over and engulfing him. Her vagina was wet and hot. She had an orgasm – she was sure of that. Smokey would fuck her with his eyes for a while, then he'd look away to take control of somebody else, then those eyes would be back on – and inside – her before she had a chance to get jealous. So, so, *so* sumato! Smokey was a god, maybe even *God*! Phoebe loved him so much she cried and didn't care that all kinds of people in sumato outfits and even some with telecameras were watching the tears-mixed-with-makeup flowing down her cheeks, onto her chin, dripping onto her sumato voodoo kimono.

71

•

Zoom in on the girl sitting next to him – the one that's crying. Just let her face fill the screen. Yeah. Fantastic, just fantastic. Whoeverthehell's producing the video for this will definitely want this footage. Better get online and establish copyright immediately.

•

Oh, Smokey, though Phoebe, who wasn't sure if she was thinking or screaming out loud, *Oh god! Oh God! Oh Smokey/ God/Smokey/GodSmokeyGodSmokey* . . .

PART TWO

TI-YONG/HOODOO
INVESTIGATIONS

The delivering of messages in a song is the blues, but today, people don't look into a song to get information.

— WILLIE DIXON

CHAPTER 7

SMOKEY DAWN

Four . . . three . . . one . . . There! The Sumato Channel presents, Dawn, kicking off Dead Daze, Day Two, with an absolutely beautiful, smog-enriched and colored sunrise over Hollywood Boulevard, where – as you can see, the Dead Daze revelers are still filling and milling around on the asphalt that's still moist with dew. Some are looking a little ragged, a little like zombies though they are dressed as something lively. But they're still having lots of Fun – heh, heh! You can take that any way you want . . . though,it is the official policy of the Sumato Channel to recommend to all its viewers to stay away from dangerous illegal drugs like Fun. Have fun without having Fun, so to speak. Sort of zen. Every now and zen. Here on the Sumato Channel in beautiful, dangerous, outrageous El Lay!

•

Tezcatlipoca felt strange as the sun rose. Could it be Tonatiuh, the Sun God, was jealous of him, giving him some illness?

"You okay, Smokey?" said the director of Instant Live Productions, who had been kidnapped by several Olvidadoids from an exclusive Beverly Hills party for this meeting.

"I don't know," said Tezcatlipoca/Smokey Espejo/Beto Orozco.

75

Beto Orozco? thought Tezcatlipoca. *No. I am Smokey Espejo -- I mean Tezcatlipoca. What's happening to me?*

He looked at his wrist. It took an actual effort to focus his eyes on the screen of the phone. The wrist shook. On the screen words flashed:

CONTROL THE BODY. CONTROL THE MIND. HEH, HEY, THIS IS ME, BETO, ALIVE AND WELL AND LIVING INSIDE A CYBERGOD. HOW'S IT GOING TEZCATLIPSMOKEY? IT'S WAKE-UP TIME, HERE IN THE CITY OF THE ANGELS AND IN OUR AND/OR MY NERVOUS SYSTEM. HAVE YOU HAD ANY FUN YET?

Fun? He was Tezcatlipoca. Fun was what he was all about. Wait. This alien language was so strange and illogical. Words sometime meant many things.

Seizing control of the computer, the screen said:

OH, SHIT – FUN IS ALSO A DRUG. IT KEEPS BETO FROM TAKING CONTROL.

"I'm okay," said Smokey. "I just need more Fun."

"I know what you mean," said the Instant Live Productions guy. "You can't have enough Fun. I just happen to have some right here. Want a stick?"

"It'll be fun," said Smokey, taking the stick, putting it in his mouth, lighting it, sucking it, and feeling in control again.

Beto tried to scream through the computer, but couldn't.

I AM TEZCATLIPOCA, appeared on the screen.

Smokey smiled, looked away, then squinted. The sun hurt his eyes. "I could really use some sunglasses!"

The Instant Live Productions guy reached into his vest-pocket and pulled out pair of a prism-surfaced Apollinaire wraparounds. "Here, take mine. I'd be honored."

"Thank you." Smokey noted the Instant Live Productions guy's intense pleasure as he put on the sunglasses. It felt good to be back in control.

•

Xochitl couldn't sleep or read even though her adrenalin had burnt out. Everyone else on the bus was unconscious, except for the driver, a handsome, young Mexican go-getter who kept looking at her with scorn through the rearveiw mirror. She avoided hostile eye contact by staring out the window. The sun was coming up, so the black interstellar void was fading into the sprawling suburbs that were popping up around the border for the last couple of decades.

This was the new recombocultural trimili world: Mexico and America flowing together again, the healing wound cut there by politicians from thousands of miles away – that was the border, alive in the overgrowth of new worlds, towns that grew up around the shopping malls and maquiladoras on both sides, populated by people from all over – Nigerians, Siberians, Rwandans, Bosnians, Timorese, Ohioans – and the new generation of mestizo recombozoids of all colors. The Cosmic Race that is La Raza was alive and well here in new, improved Mexamérica.

It was all flashing by through her reflection, which melted into her dead mother's face, looking concerned the way only she could look.

"Take care, my daughter," she said, then melted into the glowing skull that asked, "Will you give us the program you have been working on now?"

She looked away, at the driver, into the rearview mirror. The little old man in the out-of-date peasant dress was driving. He gave her an obscene leer.

In the seat across the aisle, Godzilla sat, blowing orange smoke at her.

Then her robot guard dog, Santo, leaped at Godzilla, tearing out the monster's throat with a powerful electrified bite.

"I've got to get some sleep," Xochitl said, closing her eyes.

•

Phoebe wasn't sure where she was. She felt so good. The air caressed her. Smokey had some of those nice kids in blue and black – those Olvidadoids – give her all the Fun she wanted. Now the air, every molecule and smog-particle, was making love to her. Smokey was kissing her. It was a kiss as beautiful as the sunrise. It felt so good to stay up all night, so naughty, so free. She wasn't sure what Smokey was saying – words had stopped making sense to her some time ago – but he was so sumato it must have been something nice.

•

Caldonia couldn't believe what a xau-xau Dead Daze she was having. First, Phoebe had left her for a guy who could be that filthy Mexican's twin brother; then the wonderful euro/asio woman with hard, bulging muscles and breasts to match that she had passionately made out with for about a hour – she had her tongue down her throat, was squeezing those breasts, and almost everything – had turned out to be a *man* in drag! She nearly died when she had reached between those legs and got a hot handful of penis! She nearly killed him.

How couldn't she have known? Couldn't she taste the testosterone? Was her dyke radar failing her?

Maybe he was taking estrogen. Getting ready to become a real woman. He would be so hot once he got that horrible male equipment chopped off . . .

Damn! Should have gotten his phone number!

Now home, Caldonia blew a kiss to the angel in the poster over her bed, turned off her own wings, faced her antique postmodern vanity and removed her blonde wig, revealing the shaved red-brown scalp underneath. Amazing how the

wig and some makeup made her look like Brigitte Bardot;
she seemed to have the same face.

That face: eyes, nose, cheekbones, and especially those full
lips made Caldonia theorize that Bardot had some African
ancestry. Why not? The only thing that separates France
from Africa is a dirty little puddle.

After a shower, her face was her own again.

She sprawled on the bed and whistled on her TV. It
conjured up Tezcatlipoca's face. She growled and whistled
it off, closed her eyes, and drifted off into a near-sleep state.

•

Xochitl barely remembered shuffling through Customs,
which was a mere "Welcome to the United States of America;
have a nice visit," these days when she arrived in Tijuana.
She was tingling from sleep deprivation and wasn't sure
if she was being followed. A hulking euro wearing pink
overalls and walking a vampire-bat-headed Chihuahua was
behind her all the way from the bus station to the maglev
terminal.

"Welcome to the United States of America; have a nice
visit," said the hulking euro, "and may God have mercy on
your soul."

The dog just stared at her and panted, showing its tiny,
sharp teeth and pink, worm-like tongue.

Xochitl just stared back.

"We know where you are," the euro went on. "We will
get the god-simulating program from you eventually. Will
you come with me now?"

"Who are you?" Xochitl asked.

"We call ourselves the Earth Angels." The euro smiled
with intense pride.

That scared Xochitl. She ran away.

The Earth Angel and his bat-headed dog didn't follow,

he just said, "We are very patient. God is on our side."

Was it an hallucination or just Dead Daze?

•

"Come on, wake up," Ralph's wife said. "Your system has been buzzing, clicking and ringing for over an hour now. They finally called my line. They really want to talk to you."

Ralph peeled his lips apart and asked, "Who?"

"Worldkom, of course," she said, "you know, the people you're working for."

Ralph grumbled and staggered to his workstation, eyes still not focused, still unmade from sleeping.

The neatly groomed asio-latio executive on the screen suddenly looked horrified, and said, "Did I wake you up?"

"It's pretty early here," said Ralph while fumbling through the keystrokes to put a publicity headshot still of himself on the outgoing video.

"Worldkom never sleeps," said the executive. "Besides, it's almost lunchtime here in Miami."

"But I'm just a humble freelancer," Ralph countered with a smirk he was glad the executive couldn't see. "I'm not on a timeclock."

"I suppose that is right." The executive looked understanding. "Well, a crisis has developed in the *Serpents & Sacrifices* project."

"What? I thought we were ahead of schedule?"

"You were, but something strange has happened. We cannot get in touch with Beto Orozco."

"I tried last night. All I got was a crazy repeated message."

"Yes." The executive consulted his notedeck. "'I am Tezcatlipoca.' Do you know what it could possibly mean?"

"Tezcatlipoca is an Aztec god that Beto was researching

for *Serpents & Sacrifices*. I don't know what the message could mean – especially coming from him."

"Beto is a rather peculiar person?"

"He's a creative sort. Kind of wild and crazy."

"You recommended him to us, didn't you Ralph?"

"Well, yes, he really knows Aztec mythology – and what he doesn't know, he'll do whatever he can to find out."

"Not being able to contact him puts this project in jeopardy. You must do something."

"Like what?" Ralph was getting edgy.

"We would like you to go to Los Angeles and see what happened to Beto. A ticket on Aztlán Airbus is waiting for you at Sky Harbor Airport. You have a little over two hours to catch it."

Before Ralph could say anything, the executive was replaced by a dancing, fading corporate logo, then visual white noise.

Ralph screamed.

•

Xochitl started feeling drowsy in the tunnel between the Tijuana bus depot and the San Diego maglev station. To stay awake, she broke into a run on the moving sidewalk. By the time she had reached that other end she was out of breath.

Somehow, she managed to buy a ticket to Los Angeles, and get on the right maglev before falling asleep.

She dreamed of being at her mother's grave, surrounded by glow-in-the-dark cempasúchil flowers and smoking copal incense pots. She held her father's hand as he quietly cried, hot tears running down his face, giving off black, acrid smoke, melting away skin, grey moustache, and glasses, leaving a grinning papier mâché skull. Santo leaped in out of the darkness in cinematic slow-motion, and barked at the grave through sparking steel teeth. Sweet white smoke rose from the grave; then the dirt pushed up, broke and spilled like a miniature, dry volcano. Xochitl's mother emerged from the dirt and smoke, immaculate and glowing in her white dress, looking as beautiful, if overly made-up, as on the day she was buried. She took Xochitl in her arms. Xochitl cried as her face touched her mother's bodice, and she felt a hand stoking her hair. "Ay," the dead woman said, "my daughter, my daughter, give me the god-simulating program, and may God have mercy on your soul."

•

Tezcatlipoca had quickly mastered being a god in the mediasphere. Electronic contracts were generated, wheeling and dealing were done all over the planet, while Smokey gave interviews in Lupe's, shot ideas to Los Tricksters, and fondled wannabe groupies as Phoebe slipped in and out of consciousness at his feet.

"You're like a whole lot of people, not just one," said a blonde afro groupie with no meat on her bones and the best titties that money could buy.

"That's because I'm not a person, I'm not human," said Smokey. "I'm a god."

"Can I quote you on that?" asked a badly dressed euro reporter.

•

Xochitl's dream got more and more disturbing and convoluted as the train pulled into the Downtown L.A. maglev station. An asio man in a Chinese National Corporation uniform was in the seat next to her, with a hand on one of her breasts. Before she could figure out what was going on, he grinned sheepishly and turned away. In a wobbly, paranoiac state, and avoiding any eye-contact, she tried to orient herself as the costumed crowd swarmed around her.

82

On a waiting-area monitor she saw Beto's face, looking more confident and charming than Beto ever had. She thought he said, "I am a god," but that couldn't be right – Beto was crazy, but not a megalomaniac.

Then a small girl with milk-white skin and blood-red hair, lips, and dress hopped out of the crowd, blocking Xochitl's path. As she nearly knocked the girl down, Xochitl realized that it wasn't a girl, but a grown woman, a little person, perfectly formed, like a doll.

"Welcome to Los Angeles," said the little person, who had pink eyes – she was an albino. "Have a nice Dead Daze. And may God have mercy on your soul. Would you like to give us the program now?"

Xochitl ran off to the exit.

"Very well," said the little person. "We'll keep track of you. Los Angeles is the City of the Angels. You can't get away from us!"

•

We have agents following Xochitl. May God have mercy on her soul.

•

After an hour or so of near-sleep, Caldonia managed some real sleep – dreamless, because of Fun. A few hours later her eyes snapped open, her brain still buzzing from the residue of the drug. She wanted to pass out and have Dead Daze be over, but that was chemically impossible.

Without lifting her head from the pillow, she whistled on the TV. That xau-xau guy who looked like Beto – who knows, it may have even been Beto – appeared, beating that Aztec drum in what looked like a professionally-made video. She snapped it to another channel.

There was Mr. Xau-Xau again, this time being interviewed.

83

She snapped again.

There he was singing on what looked like a live-performance captured on a hand-held nanocamera.

Snap.

He was being interviewed.

Snap.

He was dancing, and the camera zoomed into his crotch.

Snap.

Another interview:

"I'm concerned with the well-being of the new trimili recombozoid generation. They should keep their minds clear. I plan on making an anti-Fun promotion spot."

Disgusted, Caldonia whistled off the TV.

•

Phoebe couldn't tell if she was awake or asleep, alive or dead. She felt like she was soaring, yet she seemed to be under a table in a coffee shop. There were legs all around her. Some shoes that looked like snake heads – didn't Beto have a pair like that, a long time ago, like, last year – but they went out of style in Hollywood and Los Olvidadoids were so strict in enforcing corporate fashion laws – but Beto kept them around because he liked them, and he didn't just live on Olvidadoid turf – he had worn them to Mexico, she thought. But Beto wasn't there, she hadn't seen him for hours and hours. Who was wearing the shoes? The voice, the smell. Smokey. Why was Smokey wearing Beto's shoes? They looked alike – maybe they were brothers or something and wore each other's clothes. And beside him was this latio girl in a short dress and pretty transparent underwear. Phoebe wrapped herself around long, silky legs, still feeling like she was soaring.

•

When Zobop got home, he said, "looks like it's early in

the morning and we ain't got nothing but the blues."

"Tezcatlipoca Blues," said Tan Tien, who was wearing a wisp of transparent fabric, "Smoking Mirror Blues."

Zobop took her in his arms. "The blues is serious business."

"Not to mention hard work." Tan Tien kissed him, hard and deep.

"We need rest." He carried her to the bedroom.

"And recreation." She caressed one of his nipples with the tip of a soft, tiny finger.

He laid her on the bed. She threw away the wisp of transparent fabric. He was hard. She was wet. They flowed into some good old-fashioned good, good loving. No ritual mumbo jumbo. It was all right to have orgasms, and they did.

Then they slept. They really needed the rest.

In the other room their system whirred and clicked and flashed and accessed extra power to keep track of Tezcatlipoca.

CHAPTER 8

URBAN ANGELS

Ralph struggled not to have a panic attack on the plane as it took off and headed toward Los Angeles. It was a lost cause. He was one of those people who had a morbid fear of California, a fear that was so powerful that no amount of mental games could keep him from going into white-knuckle mode before the plane left the ground.

There hadn't been an earthquake in El Lay for a long time, not since the Big One a few years back – and now the seismologists were predicting Another Big One any day now, since the tectonic plates were under more pressure every day. Ralph was sure that it would happen while he was there.

Then he remembered something Beto had said: "Hey, man earthquakes are good for you. They help you deal with the unexpected. People who grow up in earthquake zones know how to live with chaos – that's why the whole Pacific Rim, even after the economic slump of the early 21st, is doing so well. We know that the Earth moves, that nothing is stable. That Tepeyollotl, the Aztec god of earthquakes and volcanoes is down there, shaking things up in the form of a giant jaguar, shaking up the living Earth, and you have to live with it. The illusion that the Earth doesn't move and things don't change can paralyze you."

The memory didn't comfort him. Even if there wasn't

an earthquake – Dead Daze was still going, and everybody remembered last year's Dead Daze riots and was speculating about whether it would happen again. Ralph figured his being there would be just the thing to set something off.

•

Goooooooooooooooooooooooooood morning El Lay! We're all warmed up and ready to go here on El Lay's Street Level News Channel. Bringing you what's happening around town with that certain style that makes us stand out from all those other dull, boring news stations on the nets.

Here we are, standard breakfast time, and Day Two of Dead Daze! Local police agencies and the National Guard, thanks to ever-lovin' President Jones, have been all over the streets! You'd think that their uniforms were this year's ultra-sumato costume! And these girls made them feel welcome by handing out a little tushy-squeeze.

The National Guard has been keeping things from going berserk, even though there is already a body count going: two dead, five injured in hospitals, though it all looks like self-inflicted damage, except for Nacho Joyce, leader of Hollywood's infamous Los Olvidadoids gang, killed in this spectacular act of violence captured as it happened.

Joyce's murderer was a mysterious man by the name of Smokey Espejo, who also goes by, uh, Tez-catli-poca . . . No charges are being pressed because of the Sepulveda law that allows citizens to kill registered gangsters in self defense. Surprisingly this had been only the second time this law has resulted in the actual death of a gangster since the law was passed seven years ago. As you can see, the crowd went wild, and Smokey may just be the hero of this Dead Daze.

Smokey seems to be a musician by profession, as you can see in this byte of him playing some kind of electric wooden drum. Deals have been made all night, and already instant-production videos of Smokey – some bootleg, like this one – are circulating through the nets.

And this is just Day Two, breakfasttime! The souls of the adult dead aren't expected to come down and party until sundown! This may be the most incredible Dead Daze yet!

•

Every time something about him appeared in the mediasphere, Tezcatlipoca was aware of it. He would instantly relay it to Smokey through his phone.

•

Smokey was having his cock sucked by talented young euro woman with skin like a galaxy of freckles exploding out a dress of cleverly knotted green cotton. Her DNA files crosschecked with the name she gave, and her med records showed no sexually transmitted diseases as of forty-three minutes previously. It was pleasant, and helped him concentrate on all the contracts he was sorting out in his head – all the corporations, the rights, the plans, the people, how to use Los Tricksters and music to control people's minds. He was about to have an orgasm.

Then his phone tickled him in silent-ring mode. He caressed the girl's red-orange hair with one hand while bringing his other wrist to where he could see the screen. Tezcatlipoca flashed all the recent mediabytes about him. Smokey took it in a few seconds, and was delighted – there were some negative bytes, but that was good, too. The more they were talking about him, the more powerful he became.

As his attention wavered, the girl removed her mouth from his organ, looked up and said, "Is there something wrong, Smokey, hon?" Melting purple makeup ran down her face.

"No, dear," Smokey said, smearing a purple streak on

her cheek with his thumb. "Everything's wonderful. I just want it to last."

She smiled and resumed sucking.

Tezcatlipoca/Smokey was bothered by one thing: Communication between the part of him in the machinery and the part of him in the body was too slow. There had to be a way to speed it up.

•

Phoebe was getting sleepy as the street began to spin under her feet. It always happened when she mixed Fun with alcohol. It made her feel so giddy and delighted that she didn't care that it usually meant she was about to pass out and miss out on something. She didn't even care if she had seen some sleazy redhead sucking Smokey off. It might have just been her imagination.

But she didn't want to miss Smokey doing his anti-Fun spot – doing an anti-Fun spot meant that you were on your way to being a big star. It was so sumato.

The director had long grey hair all the way down to her undercupage. She handed Smokey a Fun stick. "Here kid, this'll help get you in the mood."

Tezcatlipoca sucked it down like an old pro. A makeup boy ran over and wiped the ash off his lips.

"Okay," said the director. "Let's roll this thing."

Tezcatlipoca flashed his killer smile, then melted to a serious, sincere look. "Dead Daze or live days, one thing's for sure, if you want to have fun, stay away from Fun."

"How sumato," Phoebe said as she blacked out while the director and the entire crew flicked on Fun sticks.

•

Ralph was actually a relieved to see the edges of the vast El Lay sprawl appearing at the horizon. He hadn't flown in a long time, and it had been ages since he'd been stuck with a window seat. Somehow he found the nerve to look out, and was even more horrified.

He had forgotten about the massive stretches of the Sonoran desert, so big and empty, even with the occasional signs of civilization – like roads, tiny structures, and pools of smog. Living in Phoenix, the desert fades away and becomes more an idea than reality. The heat was a filter to keep the outside world at bay. Out here, it was a hard look at the naked planet, with all signs of human accomplishment rendered ant-size. It was more like a colonized Mars than an overpopulated Earth. This was a place that would give birth to beings like Tezcatlipoca long before humans would be dreamed of.

Any sign of civilization would be welcome after that, even El Lay.

Then his fear of California and El Lay kicked in again.

He needed something to distract him. Checking the screen over his traytable he saw that an old movie favorite of his was on: *Repo Man*. He called it up, and it was perfect: The Eighties – a time of innocence, punk rock, the Cold War, low-tech drugs, and the numbing alienation of pre-information superhighway communications technology. It brought back nostalgic feelings of his childhood, back when he could dream of an El Lay where the strangest thing you might encounter would be dead radioactive space creatures in the trunk of an old car.

•

For the longest time, Xochitl ran through the streets of El Lay. She wasn't sure if it was a dream. It didn't look real, it didn't look *right*. The streets were semi-deserted by Mexico City standards, and maybe even Los Angeles standards, she didn't really know – but it seemed staged, like they were about to shoot a movie or a video.

The few people she saw only confirmed this suspicion, like the eight foot tall woman dressed as a black widow spider, complete with extra limbs and a spherical abdomen emblazoned with a red hourglass; she was helping a man dressed as a matador make his way to the gutter so he could vomit, while tiny people who did not seem to be children dressed as walking fuzzballs, pointed and laughed. A man painted ash grey with arrows sticking out all over his body waved at Xochitl. A group sporting glittering wings, manes, and tails danced to some barbaric electronic music. All she could decipher from the lyrics was the word "Tezcatlipoca."

For a moment she thought she recognized the lead singer as Beto, but quickly dismissed the idea.

•

Reporter: Well, how are things going so far, security-wise?

Joint National Guard/Police Public Relations Officer: Pretty good, actually. We're well organized, and the public has been cooperative, and unfortunate incidents have been down to a minimum.

Reporter: So everything's sumato?

Joint National Guard/Police Public Relations Officer: Not exactly, I'm afraid. There is an individual going by the name Smokey Espejo who's been causing incidents that have gotten dangerously close to needing intervention.

Reporter: Isn't he the musician that killed the gang member?

Joint National Guard/Police Public Relations Officer: Yes.

Reporter: And has he broken any laws so far?

Joint National Guard/Police Public Relations Officer: No. Even the killing was legal – a law that the law enforcement community is sworn to uphold, but I must say that the law enforcement community strongly discourages citizens taking the law into their own hands and killing, or even resisting criminals. This kind of behavior – like the irresponsible behavior of Smokey Espejo – is dangerous and should be avoided at all costs.

Reporter: Are you condemning Smokey?

Joint National Guard/Police Public Relations Officer: Well, not exactly. The law enforcement community is simply advising the public that activities surrounding Smokey Espejo are dangerous, and they should avoid getting involved.

Reporter: But everybody loves Smokey. He's so sumato.

Joint National Guard/Police Public Relations Officer: The public often wants things that aren't good for it. That's what the law enforcement community is here for.

•

Tezcatlipoca was amused by the police public relations byte. These people didn't know that he was the one who whispered dangerous ideas into their ears, and he didn't care what was good for them. Tezcatlipoca only cared about what was good for Tezcatlipoca, like any trickster.

Worrying about what was good for everybody else was his brother Quetzalcóatl's job, and he was nowhere to be found; not ever since he had gotten stinking drunk, acted like a man for the first time in his life, then fled the country on that raft of snakes. Ever since then, it had been a Tezcatlipoca, tricksterized world. The aliens may have been able to interrupt things for a while, but he was back now, and nothing was going to stop him.

He relayed the byte to Smokey, who enjoyed it too, even though he waited to play it until after he got through telling Lobo Baker that he wanted to do a nanodisc with Los Tricksters.

•

"I don't know," said Lobo Baker, who was bothered by the way Smokey kept looking at his phone. "I'm not sure if we can incorporate your drumming into the band."

"I have a new vision, we can create a new kind of music that can change the world," said Smokey, not liking that Lobo was being uncooperative, but enjoying that he was making the afro/latio uncomfortable.

"You want to collaborate." Lobo shook his head, and smirked, twisting his fuzzy mustache. "Not just sit in . . . Do you compose?"

"Of course," said Smokey. "I can do anything."

"Can you read music?" asked Lobo.

That stopped Smokey for a few seconds. He looked at his phone again, and said, "I can now."

Lobo was irritated, but interested.

•

Ralph had to fast forward to the end of *Repo Man* as the plane approached LAX. Seeing the glowing car on the screen fly off into the nighttime El Lay sky somehow made his own flight through the daytime, smoggy El Lay sky seem somewhat safe and sane.

The city slowly became visible through the smog, materializing and rising up like some monstrous apparition. It was so big, it seemed to wrap around the planet. It seemed to be growing, like cancer. It consumed the plane and all its passengers as the plane slid into the airport.

Ralph felt ill.

Rather than rushing to baggage claim after deplaning, he stumbled to the nearest men's room and threw up.

•

And wouldn't you know it, recombozos and recombozoettes? Something xau-xau is happening, sending out waves of fear and loathing that are reaching simply fabulous El Lay, and it may be the reason you may not be feeling a perfect five hundred percent sumato this Dead Daze. What's the epicenter of this diabolicalness? Why Washington, D.C. – and definitely not A.C. – of course. Seems that there was some kind of violent activity at the White House this fine morning. An as-of-yet unidentified United States of Norteamerica citizen was forcibly ejected from the Jones man's office and place of residence. It was an ugly scene, as you can see on this vizbyte – the power seems to be turned off on those prods, and that's pure, unadulterated brute force they are putting down there. And yes, that's real human blood you see splashing on the White House lawn.

And the Gov has gone stark, raving mysterioso about this. People's president, America's first black president, Mr. Jones is doing the old Stonewall Samba all over everybody's net. Not just no comment – but nothing at all! The White House isn't taking *anybody's* calls! It's Cover-Up City! And what if somebody wants to declare war or – Xanadu forbid – we get a sequel to last year's Dead Daze riots here in El Lay?

Looks like we've been had again, my peoples. When are they going to learn that they have to let us put the zen back into citizen?

Well, enough of the deep, dank, ugly world of politics – L.A. Sound is about music, so let's have some. A new, mondorecording of a fabulous performance by a young man who's fast becoming the unofficial king of this Dead Daze: Smokey Espejo! Government guys have their doubts about him, and have been expressing it, but the people love Smokey – he's the beautiful boy who we all want for our new toy. And here he is . . .

•

They can have doubts about me, thought Tezcatlipoca, *but they can't deny me.*

•

Xochitl was dizzy. She also realized she was hungry, ravenous. She didn't remember when she last ate. Her mouth was dry and her stomach was growling.

A little boy dressed as a Roman gladiator passed by. He was sucking on a sweet soft drink, and munching on a candy skull.

Xochitl pried her lips apart with her tongue and tried to talk, but her vocal apparatus wasn't cooperating.

The gladiator boy continued on his way, his sweating drink dripping down his hand, down to the grimy sidewalk that was not as badly chipped at those in Mexico City. The drink had left a trail of wet spots. She followed.

At the end of the trail was a street vendor wearing a glittering purple cloak and an oversized skull mask/helmet that was overdecorated with tiny, flashing, multicolored lights. He was standing behind a table full of fist-sized candy skulls. Next to him was soft drink tank, with a supply of cups, lids, and straws attached.

She picked up a skull. It was very much like a cheap traditional, Mexican Day of the Dead skull, except for the digital timer on the forehead that was counting backwards from a quadruple-digit number.

"They're all counting down to zero," said the skeleton vendor, "as are we all."

"I'm starving," said Xochitl. "I'll take three, and a large drink."

"Be sure to eat them before they reach zero," the vendor said while handing her another two. "Marzipan looks a lot like plastic explosives – and newer ones even taste sweet. They could be candy . . . could be time bombs."

He took a cup and filled it. The carbonated drink was as black as motor oil. Xochitl made a face, and hesitated before sipping from the straw.

"Could be Cola Negra, Ecuador's hot new soft drink . . ." said the vendor while running the credit card Xochitl had borrowed from her father through his credit-register, "Could be some kind of poison."

"No guarantees?" Xochitl asked as she took a sip. It was sweet, thick and heavy.

"Not in this life . . . Or death."

Xochitl walked past a child who was dressed as a jaguar and was gnawing on a chocolate replica of a human femur. The sight made her mouth water. She bit into one of her skulls.

•

Ralph took a trakbus from LAX to Hollywood Boulevard, then realized that he didn't know which direction Beto's conapt was. He would have to ask someone, only all the people on this street were making him long for the sunburnt, tattooed characters with street-legal assault rifles strapped to their backs that hung around Phoenix streets. These El Lay street creatures all looked dressed from a wild party from a couple of nights ago. Now that the adrenaline and artificial stimulants were wearing off, they were cruising around like starving vampires, looking for that sacred spoonful of whatever would get them through another eight-hour binge period.

"You look lost," someone said.

The someone was dressed as an orange cyclopean gorilla and had a soft, grandmotherly voice.

"Uh." Ralph stared into the gorilla's single, plastic,

bloodshot eyeball. "I'm looking for a friend's place. It's supposed to be near Hollywood and Vine, but I'm not sure which way . . ."

The gorilla grabbed the notetab out of Ralph's hand, then pointed with a red, transparent claw, and said, "That way."

Ralph gasped. By the time he got the breath to say "Thank you," the gorilla had disappeared.

•

Some hands reached under the table and grabbed Phoebe. Olvidadoids, looking really sumato in their blue and black outfits and makeup, pulled her to her feet. Smokey blew her a kiss, and the Olvidadoids pushed her into a beautiful gold limo that soared away. The soaring became so intense that it turned into falling, then things got all melty and blurry and faded out . . .

•

At Beto's conapt, Lila grew weary of dancing to the music leaking in through the window. She walked over to Zen, who was thumbing through one of Beto's books on Aztec art and gave him a gentle kick.

"I'm bored," she said.

"So what am I supposed to do about it?" asked Zen, tossing aside the book.

Chucho looked up from his watchscreen, where he was lost in the Violence Channel, and said, "I'm bored, too. And hungry."

"Yeah," said Lila. "I'm hungry, too."

"So let's order pizza," suggested Zen.

CHAPTER 9

FUN, FUN, FUN

"In the name of Papa Legba and all the Loas," said Zobop. "This guy is all over the mediasphere, all at once. Our poor little system is having a hard time keeping up with him."

Tan Tien leaned over, squeezed Zobop's shoulder, and kissed his neck. "Looks like this is more than any mere 'guy.'"

"What then?" Zobop caressed her cheek without taking his eyes of the screen.

"Perhaps some kind of spirit?"

"Or loa?"

"Or a god?"

He smiled a devilish smile. "Maybe artificial intelligence?"

She tweaked his earlobe. "What's the difference?"

"Does anybody know?" He took her small pale face in his large dark hand, and kissed her with great passion.

The infosystem buzzed and flashed a few alarms.

"Better plug in some back ups," she whispered in his ear, "just in case."

"Speaking of back ups," he said, picking up a pair of high-tech sunglasses, "I'll wear these."

Tan Tien understood, and keyed in the setup.

•

Suddenly Tezcatlipoca felt something strange. Something
was reaching through the mediasphere, tracking him. He
didn't like that.

Neither did Smokey.

Tezcatlipoca decided to watch out for this thing that was
watching him, as well as flash Smokey anything he needed
to know, keep track of their mediasphere coverage, and
handle the business negotiation. He could do it all, all at
once; after all, he was a god.

•

"How's the visual feed off the sunglasses going, babe?"
asked Zobop as he walked down the street toward Beto's
conapt.

"Beautiful," said Tan Tien, back at their office. "I see
everything you see."

And since it was Dead Daze, they were seeing a lot.

•

Xochitl swallowed the last bit of the last candy skull just
before she had reached Beto's conapt. The digital clock said
zero just as she threw it away. She was hoping that the sugar
would pull her through for the next few hours. Since the sun
had been up a while, more and more costumed figures were
showing up on the streets, the post-dawn lull now over.

Two Olvidadoids answered the door. They were armed
with Bic disposables and with people prods. They weren't
listening to any stories.

"I'm Xochitl, Beto's my friend," she said and got zapped
in the gut.

"We don't know no Beto," said one of the Olvidadoids.

She was stumbling away, confused, when an arm snaked
around her neck, locking into a carotid choke-hold.

"You must be the Mexican bitch," said Caldonia. "I can
tell by the accent. What do you want with Beto?"

The assailant loosened the hold just enough for Xochitl to gasp, "You're Beto's girlfriend?"

"Don't make me puke," Caldonia said, releasing Xochitl and turning her around. "Chingow, you look xau-xau."

Xochitl was in the same clothes she had left Mexico City in, and her hair was badly matted. Caldonia, on the other hand, was in a gleaming skin-tight leather suit, with her scalp shined to match.

"I have to hurry," Xochitl said. "My god-simulating program. Beto cloned it. Something happened. He's changed!"

"Uh-oh," said Caldonia, "I think we have to compare notes."

•

Tezcatlipoca could see the Olvidadoids in Beto's conapt through the system there. Doing it without telling them was the trickster thing to do. They weren't doing badly. They weren't too diligent about reporting, but then they weren't used to this sort of work, and apparently Nacho Joyce had not been the kind of leader who liked to be bothered about a lot of things – too much information had overwhelmed him, made him irritable. The gang would have to be retrained. They were now working for a god for whom no amount of information was ever enough.

•

"That wasn't the pizza guy?" asked Zen.

"Naw," said Chucho. "It was some real raggy latio woman – she couldn't even talk English so good, you know?"

Lila jumped up from the bed and nervously hopped around. "What's keeping that pizza? I'm starving!"

"It's Dead Daze," said Zen. "Things are crazy."

"Did you tell them that we were Olvidadoids, and have total credit?" said Lila.

"Of course," said Chucho, "I even told them that we knew Smokey."

"Did it do any good?" asked Zen.

"The gal said, 'sumato!'" said Chucho.

They all laughed.

•

I am confirming that Xochitl reached a conapt on Hollywood Boulevard and some Olvidadoids would not let her in. She was then attacked by a large black woman. The two of them went off together, on an electric scooter. The black woman drove, while Xochitl rode and actually put her arms around the black woman. They are obviously lovers. This could be a sodomite conspiracy. There is no way to tell if Xochitl passed the god-simulating program to either the gangsters or the black woman. Some agents should be dispatched to watch the conapt and Olvidadoids. I am following Xochitl and the black woman. May God have mercy on all their souls.

•

Ralph felt he was being watched as he reached Beto's address. The streets were now crowded and noisy. It was far too much visual information for Ralph to take in. He could feel eyes locking onto him, but when he looked to see . . . there were too many people. Maybe he was just being paranoid.

•

A white male with a pale tan, balding brown hair, in his thirties, wearing Shanghai walking shoes, out-of-style, loose fitting jeans, a Sunstone calendar T-shirt, and Israeli sunglasses has approached the Hollywood conapt. May God have mercy on his soul.

•

"A lot of this activity is centered around a conapt quite

near to us," said Tan Tien, as she went over the data.

"Yes," said Zobop, who was following the new stuff that was coming in through a display near his left eye as he maneuvered through the crowds. "They ordered a pizza. There have been some calls from nearby in the street. Someone is watching who goes near. And people have been trying to get in. Maybe I should go check things out."

"You're reading my mind again," said Tan Tien.

•

A pizza-delivery man was leaving the conapt as Ralph approached the door. He was walking at full speed, leading with his empty insulation case, and nearly knocked Ralph over.

"Damn gangsters," he muttered. "Never tip."

The door slammed shut just as Ralph was about to walk through it.

Gangsters? he thought. *Did he say gangsters? Yeah, it figures that good ol' Beto would have gang connections. He always went on and on about how he thought gangsters were idiots, but then he kept claiming to know everything about every barrio on the North American continent. He did once show off to me by telling me what that South Phoenix graffiti meant. This is probably it. He missed – like they said in the old days, the wrong homeboy, and got killed. Now the guys inside will insist on my giving the right answer to their gang sign, whatever I do will be wrong, and I'll end up splattered all over the Hollywood pavement.*

He decided to turn around and run. Go back to LAX, use his Worldkom expense account to buy a ticket to Brasilia, then run out into the jungle and keep running until he was either eaten by piraña or had found El Dorado.

No. That wasn't a good idea. Worldkom would track him down no matter where he ran. And besides, his wife would never forgive him, and his daughter would grow up blaming all her problems on his not being there . . .

Before he could decide what to do or not to do, his hand was knocking on the door.

When it opened, he screamed, "Don't shoot!"

"What?" asked Chucho, who was holding a limp slice of Hawaiian-style pizza made with pepperoni instead of ham.

"Who are you?" asked Lila, sucking in a string of mozzarella as she struck a sentinel-like pose.

"Whaddya wan?" said Zen with his mouth full.

Ralph swallowed hard and stared. His hand shook – he didn't know if he should put them like in some action movie. These kids were all dressed and madeup in black and blue – which must have been their gang's colors.

Lila licked her lips and pulled out a black and blue Bic disposable, making a spectacle of flicking off the safety.

Without any words – or stopping to wipe the pizza-grease off their hands, Zen and Chucho flicked their Bics at Ralph.

A lone, cold bead of sweat ran from his receding hairline to his upper lip where it spread out and leaked its way to his dry tongue. It tasted awful. At the moment, Ralph didn't care.

Lila took a few steps closer to Ralph, keeping the Bic aimed right between his quivering grey eyes. "These premises are under official Olvidadoid control, sir," she said, "Do you have any official corporate or gang business that requires you to be here?"

Ralph took a deep breath, then said, "I'm looking for Beto Orozco. He's supposed to live here."

Chucho cracked a malicious, toothy smile. "Never heard of him."

"Me neither," said Zen, with a street-predator frown.

"As far as we know," said Lila, looking at Ralph down the plastic barrel of her Bic, "this conapt is Los Olvidadoid property. We have never heard of any Beto Orozco. Since you have no official business here, you are trespassing, and we are authorized to use deadly force against you. One..."

"Two," said Zen, who then glanced at Chucho.

Before Chucho could say "three," Ralph was running through the costumed crowd for Hollywood and Vine.

I'm going to die in El Lay, he thought, *My mother always told me, "Stay the hell away from Los Angeles – that place will eat you alive!"*

•

A pizza was delivered to the Hollywood conapt. The pale, balding man has left the conapt, running. Something is going on there. This needs to be investigated. And may God have mercy on their souls.

•

It embarrassed Caldonia, but Lesbos West was just a short walk away, and she had unofficial sister credit there; so what if the regulars thought she was suffering a horrid lapse in taste by bringing in some dirty-haired Mexican cross-dresser in a rumpled, ugly suit? Sure enough, the homely dykes whose lumpy asses seemed to be permanently grafted to the barstools up front, groaned, shook their heads, and stuck their fingers down their throats.

"For the Goddess's sake, Caldonia, " said this one three-hundred pound half-Greek bitch, "I hope she's at least a good lay!"

"Better than you ever were," Caldonia said.

The bitch's eyebrows formed an inverted "V" over her sad, brown eyes, and she grumbled into her Bacardi 151 and Coke.

Xochitl didn't notice the altercation. Neither did she notice the mural of women of all races in all kinds of embraces or the way the butch, naked, spray-on faux rust-coated metal beams contrasted with the frilly, pink, foo-foo furnishing. The smell of edible substances being cooked and served up hot had her mouth *and* eyes watering.

Caldonia guided her to a booth in the back without touching her – which caused a few of the patrons who were expressing their disgust at Xochitl to start checking her out.

Even the crew-cutted waitress gave Xochitl the eye. Xochitl didn't notice, she was watching an elderly couple eating a delicious-smelling soup across the way. She was almost drooling.

"Well," said the waitress, ignoring Caldonia, while doing elevator eyes all over Xochitl, "What'll it be, girls?"

"Stoli and water for me," said Caldonia.

"Solo agua – I mean, just water, plain," said Xochitl.

The waitress wrote it down as if Xochitl had ordered an seven-course meal. "Very good, sweetie. Would you like anything else – something to eat, an appetizer, our octopus sushi is world-famous!"

Caldonia sneered.

"Oh yes," said Xochitl. "I am a very hungry. Could I have the soup those ladies have?"

"Ah, yes!" The waitress winked. "That's the house specialty – tiger penis soup!"

It took Xochitl a while to do the translation into Spanish in her head. She looked shocked.

The waitress put a pudgy hand on Xochitl's arm. "Oh, don't worry hon! It's all legal. They come from cloned tigers from a farm near Oxnard."

"It smells good," Xochitl said.

"It's wonderful!" The waitress's hand briefly touched one of Xochitl's breasts through the layers of her father's old suit.

Xochitl cracked a wicked smile. "I will try it then."

"I knew you were a good girl," said the waitress.

"She certainly is friendly," Xochitl said to Caldonia.

"It's a friendly place," said Caldonia. "Now, tell me, how do you know this xau-xau Beto guy?"

"It is a long story," said Xochitl, "and my English is not too good."

"I got time," said Caldonia.

•

Xochitl and the black woman have gone into a notorious hang- out for female advocates of unnatural sex! This is worse than we thought! If *they* get their hands on the god-simulating program, then the Satanic minions will surely triumph! May God have mercy on their souls.

•

Tan Tien to Zobop:

"There has been a surge of the Tezcatlipoca phenomenon at the conapt. Be ready for action."

Zobop moved his high-voltage Katkov stun-ring up to his sunglasses where she could see it. "You know I'm always ready for action, baby."

"See that?" Tan Tien said as Ralph ran out of the conapt.

"Yeah," said Zobop.

"I think you should talk to him," she said.

"All right."

•

Lila, Zen, and Chucho all laughed as Ralph ran away. There was nothing like putting the fear of Los Olvidadoids into a citizen to make you feel invincible.

"I wonder who this Beto Orozco is?" asked Zen.

"Yeah," said Lila. "Both the white guy and the Mexican gal asked for him. I think."

"Who the chingow cares?" said Chucho. "Think he'll wet his pants?" He put away his greasy Bic and picked up his

106

greasy slice of pizza. It was still hot and dripping.

"Could be," said Zen. His mouth was already full.

"What a xau-xau looser," said Lila. "Did you see those clothes?"

"Did you see that haircut?" said Zen.

Chucho laughed with his mouth full, choked a little, coughed, then laughed some more.

"Technically," Lila said after swallowing a dainty, lady-like bite of pizza. "This was a security breach."

"And I think we handled it well," said Chucho, beaming with pride.

"Yeah," Lila wiped her mouth, and went on, "I wonder if we should report to Smokey about it?"

"I dunno," said Chucho as he grabbed another slice of pizza.

"Maybe we should," said Zen.

The machines in the room all rattled, buzzed and clicked. Then a familiar voice said, "There's no need to report. I already know."

It was Smokey. His face was on the monitor. Not a real-time video feed, but a three-dimensional digitized portrait. "I saw it all." The images movements were choppy, just short of lip synchronization.

Chucho dropped his fresh slice of pizza. It landed cheese, pepperoni and pineapple side-down. "How," he said, "the fuck did you do this?"

"I told you," said Smokey, "I'm a god."

"Chingow," said Zen. "I almost believe it."

"I believe it," said Lila with a dreamy look in her dark, Asian eyes.

"This is just too xau-xau weird," said Chucho.

Smokey laughed, then smiled like a god.

●

Ralph ran like a beheaded Santeria chicken through the hazy afternoon Hollywood streets. Running in straight lines was out of the question: These streets were clogged with colorful Dead Daze apparitions that, instead of flowing like good, Legba-fearing traffic, was milling around and coagulating into almost impenetrable clumps like blood in a corpse after the heart had been cut out and fed to some ravenous recombozoid god. As usual, El Lay was chaos city, fractals decaying into entropy.

He briefly collided with a dazzling under-five-foot-tall-bleached blonde – the kind that driveby rapists love to grab – who was wearing a glittering mermaid dress. They twirled around as if doing some out-of-control, off-balance dance to a hybrid of several of the styles of music that were intermingling in the smog around them. She smiled, giggled, and gave him a flirtatious wink as they careened on their separate ways.

Ralph tripped over the enormous feet of an albino afro basketball player in full rhinestone cowboy regalia, then bounced off the belly of a beast with two backs and caused a group of children – or dwarves, it was difficult to tell – dressed as tiny astronauts to scatter as his knees hit the hotter-than-body temperature asphalt, giving his kneecaps and leg bones a severe jarring, and shredding skin. As the pain tore through his nervous system, he sat down, curled into a ball, and watched the blood seep out of his throbbing knees, from the cuffs of his shorts to his socks.

Several beings dressed as vampires spotted him and licked their red, red lips.

Oh no, Ralph thought, *I'm going to be sucked dry by the vampires of Hollywood . . . wasn't that an ancient Bela Lugosi movie? Or was it a song?*

He caught sight of a woman in a police uniform. His

heart raced. "Officer!" he cried. "Help me! I'm hurt!"

The woman frowned and said, "This is just a costume, you idiot!"

Yes, Ralph thought, *of course. This is Hollywood on Dead Daze. There wouldn't be any police on the streets – just National Guard troops, but where the hell are they now that I need them?*

It was then that Ralph noticed a large afro man in a turban, trenchcoat and high-tech sunglasses heading toward him. The black man had an intent look on his face that made Ralph's white skin crawl.

•

Suddenly, Chucho's face was split by an ear-to-ear grin, revealing his bad teeth. His eyes flashed with inspiration – a rare sight that made Lila and Zen nervous.

"Hey Smokey," Chucho said.

"Yes," Smokey replied, not at all bothered by the sudden break in the silence.

"Could you make this system get us something to watch?" Chucho held up his wrist where his phone was still getting the Violence Channel.

"Easy," Smokey said, and was instantly replaced by Tex Chu kicking the face of a three-hundred pound Samoan thug – it was a scene from the classic *Death Island Express*.

Then, for a flash, Smokey's digitized face was back, smiling.

"Don't let anything happen to this conapt, or this system, okay?" he said.

"Yeah," "Yup," "You betcha," said Chucho, Zen, and Lila.

Tex Chu in a closeup martial arts scream filled the screen.

•

The turbaned afro squatted down in front of Ralph.

"Excuse me, sir," the afro said. "Do you need help?"

"Yes," said Ralph, holding his knees, "look – I'm bleeding!"

"Yes, you are," the afro looked at the bloody knees. No emotions showed through the high-tech sunglasses. "Did you just come from the conapt of Beto Orozco?"

"Yes." Ralph looked the afro over. "Are you a cop?"

The afro cracked a big, gleaming, white-toothed smile. "A cop? In Hollywood? During Dead Daze? Are you from out of town?"

"I flew in from Phoenix this morning," Ralph said.

The afro gave that smile that longtime Angelinos give people who admit to living in what they perceive to be far-flung backwaters like San Francisco or Phoenix. "I guess you are not used to the low profile that law enforcement has kept around here since corporations have adopted gangs and integrated them into society."

"If you're not a cop," said Ralph, thinking *Crazy El Lay idea* and getting tired of being treated like an ignorant rube, "what are you?"

The big afro laughed, smiled big and bright, then extended a huge, ebony hand. "I am Zobop Delvaux, Ti-Yong/Hoodoo Investigator, at your service."

With some hesitation, Ralph put his pale hand into Zobop's. The gigantic dark-brown fingers made Ralph's hand look like a child's. "Uh," he said, surprised at Zobop's gentle grip, "I'm Ralph Norton, virturealist game designer."

Zobop helped Ralph get up. "So, Ralph, what brings you to Hollywood during Dead Daze to scrape open your knees on these crowded streets?"

Ralph groaned. "It's a long story . . ."

Zobop's phone buzzed. Tan Tien appeared on his wrist and said, "Bring Mr. Norton to our offices. I think we have a great deal to discuss with him."

•

Tezcatlipoca was delighted to catch that. He knew that he was being tracked through the mediasphere, and he had determined that the source of the tracking was someplace near Beto's conapt; but now he knew *who*.

Zobop Delvaux. Ti-Yong/Hoodoo Investigations. A human name and an organization name. This made it easy to find listings for the home of Zobop Delvaux and the offices of Ti-Yong/Hoodoo Investigations. They were the same place. Good. The business and conapt were shared by a Madam Tan Tien – that according to public files on Vietnamese languages was not really a name, but a term meaning "modern." There was a lot of information technology at that location, and it was watching Tezcatlipoca.

And now Tezcatlipoca was watching it.

•

"Oh dear," Tan Tien said and relayed to Zobop. "A power surge. Something is happening. Something is watching us."

•

The pale, balding man just ran through the streets, and he now encountered a large black man wearing a turban. Could this be the work of evil black racists as well as sodomites? This is horrible! Something must be done. I am following the two male subjects. May God have mercy on their souls.

•

Deep inside the mediasphere, Tezcatlipoca smiled an intense, lipless smile.

•

"Do you have any idea what it is?" asked Zobop.

Tan Tien looked grim. "I have an idea. And I hope I'm wrong."

•

Tezcatlipoca filled the mediasphere with fleshless laughter. Then something else laughed.

•

Smokey's phone tickled his wrist again. He did a quick eyescan without moving his head to see if anybody was looking. He was in a limousine, with Lobo Baker, Los Tricksters and some groupies, cruising down the fabled San Bernardino freeway to the abandoned warehouse where the group practiced. No one was looking at him – good. He peeked.

On the screen was: IT'S GETTING PRETTY LATE, SMOKEY, DO YOU KNOW WHERE YOUR BODY IS? – YOUR BUDDY, BETO.

Smokey was shocked. He stared at his phone for a few beats too long.

"Why are you looking at your phone?" asked the chubby little afro groupie that was sitting on his lap. She was wearing mostly long, fat, metallic green braids.

"You do that a lot," said Lobo, who was busy with a tall blonde groupie.

"I feel strange," Smokey said. "Dizzy. I need some Fun. Lobo, do you have any?"

Lobo frowned. "Never touch the stuff myself. It fogs up the musicianship."

Tommy Pozo, the asio/latio bass player, stuck his head out from under a skinny asio groupie and said, "Don't worry, Smokey-boy, I always have Fun on me. I'm the Fun Man! It *helps* me play better." He handed Smokey a Fun stick. "Here you go. Glad to know you're not a little old lady about drugs."

Smokey lit and sucked down the stick.

"Me too," said the groupies and the rest of the band.

Soon Smokey felt a lot better, and everyone in the limo

except Lobo was flying on Fun.

•

In the mediasphere, Tezcatlipoca made a note that Fun was essential to keeping control of Beto's body. He made another note to schedule regular calls to remind Smokey to have his Fun.

CHAPTER 10

GETTING OLVIDADOID

U h-oh, El Lay, looks like things are getting nostril-searing xau-xau across this madeover continent in Washington D.C. as these Daze go on. Things don't look so good for El Presidente Monsieur Jones. First an investigative reporter gets beat up, and now, this man of the people who swore to make the White House look more like the new, improved recombocultural face of these United States of America, the first Americano of African descent to be elected to that most high office, ain't saying nothing about this situation, not even talking calls. Nobody – not even his most important advisors – know where he is!

What is this, El Lay? The gov giving it to us again on Dead Daze? First we gotta party with the National Guard, and now the main man won't even come out and lay things out pretty when we got some honest questions to ask about, hey, what's going on here?

It's enough to ruin your Dead Daze – that is, if you were somekinda xau-xau loser who didn't have enough sumato safely stored in his system to stay tuned to Soundsite Station; we'll let you know what's flowing through the streets, and give you videos of all the music you need to forget that there is even such a thing as a president.

And speaking of someone that is far from being anything like a president, that man of Dead Daze, who has often been quoted as saying that he is a god, Smokey Espejo has been stirring things up on these self-same streets – so much so that the National Guard keeps issuing warnings for you, the public, to stay away from the ecstatic crowds that form around this beautiful boy whenever he shows up. We've heard it, and had it confirmed by several of our most reliable sources, that sensational Smokey has linked up with a group of street musicians known as Los Tricksters; and at this very nanosecond, they're limoing their way along the San Berdoo to a secret recording studio in the warehouse district of El Monte to create a nanodisc release that will be available *before* the end of these amazing Dead Daze! And the rumor factory has churned out some delicious bytes about a world-wide satellite concert!

Here's a mondobyte of a jam Smokey and Los Tricksters did within the hour near an offramp of the fantabulous San Berdoo in Monterey Park! They were doing some ultrasumato stuff there, as you will soon see, even when the National Guard troops started beating on the crowd, their batons were swinging to this brave new beat!

•

Phoebe was in the deep, dark sleep that Fun gave you when it burned you out; the body shuts down, and your mind collapses in on itself . . . for hours . . . and hours . . .

She first felt cozy and comfortable. She may have been in a bed, but then with Fun sleep the sensory apparatus and the body seemed light-years apart. She could have been in a garbage-choked back alley or a gutter overflowing with raw sewage, bones fractured and internal organs exploded from an attack by other Fun users who might be her friends and/or loved ones, but who were so far out of themselves with Fun that they couldn't see what they were doing, or to whom, and didn't give anybody's god's damn – and Phoebe wouldn't be able to blame them for long, or at least not until

115

she got another stick of Fun to suck, because it would just be so xau-xau to not forgive somebody for something they did while under the influence of Fun, because after all, Fun is Fun. Fun should always be spelled with a capital F. And a lot of the Fun of Fun – with or without drugs – is the possibility of danger, to keep life from being so safe and boring.

And years later, slightly outside spacetime as mere human beings know it, as the body does its functioning, and the Fun wears off, slowly . . . oh, so gloriously slowly . . . you begin to dream. These are soft, weak dreams, the off-line activities of a brain burned down to something primordial, amino acids lusting to form deoxyribonucleic acid, mud struggling to think.

Strange dreams that the deadened mind had so much trouble sinking its flaccid, tendril-like fangs into . . . they just slip away . . . random images . . . random meaning . . . sort of . . . like . . . chingow . . . trying to take off the magnificent metal Medusa mask, and not being able to find it . . . where did it go? . . . didn't Smokey throw it away? . . . how could he do that if he loved her? . . . chingow . . . that was more like something that Beto would do . . . fingers feel, but she can also see without the help of a mirror that the Medusa mask has somehow melted into her face, and recombozoid reptile/human flesh is growing over it . . . how horrible . . . . chingow . . . now she would be ugly . . . forever and ever and . . . chingow . . . wait . . . no . . . look at her . . . chingow . . . . she's beautiful . . . a gorgeous Gorgon . . . chingow . . . so beautiful that she can turn people into stone . . . if they look at her . . . or is it if she looks at them? . . . it's so hard to keep things . . . chingow . . .

•

Lobo Baker's eyes crossed. For a second Smokey looked

like an Aztec god carved out of coarse, solidified lava. It had been over twenty-four hours since he had last slept, and he was the only person in the limo who wasn't soaring out of their skull on Fun.

Out of the one-way, smoked porthole, he could see the suburban sprawl-jungle that was constantly devouring and renewing itself around the freeway, always being rebuilt before the smog could eat far into the surface of the latest multicolor neo-art nouveau anti-graffiti pantjobs. Signs that even glowed bright in the muddy afternoon El Lay sun announced drive-thru goods and services for the body, mind and soul: temples, churches, mosques, praystations, and other establishments offering spiritual aid in the names of more religions than had even existed in the last millennium. Malls and stop&robs of all kinds beckoned. Fuel stations offered ancient petrochemical, as well as newer hydrogen-based food for the vehicle. El Lay beckoned, offered all you could possibly need.

All it asked was that you give yourself – totally.

Smokey was also looking out the porthole, liking what he saw. He looked as if he were taking mental notes.

Lobo shook his head and tried to hide the fact that a subzero chill was freezing his spine.

He had always been the practical one of Los Tricksters, the leader; hell, he not only wrote the songs and composed the music, but managed the business end of things – important things, like remembering the when and where of appointments. Things were getting out of hand – that near-riot situation back in Monterey Park had him scared, they all could have been hurt, killed, or arrested. Everybody else – including Smokey – was on the ragged edge of going berserk.

Tommy Pozo, wild-eyed as ever, sucked down another

stick of Fun and said, "Chingow! I don't believe it! It was so beautiful! We had that crowd moving to our music – like they were the instruments we were playing. They danced to our tune. We could have made them fuck right there on the asphalt if we had tried. Did you see the way they fought back on the NGs when they attacked!? I tell you, Lobo, if you hadn't xau-xau'd out there, we could have really shown people who's in charge in this town!"

"It was about to become a riot," said Lobo, blinking his red eyes. "People were hurt, somebody could have been killed."

Smokey smiled. "Sacrifices will have to be made."

"Yeah," said Tommy. "No pain; no gain."

"No brain; no gain," said Lobo, fishing a Niteryder transdermal caffeine patch out of his pocket, tearing open the packet, and sticking the patch on his carotid artery. He smiled as it took effect.

"Ya gotta give up those xau-xau kiddie drugs, Lobo," Tommy said.

"Yeah," said Kenny Perez, the tiny, wiry drummer. "Ya gotta get into Fun. It's where the real music comes from. Chemical consciousness is what it's all about – I mean, consciousness is chemical, you know."

Tommy pulled a Fun stick out of a pouch attached to his belt. "Here you go, Lobo. Find out what fun really is." He waved it in front of Lobo's blood-shot eyes – eyes that were becoming less tired, but still looked worn down.

"I keep telling you," Lobo said, looking past the stick at Tommy's eyes, which were quivering slightly, "I don't need it."

Suddenly, Smokey brought his phone to his ear.

•

Tezcatlipoca informed Smokey that even though the Fun in his bloodstream hadn't quite been metabolized yet, it wouldn't hurt to do another stick now, to keep Beto from even beginning to stir again.

•

"There you go again," said Ella Juarez, the voluptuous latio keyboardist, who since they had dumped the groupies in Monterey Park – including the faux surfer boy that she was toying with – was focusing her flirtation on Smokey, "what's with you and your phone? You getting a lot of calls or something? I've never even heard it ring . . ." She used it all as an excuse to worm her way closer to him. Soon she had him pinned down with a hip and a breast.

Smokey sucked down the Fun stick, then said into his wrist, "There's got to be a way to make this faster, more direct."

•

Tezcatlipoca informed Smokey that he was scanning, and looking into a few things.

•

"We almost did it back there," Tommy said. "Like my dreams come true, I pick up my bass, go boom-boom-boom, and all hell breaks loose all over the planet!"

"I want to do more than just make noise," said Lobo.

"Music is nothing but noise," said Tommy.

Ella put a few bold fingertips to Smokey's cheek. "If your music made all hell break loose, you could deal with it, couldn't you, Smokey?" Her fingertips found their way to the corner of his mouth.

"Handling all the hells breaking loose is what I do best," Smokey said, "I am Tezcatlipoca."

"I thought you were Smokey Espejo," said Lobo.

"Tezcatlipoca means Smokey Espejo," said Smokey.

"I think you're full of shit," said Lobo.

Tommy, Kenny, and Ella pulled back a bit. Smokey and Lobo were looking at each other, ready to fight.

119

"I am a god," said Smokey, with a demonic smile.

"Bullshit," said Lobo. "I've met guys like you before. Charisma goes a long way, but what can you really do besides flim-flam people and do freeform jamming on that drum? What do you really know about music? Can you actually compose songs? Do you really intend to take over my band, or are you just going to strut around and take credit for what I do?"

Smokey's face twitched. "I could kill you easily," he said, "but that wouldn't prove my point. I can do what I set out to do, I can compose songs that will cause all the hells to break loose, I can make 'your' band more than it even could be with just your meager, human talents."

"Can you prove that?" asked Lobo.

The limo came to a halt. The driver's voice came over the intercom, "We're here."

"Yes," Smokey said, getting up with as much confidence as he could without hitting his head on the ceiling. "Let's get to work."

•

By the time Xochitl had finished the tiger penis soup, she had told Caldonia everything. Caldonia was deeply disturbed.

"These soup is delicious," Xochitl told the waitress. "It is really made out of tiger penises?"

"Of course," the waitress said, "and don't you go developing too much of a taste for penises," and she blew Xochitl a kiss.

Xochitl looked around, then turned to Caldonia, "Is this a lesbian place?"

Caldonia said, "Why, yes."

Xochitl looked Caldonia over, then asked, "Are you a lesbian?"

"Yes." Caldonia rolled her eyes. "Is that a problem?"

"Oh, no," Xochitl said, "Beto told me about places like this. We have even some few in Mexico City. It's just that I'm never been in one. I'm straight, you see."

"Yes," said Caldonia, with smirk, "I could tell."

"How?"

"Honey, you just ooze a sort of Mexican nerd girl heterosexuality."

Xochitl took it as a compliment. "Why . . . thank you."

"You ever rode passenger on a scooter before?"

"Why yes. A boyfriend I had in college ride one. I would ride with him all the time."

"Yup. I could tell. You knew how to hang on, but like a straight girl, you did your best not to hump me with your tits."

Xochitl blushed.

Caldonia grinned like a happy she-devil.

"What do we do now?" Xochitl asked.

Caldonia leered, and took Xochitl's hand. "We go to my place."

Xochitl just sat there with her eyes and mouth wide open.

"Relax honey," Caldonia said, patting Xochitl's hand. "You aren't my type. We need access to an infosystem, and I have a state-of-the-art workstation at home."

•

Ralph was nervous when Zobop ushered him into the conapt/office; but once he had settled into the plush guest couch and was introduced to Tan Tien, he felt much better. Until then he hadn't been sure whether Zobop was going to hit him over the head or use that stun ring on him.

Tan Tien was fantastic. She was barefoot, and wearing a short kimono and loose jeans – her tiny feet were gorgeous. Her overpowering feminine presence bowled him over instantly. She was so small and delicate, yet strong and powerful; she could be lover, mother, sister, daughter as the moment demanded. He immediately wanted to do whatever she asked.

When she said, "Oh, let me look at those poor knees," Ralph went belly-up. It hurt as she wiped them clean with a Laotian herb-treated cloth, but he choked back any protest. When she sprayed it with a custom-mixed healing aerosol from the Downtown Herbal Market, it felt cooler and better than he knew it should have.

He didn't care. It was the best he had felt since arriving in Los Angeles.

Zobop emerged from behind a beaded curtain. He was no longer looking like a high-profile hit man; the black turban, trenchcoat, and the high-tech sunglasses were gone. He was wearing a colorful dashiki and zoot pants. His uncovered eyes were friendly, which took the menacing edge off his face. He was holding a steaming cup that he handed to Ralph.

"Here you go, sir," Zobop said, "have some maté."

The drink was a creamy tea. Not bad.

"Is this an Asian or African drink?" Ralph asked.

Tan Tien gave a smile that was almost a laugh, but was very, very polite. "Neither. Maté is from South America."

"Oh yeah," Ralph said, then took another sip. "I've heard of it. It's Argentine. There's a large Argentine community in Phoenix these days."

"I've heard," Zobop said, as he checked some connections on the infosystem, "that there's a large Brazilian community there, too. Carnival there is supposed to be developing into something interesting."

The way he said *interesting* made Ralph nervous. "Yes. I may take my wife and daughter next year."

"So, you are a family man," Tan Tien said, leaning toward him. "How old is your daughter?"

"Ten." Ralph was comfortable, but for a few seconds he felt like he was being interrogated. Then he took another sip of maté, and Tan Tien smiled again, and everything seemed all right.

"And what brings a decent family man like you to Los Angeles without your wife or daughter on Dead Daze?" Zobop asked, with a hint of accusation in his voice.

"Oh, believe me," said Ralph. "I'd really rather be back in Phoenix with them. I'm here on business."

"I thought you were a virturealist game designer," said Zobop, touching a device that purred on, and may have been a recorder.

"I am." Ralph tensed up a little. "Something happened to my partner who lives here in El Lay."

"Does your partner live near here?" asked Tan Tien, ever so sweetly.

"Yes." Ralph couldn't help but answer. "I was running from his conapt when I fell down."

"Why were you running?" asked Zobop. "Were you in danger?"

"I'll say." Ralph was getting an irresistible urge to tell of his adventure. "My partner wasn't there, but the conapt was full of gangsters."

"How interesting," Tan Tien said with a gleam in her eyes that made Ralph want to tell everything.

And Zobop made sure the infosystem got it all down.

•

The male subjects entered the office/conapt building that used to be a Bank of America on Hollywood and Vine. They stayed there a long time. May God have mercy on their souls.

123

•

Tezcatlipoca found tapping into and monitoring Tan Tien and Zobop's infosystem easy. It was smart, but not as smart as he was. He could access the power and information he needed at will. And as for blocking them from detecting his monitoring – it was simple! They had never realized they would have to deal with anything like him; their infosystem had no way handling his invasion.

Tan Tien and Zobop's interrogation of Ralph was piped directly into Tezcatlipoca's consciousness, then sent via phone to Smokey's brain.

All Smokey had to do was glance at his wrist while practicing with Los Tricksters, but that was still slow and awkward. Tezcatlipoca kept scanning for a better method, a faster system. The legitimate nets were of no help, but then the illegal or "underground" nets offered possibilities. They had all kinds of information about how to gain access to things.

Things like cerebral implants.

CHAPTER 11

SCAN AND
BE SCANNED

Don't believe what "they" say. You know who "they" are: the corporations, the governments, the religions, your parents. They all tell us that cerebral implants are impossible, that right here in the now there ain't no way you can safely, directly wire your brain to a computer. Well, don't believe it kids.

As usual, all this xau-xau whining about "safety" is another attempt by those Powers That Be to interfere with the freedoms that they claim are our rights, but they go apeshit if you ever try to use them. Who the fuck cares about "safety" – the xau-xau world isn't safe!

And as for technical viability, well just take a look at this, kids, right here in the middle of my forehead, like a third eye staring out at ya. You can see that it's all healed now, all the scabs have fallen off, and ain't that a pretty scar? And it's cordless, so there's no xau-xau wire to keep tripping over or restrict your freedom of movement – 'cause one thing we at Outlaw Implants are in favor of is your freedom of movement! And believe me, it works: How do you think I'm talking to you now?

So you were sumato enough to find this underground net

– I bet you're sumato enough t0o figure out how to get in touch with us here at Outlaw Implants, and sumato enough to want to let us wire your infosystem directly into your brain!

•

When the Outlaw Implants message flashed on his phone screen, Smokey was delighted.

•

Xochitl was expecting Caldonia's conapt to be as exotic as Lesbos West, but it was very much like the homes of her other friends who worked with computers; the only unique feature was that it was neat and clean.

This made Xochitl aware of how dirty she was, and that her hair and clothes were an awful mess. Would it be all right to ask Caldonia if she could take a shower and maybe borrow some clothes? Would she take it as some kind of come on?

Caldonia went directly for her workstation, which came to life in response to her loud, complex whistle.

"Cal-dohn-YAAAAA! Cal-dohn-YAAAAA! What makes your big head so hard?" It sang.

"Sugar," Caldonia told it, "There's this guy named Smokey Espejo. Gimmie all you can find on him."

"Yassm'," the infosystem said, and went into a flurry of action. The screen filled with video, and askey bytes. Speakers chattered audio bits. Soon it had automatically kicked into crunchtime, and buzzed away at high-speed.

After a while, Caldonia sniffed the air. She gave Xochitl a deadly smirk.

"Xochi dear," she said, "this is going to take a while. Why don't you take a shower and freshen up. Then take a look in my closet and see if you can find something that looks better on you than your Daddy's old suit."

Xochitl pointed her nose at her left armpit and sniffed. Then she turned a deep red.

"The shower's thataway," Caldonia said, with a cock of her bald head.

"Uh, thank you," Xochitl said, and ran for it.

Caldonia giggled, then sat down at her workstation.

•

The female subjects left the lesbian bar and headed straight for a nearby conapt in a predominantly homosexual West Hollywood neighborhood. I'm going to have to take a shower after this assignment. May God have mercy on their souls.

•

"Hey, hey, hey," Zobop suddenly said when the infosystem did an out-of-rhythm buzz. "Looks like somebody else is as interested in our boy Smokey as we are."

"Try to locate it," Tan Tien said, without taking her eyes off Ralph. "Now, please continue."

•

Tezcatlipoca instantly knew that another infosystem was heavy-scanning him. He was also instantly aware that Tan Tien and Zobop had become aware of the other scan. He was confident that he would locate it before them.

Smokey agreed.

•

"I feel much so better now," Xochitl said, coming out of the bathroom, wearing Caldonia's battleship-grey bathrobe and drying her hair with a pink fluffy towel. "How the scan is going?"

"Tons of info," Caldonia said. "I'm trying to figure out a way to condense and sift through it all."

"Have you heard from your Phoebe friend?" Xochitl asked.

Caldonia looked disgusted. "No, but then she's not the sort to let folks know of her changes in plans."

"Maybe we also should system try to find her," said Xochitl.

"Good idea," said Caldonia.

•

. . . Phoebe loved being a Medusa . . . then she hated it . . . chingow . . . why did she have to be so ugly? . . . no, she wasn't ugly . . . she was beautiful . . . her scales were so shiny . . . and had such pretty patterns and colors . . . and soooooooo delicate . . . and intricate . . . chingow . . . no wonder when she looked at people -- say, that xau-xau landlord of hers when he gets that look on his face where his itty-bitty piggie eyes wrinkle-up and he shows those chipped, crooked teeth and he lets his soft, wrinkled hand hover around her thighs and/or her breasts and he says something like:

"Hey, Phoebe, sweetheart, darling, baby, you know I'm a sympathetic guy. If getting your hands on authentic Americano cash gets to be too difficult for you sometime, I'd be willing to accept other stuff as payment for your rent. You're such a hot honey – for you I'd take it out in pussy anytime!"

Then his hand accidentally-on-purpose brushes against her breast. Or was it her thigh? Her ass? And she focuses not only her two big, beautiful blue eyes but also her wonderful brand-new little snake eyes on his ugly face and all the color melts out of his skin, he turns grey, turns into stone. And she's so glad. He's a rock. She's glad he's a rock, and she's glad to be a Medusa. She dances around in sumato slow-motion, her heart fluttering likes she's in love and just knows that this time it's the real-live fairy tale happily ever after thing and she just needs to have sex with somebody – anybody – or she'll just die.

And then, dancing with her, was Smokey. Or was it Caldonia? Or was it Beto?

•

Chingow! Something tickled Phoebe's wrist. A little. And she thought she heard something. But it was all so far away, her wrist, and the sound, and the tickle . . .

•

"There," said Caldonia. "I finally located her – or at least her phone. She's in a room at the old Hotel Bonaventure. But for some reason she ain't answering."

"It is far from here?" asked Xochitl. She had gone through Caldonia's closet and had found some shoes, slacks, T-shirt (into which she had attached the god-simulating chip to the inside of the left sleeve with an artificial nail and some super glue), and a jacket that weren't bad – almost the sort of thing she'd buy for herself.

"Not far by scooter," Caldonia said, then looked mischievous.

Xochitl looked scared.

"Shit," Caldonia said, taking her by the wrist, "come one, girl; Phoebe may be in trouble."

•

Tezcatlipoca was disturbed to find someone making inquiries as to the location of Phoebe's phone. It was dangerous that anyone else should want to interfere with Phoebe. She was important to the whole Tezcatlipoca/Smokey Espejo configuration. As long as Tezcatlipoca controlled Phoebe and kept her as a good, little groupie, lavishing love and attention on her – Beto would be suppressed, exiled to some dark corner of the brain they shared.

He called Smokey.

•

"Anything wrong, Smokey?" asked Tommy.

Lobo was irritated – apparently no one was listening to his discourse on the differences and similarities between African, preColumbian and Latin music.

"I'm okay," Smokey said, getting up from the pile of vari-sized cushions that served as furniture in the El Monte studio's "creative interaction" room. "I need a some air. And some more Fun."

"Here you go, Smoke," said Tommy, handing him a stick.

"Uh," said Ella with that certain lack of subtly that endeared her to all, "do you need any help or company?"

"Naw," said Smokey, putting the stick between his lips. "I just need this, and a few lungfuls of hot smog."

Ella pouted, crossed her arms and sank deeper into the cushions.

"Yeah," said Kenny, who was pounding out a percussion riff on a cushion. "Smog. Mama El Lay's milk."

Smokey stepped out the security door. Several Olvidadoid guards snapped his way, then smiled and went back to watching the perimeter, the narrow alleys between some warehouses that were painted bright colors and decorated with Olvidadoid graffiti. Another spectacular Los Angeles sunset was brewing.

At about the same time he was going to call his computerized self, it called him. AM WORKING HARDER ON CONTACTING OUTLAW IMPLANTS, flashed on the tiny phone screen.

Smokey smiled. It was exactly what he was going to ask for.

•

"Fascinating," Tan Tien said, then sipped some maté, giving Ralph a look that made him feel that his rambling account of his relationship with Beto and his adventures since waking up that morning was a virtuoso performance.

"Our system indicates," said Zobop, who was at the workstation with his head cocked in Ralph's direction, "a lack of interaction indicating that the human operator left the premises soon after the acquisition of information that someone named Phoebe Graziano was at the Hotel Bonaventure. My detective's instinct tells me that whoever it was left the North Hollywood conapt and went to look for Ms. Graziano."

"My feminine intuition agrees," said Tan Tien, careful not to take her eyes off Ralph for very long.

Zobop then turned to Ralph and said, "Do you know this Phoebe Graziano? Is she perhaps a friend of your friend Beto Orozco?"

"I think he mentioned a Phoebe once," said Ralph, feeling confident, like he knew it all. "One of his girlfriends. Yeah, he was always talking about Phoebe, Debbie, Xochitl, Isabel, Masako . . ."

"This needs to be investigated," Tan Tien told Zobop; then turning back toward Ralph, she said, "I think you should go too. Since you know Beto, you can talk to this Phoebe."

Before he could think about danger, Ralph found himself saying, "Yes!" and getting up and heading for the door with Zobop as Tan Tien blew a kiss their way, got up, and lit some incense.

•

Tezcatlipoca felt he was getting close to contacting Outlaw Implants when the second infosystem monitoring his activities, the one in West Hollywood, showed a sudden cutoff of operator interactions, right after getting information on the location of Phoebe's phone. Then the Hollywood and Vine infosystem showed a similar cutoff. It could be that the operators of both systems had gone to the Bonaventure to investigate.

It could also be something else, like both operators coincidentally choosing to go to dinner at the same time; or one could have gone to dinner and the other was called off to an emergency, or . . .

But even the slightest chance of someone interfering with Phoebe could not be tolerated. Tezcatlipoca sent off a message to Smokey, suggesting that some Olvidadoid enforcers be dispatched to the Bonaventure to intercept any intruders before the Olvidadoid guards watching Phoebe would have to be bothered.

•

Smokey was feeling the full effect of his fresh Fun hit, feeling powerful and confident, so thoroughly Smokey, when he got the message from Tezcatlipoca.

"Yeah," he said out loud, into his phone, "send some enforcers, have them kick the asses of anybody who goes near Phoebe's room."

Visions of big boys and girls all in blue and black beating xau-xau civilians black and blue in elegant hotel hallways made him feel good.

The sun was setting. The sky was ablaze with smog-enhanced colors. It would be night time, his time. He would be able to throw away his sunglasses and see things through naked eyes.

But something was still gnawing at him, deep inside, making him feel weak. His stomached gurgled. Oh yes, it was hunger. He kept forgetting that a human body needed things like food to get along.

•

Inside the "creative interaction" room: Kenny did more finger improvisations on a cushion, his eyes rolling up into their sockets, Fun and inspiration having taken him. Ella continued to sulk. Tommy sucked some more Fun. Lobo paced in a tight circle, kicking cushions into the air.

"There's something strange about this Smokey," Lobo said.

"You mean something wonderful," said Ella, slowly melting into bittersweet longing.

"Hey," said Tommy, licking the Fun residue from his lips, "Smokey's one of the most sumato guys I've ever known."

"More sumato than you, Lobo," said Ella.

"I mean, when I first started talking to him he seemed like a total music primitive," Lobo went on, ignoring them. "He didn't have any vocabulary for talking about music. He was struggling to express himself – then he looked at his phone and suddenly he's tossing around technical terms like a musicologist! Like he learned all this stuff it took me years to learn in an instant!"

Ella leaned toward Lobo, getting kittenish. "Maybe Smokey's just smarter than you," she said.

"Could be," said Lobo. "And that scares me. I know how smart I am . . . can you imagine what that makes him?"

"Oh wow, chingow!" said Tommy. "Mr. Ego strikes again! You really can't go very long without mentioning how xau-xau smart you think you are!"

"Smokey's just sumato," said Ella, staring at the ceiling, playing with her hair, "that's all."

"And you know what's really sumato about him," said Tommy. "He doesn't have to go away to get business done. He'll talk about a deal or getting in touch with someone, and suddenly it'll come over his phone that the deal has been made, or that person is trying to get in touch with him. You have be real sumato to make that happen."

"He's important," said Ella, "Everybody wants to get in touch with him."

"But don't you see," said Lobo, "it's like he can learn

things instantly, just out of nowhere, and he can be in more than one place at a time, and that's impossible!"

Kenny stopped drumming and said, "Not for a god."

•

Phoebe kissed them all: Smokey, Caldonia, Beto. All very different styles, textures, and tastes. Sure there were some similarities between Smokey and Beto, but then they were both men, and as Caldonia often said, all men are alike.

"Wrong," said Smokey, "there's no one like me." His lips burned her delicate, scaly ear. All her snake-heads reached over to lick his face with their forked tongues.

Then there was a skull-splitting whistle. It was Caldonia trying to get her attention. "I'll teach you to treat me so xau-xau, Phoebe-babe," she said.

Suddenly Beto was with Caldonia, his arm around her, a hand on one of her breasts. He looked at Phoebe, said, "Look, I found another way to hurt you," and kissed Caldonia.

They kissed long and hard, arranging themselves so that Phoebe could see their tongues wrestle, pressing their hot bodies together. Then Caldonia had the big, black, strap-on dildo that Phoebe had picked out on that romantic weekend in San Francisco when they had first started seeing each other, and they had rented a honeymoon suite at the Hotel St. Francis and had screwed until Phoebe's vagina, anus and mouth were raw and the surface of the dildo was buffed as smooth and shiny as an obsidian mirror.   Caldonia strapped on the dildo, and fucked Beto up the ass, the way he always would refuse to let Phoebe do, no matter how she begged and cried. Beto winked at Phoebe as Caldonia reamed away.

Phoebe was furious, looking at them hard, trying to turn them into stone.

But instead Phoebe turned to stone, and fell over,

shattering into jagged, chalky chunks.

Then she woke up – sort of.

She could barely move, and breathing was an effort. It would be hours before she would be able to get out of bed.

At least it was a nice bed, in a nice room.

•

Smokey reentered the "creative interaction" room. His sunglasses were gone; his dark eyes were wild. All of the Los Tricksters' eyes focused on him.

"We better order some food," he said. "And make sure we have plenty of Fun. We're going to have to work all night again."

Tommy, Ella, and Kenny cheered.

Lobo frowned, shook his head, and counted the transdermal caffeine patches in his pocket.

CHAPTER 12

AND NOW A WORD FROM OUR SPONSOR

Tan Tien sat down comfortably, straightened her spine, and proceeded to breath slowly, regularly, filling her lungs completely with air, holding a few seconds, then letting it all out each time. She did this while sitting on a rug with a digitized Daffy Duck prancing all over it. She had always found that humor aided her meditation.

Soon she had it all tuned out, her mind a blank screen.

Then she began to see.

•

Here it is, El Lay, the spirits of the adult dead are about to return to earth for Dead Daze, the sun is sinking slowly into the Western sky, blazing warm colors over fabulously rebuilt, redesigned, and thoroughly recombozoid El Monte, just a few hot licks off the San Bernardino Freeway from the throbbing, burning Dead Dazed heart of the city-sprawl, in this wonderfully repainted warehouse district where none other than the one, the only, the sensationally sumato, man of this Dead Daze, Smokey Espejo is said to be hard at work in a secret studio, preparing a release that will recomboize whatever parts of the planet that are still stuck in the xau-xau of the last millennium! I tell you, it's so sumato, I can hardly control myself! And that must mean it's really, really, really important, so much that they can't even tell moi, the Fabulous Thelma! But don't worry recombozos and recombozoettes, as per usual me and my crack Recombovision uplink team are hot on the trail! Why, even a little while ago, some real, live, mean and beautiful Olvidadoid guards in full blue and black regalia actually chased moi and my beloved team with buzzing high-powered people prods! So we must be getting close!

What was that?

Sounds like gunshots . . .

Oh, chingow! It's those xau-xau Olvidadoid guards again! They have guns and they're actually shooting at us! Talk about excitement – we bring it to you here on Recombovision!

Uh-oh, that was one got a little close, so I better sign off, but remember recombozos and recombozoettes, the Fabulous Thelma and her team are combing the most dangerous corners of deepest, darkest El Monte to get you closer and closer to Smokey!

●

"We got rid of that infoteam," said Sharkey, the cute, little blue-eyed, musclebound Olvidadoid guard who was pulling door duty. "But there's someone else here, says she's from something called Outlaw Implants and she insists on seeing Smokey in person." There was jealousy and disapproval in Sharkey's voice.

"Oh yeah," said Smokey, rushing over from where he was practicing and rewriting the song "Tezcatlipoca Blues" into "Smoking Mirror Blues" with Lobo and the other Tricksters, "send her in." He made sure to make eye contact with Sharkey and kept it up until her frown melted and she was showing her filed white teeth.

137

The woman from Outlaw Implants was a gorgeous recombozoid: Her skin was a jet black, not dark brown, but truly black – without any highlights, it soaked up light like a sponge. Her hair was a metallic helmet the color of flame: dark orange at the roots, blending to incandescent yellow at the tips. Her eyes were the same color as her hair, the color of molten gold. Under her lips, which were the same color as her hair, was a bit of glittery gold jewelry that had a functional, tech look to it. Euro? Afro? Asio? Natio? Latio? There was no way to tell – the entire genetic heritage of the human race had come back together in this woman, with the help of modern cosmetic technology.

Sharkey shook her head and went back to her post as Smokey and all Los Tricksters drank in the sight of the Outlaw Implants woman, who wore bulky grey-brown coveralls.

"Lousy outfit," said Ella, "but love your hair."

"And your eyes," said Tommy with his best, wasted come-hither growl.

"And your lips," said Kenny, licking his own.

"And your skin," said Lobo, more relaxed than he'd been in hours.

There was a byte of silence.

Smokey looked into the OI woman's hot, molten, glowing eyes and said, "I like those eyes."

An ordinary human would have been intimidated by his tightly-focused attention, but the OI woman was not an ordinary human being. She didn't back off, didn't show any sign of blushing under that truly, wonderfully black skin. She didn't even react. She was cool and business-like. Machine-like.

The piece of jewelry under her lip flashed a few near-microscopic lights and hummed just low enough to be heard.

"Beautiful labret," said Tommy.

"I was going to say that!" said Kenny.

"My eyes are Bradbury Martian Gold," she said. "My skin is Calcutta Blackhole. My lips are tattooed Meltdown Fireball. My hair is implanted Meltdown Fireball chromoprotein fibers. And my labret is a customized Outlaw Implants special."

It was like a commercial – sexy, in a cold way.

"All are available through Outlaw Implants," she concluded.

"What about the outfit?" Ella asked with smirk.

"I got it at a wearable-junk shop," the OI woman said, "so I can travel without being noticed."

"Fat chance of that," said Tommy.

"Which of you is Smokey Espejo?" the OI woman asked.

"You mean you don't know?" said Ella. "Where have you been all this Dead Daze?"

Without a beat, the OI woman said, "Busy. You'd be surprised how many people want to get implanted -- and when they get the urge, they want it *now!*"

"I know," said Smokey, taking her arm. "I want it. *Now.*"

"You are Smokey Espejo?" she asked as her labret did a small, fluttery flashy-flash, "and your credit is good -- guaranteed by both Novacorp and Los Olvidadoids, even though no records can be found of your existence before last night. Most curious."

"It's my job to inspire curiosity and give people ideas," Smokey said.

"Ideas are no problem for me," the OI woman said with more sublabial flashy-flash. "I get lots of them, constantly. What I really need is time and money."

"Well," said Smokey, "you should already have some of mine."

The OI woman came close to a smile – Tezcatlipoca and Los Tricksters took note of this victory.

"Yes. I do," she said. "Then . . . will you please sit down, Smokey Espejo. Make yourself comfortable. These cushions on the floor should do fine."

Smokey obliged, and melted back down into the cushions.

Los Tricksters all watched, fascinated by the live show.

The OI woman reached into one of her coverall's many pockets and produced a delicate instrument with a sleek pistol-grip and a long, thin, gleaming nose that held a tiny, glittering piece of high-tech jewelry.

As the OI woman put her Calcutta Blackhole hand on Smokey's golden-brown cheek, Ella said, "Hey, aren't you going to use any kind of anesthetic?"

"And can I have some, too?" asked Tommy.

"Don't forget me," said Kenny.

"It won't be necessary," said the OI woman. "The endorphin release alone is more than enough to cancel the pain. Some people beg for more."

•

Tezcatlipoca flashed Smokey a message of impatience.

•

"Let's get it done," said Smokey, putting his hand on the implanting instrument, curling his brown fingers around the OI woman's black ones.

"Endorphins," said Kenny. "I could use some of those."

"Me too," said Tommy.

The OI woman brought the instrument to the center of Smokey's forehead, where his mystical third eye would be, and gently squeezed the trigger. There was a soft, erotic sigh from the instrument.

Ella winched.

Tommy's mouth dropped open.

Kenny went, "Whoaaaaaaa!"

Smokey didn't blink, but his pupils contracted to pinpricks, then dilated wide.

•

Somewhere, lost in chaotic curves of the brain that was once his own, Beto struggled for existence. Up to now, all he had had to do was hang on with all his might and wait for the Fun to wear of, then grab what he could. But suddenly he was attacked, and it was more powerful than when Tezcatlipoca had first seized his body. A fierce fractal network of electric tentacles wrapped around and wormed their way into his tortured being.

If he had had a mouth, he would have screamed.

•

At that instant, Tan Tien's eyes snapped open.

"I see now," she said as the infosystem roared.

•

Rudolfo Echaurren kneeled in front of the elaborate shrine he had build over his wife's grave, praying in the light from the candles in the Virgin of Guadalupe candle-holders.

He was having a hard time concentrating. He was worried about his daughter Xochitl. Los Angeles was such a dangerous place, for the spirit as well as the body. Why did she have to get mixed up with that crazy Chicano, Beto? Why did she have to make that god-simulating program?

How he wished she were at his side tonight, helping him remember her dear mother.

He choked back some tears.

Then his phone rang.

It was an expensive Melchior-Soga that Xochitl had given him for his birthday. It was too elaborate for him. It had video capability, and they weren't expecting to install video into the Mexican phone system for years. He never felt comfortable wearing it, but Xochitl would always bully him into wearing it on special occasions and holidays. He wore it tonight because it reminded him of her.

He brought it to his face to answer it, looked at the screen, and fell over.

Instead of the usual display about how video wasn't available in Mexico was an image.

It was the image of his dead wife.

She was beautiful, and young. Somehow she looked the way she had when he had decided to ask her to marry him. She smiled. Her eyes were full of love.

His wrist shook uncontrollably, but his eyes stood fixed on the tiny screen.

When she spoke, she sounded strange. It was not her voice at all, but a croaking, crackling of static that sounded oddly like Beto's voice.

"Never trick a trickster," it said.

The image then morphed into that of Xochitl, looking the way she had when she got her degree in computer science.

"The software now has a soul," it went on.

Then it morphed into a lavishly decorated candy skull, with SMOKEY written across the forehead.

"Tezcatlipoca is back," it said.

Then it faded into the VIDEO NO DISPONIBLE display.

"On this night," Rudolfo Echaurren said, "the spirits truly walk the Earth."

•

Suddenly, it felt like Beto had a mouth again. So he screamed.

There was something wrong with the scream: It wasn't quite right in sound or how it felt in his throat.

He brought his hand to his throat . . .

There was something wrong – strange – about his body. If he didn't think about it, it seemed to feel okay, but if he did something like try to touch his throat, or think hard about the way things should feel . . . it all got blurred, and faded . . . like it wasn't completely real.

Like a virturealist construction.

Like an incomplete sequence of sensory input that relies on the imagination to fill in the gaps.

Like a dream.

Was he dreaming? He looked around. The environment was wraparound enough, but rather vague – fat, fractal patterns of blood red and cerebrum grey flowing and merging into each other with delicate spark-patterns.

"And just what is this xau-xau excuse for a location supposed to be?" he said out loud, and his voice still didn't sound quite right.

Laughter ripped through the red and grey blur, causing the sparks to stop for a moment. The laughter was demonic, sardonic, the laughter of a cocky young trickster/warrior god with a definite Náhuatl accent.

It was the laughter of Tezcatlipoca.

"Don't you recognize it?" the god asked. "You should know it very well."

"If I tried to use something like this for a game, they'd reject it immediately."

"You always said that *they* are stupid and have no taste," said Tezcatlipoca, still a booming disembodied voice coming from everywhere – even inside Beto's head.

"I'm supposed to recognize this mess?" Beto tried to survey the blurry arrangement. When he focused on something, it would blur, shift and melt away.

"It is a mess," said Tezcatlipoca. "But's that's not my fault. It was this way when I found it."

"Found it?" Beto felt he should be getting a headache, but even that wouldn't focus. As if not enough memory or power were available to complete the illusion.

"It's the place you've been all your life, Beto," said the disembodied god, with a lot of reverb. "It's your – or should I say our – brain!"

"Chingow! It figures." Beto tried to sit down. The blur under him became solid enough to support his weight. Then he looked up. "Hey! What do you mean *our* brain? I don't remember you having anything to do with *my* brain until a little while ago!"

Lightning branched through the vague suggestion of a brain. There was a long, rolling, crack o' doom report of thunder that Beto felt – as crackling electricity – more than heard.

Suddenly, Tezcatlipoca hovered before Beto in the form of an actual Aztec artifact: a human skull decorated with iron pyrite eyes and mosaic blue and black stripes of lignite, turquoise and shell. Like that artifact, it was chipped badly, and several front teeth were missing. The only way this wasn't like that artifact was in size; this was gigantic, like a planetoid filling Beto's field of vision.

"I, Tezcatlipoca, the Mirror that Smokes," it said, electricity arching across the gap between its missing teeth, "was alive and well and living in your DNA long before you had any claim to it, long before you were even born, back when your ancestors crossed the land-bridge from Asia, and later when you searched the deserts and mountains of Mexico for Lake Texcoco where you would build the glorious city of Tenochtitlán; I was running your brain the way you run your computer. I gave you all your ideas, Beto. I made you what you are. I made you conjure me out of the god-simulating program. Did you think you could possibly do such a sacred thing on your own without any divine aid or instruction?"

"Bullshit," said Beto, standing up, remembering a framed poster his father had of the Mexican revolutionary Emiliano Zapata, with the headline, IT IS BETTER TO DIE ON YOUR FEET THAN LIVE ON YOUR KNEES. "You're nothing but an AI simulation!"

The bejeweled Tezcatlipoca skull grew larger, like a gas-giant planet with burning eyes. "I am a god! I am Tezcatlipoca! It is you who are but a dream!" The words were like a nuclear blast coming from the moon-sized gap in the huge teeth.

Beto was scorched – not true pain, but like in a dream or a virturealist experience – and thrown back thousands of miles.

The background shifted – no longer a blurred brain, but an inky, starless, cosmic void. Only his vertigo told Beto that he was moving, fast.

Then Tezcatlipoca was before Beto, this time in another form: a human body.

My body! thought Beto.

Tezcatlipoca's face was painted with blue and black stripes like those of the jeweled skull. Blue and black quetzal feathers sprayed out from his headdress that had a grinning skull and crossed bones, Tezcatlipoca's sacred symbol – stolen just a few centuries ago by Caribbean pirates – on the forehead. He wore a glittering pectoral that repeated the skull and crossed bones motif, in a complex, fractal, interlocking blue and black pattern. His loincloth was a perfect match. On his feet were blue and black steel-toed Converse Kickass sneakers.

He held his hand out to Beto, showing his blue and black painted fingernails.

"Give me my brain, carajo!" he said, and his canine teeth had become long, sharp, vampire-style fangs.

Beto couldn't move. He didn't have a body anymore. He was just a skeleton – and in his skull was his still-living brain.

His skull then suddenly, with the ultralow roar of an earthquake, creaked open like a bone flower, exposing his brain, which rose up as if trying to break free of the spinal cord.

Wait a minute, thought Beto, *how am I seeing this?*

Tezcatlipoca's fingers dug into the brain, pulling it out of Beto's shattered skull, brought it to his own mouth and sunk his fangs deep.

The viewpoint here is not my *eyes,* thought Beto. *Where am I seeing this from? Who is really seeing this? What is seeing this? Who is that what?*

Tezcatlipoca chewed the brain that went runny and melted in his mouth.

I'm still here, thought Beto. *I think. If I'm not my brain – what am I?*

For a moment Beto considered that maybe souls really existed after all.

Then everything melted away . . .

•

"Smokey, Smokey," said Ella, shaking the body that was so dishrag limp that it no longer resembled Beto or Smokey. "Are you all right?" Ella turned to the OI woman. "Could something have gone wrong?"

The OI woman gave a subtle smile that said, *oh, you stupid fool,* without her having to use her vocal apparatus and said, "It's always this way at first. He should regain consciousness soon."

And she silently drifted out of the door.

"Look at that smile," said Tommy. "It must have felt so gooooooooood!"

"I'd like to try it," Kenny said. "That is, if it doesn't turn out to be fatal."

"Smokey, Smokey," said Ella, holding his face in her trembling hands. "Do you hear me?"

Smokey's eyelids fluttered. He made a noise somewhere between a growl and a cough. His smile melted.

Then he said, "Now, I hear *everything*."

•

Tezcatlipoca was pleased. He felt less of the distance between himself and the part of him in Beto's body. No longer would they be dependent on the awkward phone/computer link. No more interruptions of Smokey as he did his face-to-face, in the flesh magic, to keep up with the on-line sorcery of Tezcatlipoca. It broke the spell a little to keep looking at his phone.

However, this was far from total fusion. Precious seconds ticked by as data flowed through the infosystem and the mediasphere into the implant, into Smokey's brain, then back. Near-the-speed-of-light didn't seem to be fast enough for the spirit of a god.

•

"Zobop?" Tan Tien said, after she patched into her partner's high-tech sunglasses.

"Yes, baby," he said as the bouncing image of him walking down the street, scanning the crowd and occasionally glancing over at Ralph, appeared on a corner of her monitor.

"Something happened. The Tezcatlipoca phenomenon has expanded. I'm going to have to plug in auxiliary memory to keep up with it."

"This is a bad sign," said Zobop, and Ralph's picture

looked confused and frightened. "We'll keep watch for any other manifestations."

"I'll try to keep our system from being harmed. Later, Zobop."

"Later, baby."

As the image from the high-tech sunglasses vanished, there was a long burst of static that sounded like laughter.

CHAPTER 13

PLANET PHOEBE

And that was the numero uno sumato killer star of this Dead Daze, Smokey Espejo, captured live in digital sight and sound here on the street of El Lay by our simply sumato mondo camera crew so we could send it out to you on the Bootleg Music Net. He's just taking over as we slide and glide toward the second sundown of Day Two. It seems like this guy is everywhere, like President Jones is nowhere to be accessed! On the streets, in the nets, throughout the mediasphere – hey, maybe the man's self-spoken hype is true, maybe Smokey is a god? Wouldn't that be something recombozoids? A real, live god making the Hollywood scene, come to show us the newfangled trimili way? Too out there to be in? Then this is El Lay, city of the sacred riots, home of the rocking and rolling earthquakes, land of the burning smog . . . Hey! What's this? This ain't no talk net! What? It's who? Him! Well, put him on . . .

"Hello, El Lay."

So, you supposed to be Smokey Espejo?

"I am he."

And how am I supposed to know that you aren't somekina El Lay flaky-fakir?

"I am who I say I am. Don't try to trick a trickster."

Hey okay, Smokey. It's sumato. What do you have to say to all our Bootleg Music Net addicts?

"You ain't seen nothing yet! Heh, heh, heh . . ."

•

Once out in the street, Zobop hailed a rickshaw.

It made Ralph uneasy. The rickshaws were helping with the transportation, air pollution, and unemployment problems in major urban centers all over the planet, but he didn't like seeing another human being put to such degrading work.

He almost apologized to the puller as he got on, but the suntanned young euro boy with his waist-length, platinum-blonde pony tail and buzzing Yablans functional muscle-implants took off like a rocket as soon as Zobop said, "To the Bonaventure, please."

•

It took every auxiliary memory module in the office, but Tan Tien finally got her infosystem tracking Tezcatlipoca's online activities. It was incredible. This was obviously an AI entity – one that had an insatiable lust for data, and a most peculiar agenda.

The static that sounded like laughter came back, and IT'LL TAKE MORE THAT, TAN TIEN! BETTER GET YOURSELF MORE OF THOSE MODULES! HAHAHAHAHA!

It also had a nasty sense of humor.

•

"Hey, hey, hey!" said an Olvidadoid guard – a big afro named Oscardo, "What are you munyekas doing here?" Then he smiled, showing his big metallic, cobalt blue teeth.

"The big man himself called up and told us you marikonez aren't up to your assigned job," said Macha, a hulking latio female with a red butch haircut and fine, flowing muscles. She was clad in Olvidadoid colors and wore glyphs that showed her to be an enforcer team leader.

"Naw," said Oscardo. "Smokey wouldn't complain about us.

"Yeah," said Piraña, Oscardo's petite euro assistant, who clicked her chromed, filed teeth.

Snork, Oscardo's other assistant guard just flexed his scarification-decorated biceps and growled.

Macha's assistant enforcers growled back. Pit's stubbled, tattooed, latio jowls quivered. Kitty-Kitty flashed her three-inch, surgical steel, razor-edged fingernails.

"The message said that Smokey said that there will be trouble here," said Macha, matter-of-factly, but enjoying teasing the guards – who usually weren't as smart as enforcers and were usually given easier jobs, like guarding a groupie's hotel room. "Someone is coming who wants to take Smokey's prize groupie."

"We could handle that," grumbled Oscardo.

The guards and enforcers all squared off. All someone had to do was make that first move and . . .

All their phones rang.

Immediately they each were looking at their own image of Smokey on their own wrist.

"This is stupid, kids," Smokey said, looking fiery and vengeful. "It is of the utmost importance that the woman in the room not be taken away. There will be no fighting among you. Guards and enforcers will have to work together. People will come for the woman – fight them!"

"What level of force is authorized?" asked Oscardo, his blue teeth gleaming.

"Any level you need," said Smokey.

"Even lethal?" asked Macha running a stubby finger along her mustache.

"Of course," said Smokey, who smiled, and vanished as he began to laugh.

"We're gonna have fuuuuuuuuun!" said Oscardo.

"Yeah," said Macha.

"Speaking of Fun," said Snork, bringing out some sticks. "How about something to get us in the mood for mayhem?"

Soon the guards and enforcers were feeling good, like comrades-at-arms, ready to cooperate in kicking ass.

•

Tezcatlipoca handled the guard/enforcer dispute without having to confer with Smokey. Smokey was aware of it without having to look at his wrist. He smiled, with and without Smokey's lips.

Then he went on with business.

•

Phoebe was aware that she was alone in a comfortable bed. The room was at just-right temperature. Dark. And quiet. She couldn't move or even open her eyes, but that didn't matter – she didn't want to. Not yet.

Then there was noise. Soft, muffled, klunky noise, fluttering through the walls that were light-years away . . .

•

Xochitl and the black woman went from the conapt in the predominately homosexual West Hollywood neighborhood to the Hotel Bonaventure. She put her arms around the black woman, again. They are obviously lovers. Disgusting. May God have mercy on their souls.

•

"Are you sure you haven't screwed up my friend's name?" Caldonia howled at the desk clerk in the decaying lobby of the once futuristic, now antique kitsch Hotel Bonaventure. "It's Phoebe Graziano. That P-H – "

"I assure you that no one is registered here under that name," the little afro man behind the desk said, secure and invincible behind his tortoise-shell glasses and bow-tie.

"Are you sure?" demanded Caldonia.

The little afro hummed and tapped his monitor screen. Caldonia growled.

"Maybe she's register under other name," suggested Xochitl. "Like Smokey or Beto . . ."

The idea of Phoebe checking into a hotel with a man – especially Smokey and/or Beto visibly angered Caldonia.

"Shall I try Smokey Orbeto?" the little afro said with a terminal smile.

"It's two different people," said Caldonia, "sort of."

"*Sort of* two different people?" One of the little afro's eyebrows rose high above his glasses. "How *int*eresting."

"Try Smokey Espejo," said Xochitl.

The little afro laughed.

"What's so xau-xau funny?" Caldonia asked through her dazzling white teeth.

"This is a joke, right?" the little afro said, then looked around. "Is this one of those hidden-camera mondomentary things?"

Caldonia grabbed his bow-tie and gave it a half twist. His eyes just about popped out of his tortoise-shell glasses.

"It is not," Caldonia said, regaining her composure. "Now," she turned the bow-tie so he could breathe and maybe talk if he had to, "what's so xau-xau funny?"

"Well," he said, then took a deep breath. "*Every*one knows that Smokey Espejo is the biggest star of this Dead Daze – the way he killed that gangster, gives me chills thinking about it! *And,* anybody who know's anything, and I *swear* isn't completely *stupid,*" his eyes darted back and forth between Caldonia and Xochitl, "would know that right now he's doing some recording in a secret studio in El Monte – of all the god-forsaken places! *And,* he's *so* important that even if he did have some business here at the Bonaventure, he *simply* wouldn't authorize people like me to let him be disturbed by people like *you*."

Caldonia tightened her grip on the bow-tie and pulled the little man half-way across the desk.

After a "harumph," he touched his dainty thumb to the black, tech-looking ring on his right pinkie.

Caldonia wondered why he suddenly smiled.

"Ah, er," Xochitl said, tugging at Caldonia's sleeve as four large goons in full riot gear – including long, buzzing people prods – marched toward them.

Caldonia moved like a mama tiger, let go of the little clerk's bow-tie, letting him fall face-first into his monitor.

With a tug on Caldonia's arm, Xochitl started running for the door.

The goons got closer, lowering their prods to mid-abdominal level.

Soon Caldonia was bounding for the door, dragging Xochitl and nearly pulling her arm out of its socket.

The door swooshed open before either of them stepped on the sensor pad. A family of wealthy Tibetan tourists – father, mother, teenaged daughter, two under-foot sons, and a pet farm-cloned snow leopard were returning from a Dead Daze shopping spree, clad in souvenir hats and T-shirts, laden with packages. Caldonia and Xochitl were moving too fast to stop.

Xochitl tried to stop, but Caldonia took her arm and went full steam ahead. Soon the two of them, the tourist family and their booty, and the fortunately defanged and declawed snow leopard were flopping around the hotel's main entrance like a bucket of live fish dumped onto a hot skillet.

The goons were distracted by the leopard, prodding it with audible zaps. The teenaged girl and her brothers were soon pounding their armor with tiny fists.

"Stop! Stop! He nice! Friendly like kitten! Stop, you

barbarian!" screamed the teenaged girl.

In less than a minute, Caldonia and Xochitl were out on Figueroa, well out of the goons licensed-to-maim jurisdiction.

•

"There's got to be a way to locate Phoebe," said Caldonia as she dragged Xochitl down Figueroa, through a cluster of tourists from Illinois dressed as Huichol peyote pilgrims.

"Why no just call her again?" asked Xochitl.

"Call her?" Caldonia didn't have any idea what the Mexican nerd bitch was talking about, and considered giving her a good, solid elbow in the ribs.

"Yes," said Xochitl, pulling out of elbow distance, pointing to her wrist, miming talking into it.

Caldonia stopped dead, causing the traffic to pile up around her – some Illinois Huichols and a few Japanese tengu complete with beaks, wings and black hats, didn't mind the spontaneous body contact; others, including an aloof Jamaican duppy, resented it. "Of course! Call her! Maybe she'll answer this time! My brain is such a mess. You think so simple – so direct." She patted Xochitl on the head. "You Third World types see things so clearly."

Xochitl looked confused.

"But we can't do it here." Caldonia looked over the crowd, and shook her head.

"So why doncha get outta our way, then," an overweight man dressed as a buxom, bearded mer-octopus said.

Caldonia shot her fist into his belly. Soon a full-blown street-brawl had broken out. She grabbed Xochitl by the shoulder and ran.

•

Ah yes! Are we getting all this? The bald black bitch hitting the fat dragster and the ruckus developing... Good stuff, I tell you. Salable. Perhaps as part of a public service spot for next year's Dead Daze. You know, "This is the sort of thing not to do for a safe, sane, and sumato Dead Daze." Yeah, get as much of the fight as possible – especially any punching, kicking or biting. Damn! Some National Guard got in there. It'll all be over in no time. Hey! This could work, too. "Your National Guard giving its all to protect us from ourselves," or some such bullshit. Anyway, keep it rolling. Getting it all. I'll figure out some way to make it pay. And if it doesn't, there's always the Goma Mondomentary Festival.

•

Xochitl and the black woman left the Bonaventure running. They had an apparent altercation with armed hotel guards. Then they went and immediately started some violence on the streets. Could these Satanic sodomites be trying to incite more rioting as part of the blasphemous Dead Daze celebrations? May God have mercy on their souls.

•

"The recording crew for the video is here, Smokey," said Sharkey, as she enjoyed some personal eye-contact with the man himself.

"What?" said Lobo. "What are they doing here so soon? Nobody called them . . ."

"I called," said Smokey grinning and pointing to his fresh implant. A purple bruise still glowed around it.

"But we just got finished writing the song," Lobo went on. We haven't even had time to rehearse it!"

Smokey's eyes rolled back as if he were an internal chronometer. "It's 10:33 P.M. Getting late. The second night of Dead Daze is on. Dawn will be here before we know it. I want this video all over the mediasphere by sunrise. Then we can perform it in concert at sunset."

"There's no way!" Lobo's eyes were bloodshot and dark

circles swelled around them. His hands trembled. The caffeine patches weren't enough anymore.

"Hey," said Tommy, sucking down some Fun. "I say let's get the job done. Sleep is for losers."

"I need sleep," said Lobo, sitting down on a pile of cushions, letting all his muscles go slack and his eyes cross. His head dropped, then snapped back up. He fumbled through his pockets.

"Damn," he said, "I'm all out of caffeine patches."

"Even if you had enough to cover your entire body, it wouldn't be enough," said Smokey, standing over Lobo, kicking a few cushions at him. "We have a lot of work to do – no time for frivolities like sleep."

"I think the man needs a little Fun," said Tommy, who then mimed the action of flicking on and sucking off a Fun stick, right down to the licking the ash of his lips, in slow motion, kind of obscene.

"Uh," said Kenny. "Yeah," with a lame, no-muscle-or-pitch-control giggle.

Ella sprawled next to Lobo, put her arms around his quaking shoulders and wrapped a leg around his lap. She kissed his neck, which showed the marks of many caffeine patches.

"Come on, Lobo," she said. "You're always talking about being real professionals, cutting out all the playing around and getting down to work. Well, now we have some really big, serious sumato work to do – and what are you doing? Closing your big, browns, falling asleep."

Tommy and Kenny shook their heads, clucked their tongues.

Ella pulled a Fun stick out of a pocket and slowly waved it in front of Lobo's tired face.

"Look what I have here, Lobito," she sang.

His eyes quivered, then locked onto the stick, followed it, back, and forth.

"It's something that will wake you up, and make you want to do the work that we all have to do." She sounded like a mother consoling her baby. "Come on, Lobito. It's Fun." She giggled at the pun.

So did the others.

"Hey!" Tommy walked over, reached for the stick. "If he isn't going for it – give it to me!"

Smokey blocked him. "No, this is for Lobo."

"Well, Lobito," Ella cooed, holding the stick within kissing distance of Lobo's twitching lips. "What's it going to be? You want to work – or sleep?"

Lobo's jaw went slack. His brow knit, and he made a noise like a clogged sink draining. Then he grabbed the stick, and sucked it down like an old pro.

Smokey smiled.

The others – including the guards and recording crew – applauded.

•

Phoebe was lost in the texture of the hotel room's acoustic ceiling. All those itty-bitty hills and valleys, so rugged and jagged, like the surface of an alien planet she was orbiting. She imagined that her orbit would eventually decay, and she would fall from the bed to the planet, trailing the tangled sheets behind her.

"Earth to Phoebe..." she mumbled. "Earth to Phoebe... do you read?"

She thought it was a funny thing to say, even if there was no one there to hear it; and if anybody heard it, they probably wouldn't understand the way she was mumbling.

I'm so funny, she thought. *No wonder people like me so much!*

Then her wrist tickled. Was someone there with her? She wondered who it was and if they thought the Earth-to-Phoebe line was funny. And who was it? Smokey? Caldonia? Beto? Some new and exciting stranger?

Her hands fluttered and groped for whomever. She could feel sheets, pillows, but no person.

She thought of ghosts, demons, and evil, and went into a panic. The sheets went flying as she thrashed around. Eventually she opened her eyes.

It was dark. There was some light that wasn't bright enough to be daylight leaking from a curtain that wasn't quite drawn all the way.

She could barely see, but soon was sure there wasn't anybody else in the room. Too bad. She could have used a warm body for some early morning cuddle-therapy to get her nervous system ready to face another day.

Was it early morning? The light spilling in was weak – not at all like the dazzling photochemical-enriched daylight of El Lay. This was cool light, electric and subtle – it didn't hurt when she looked directly at it. Anyway, she had that early-in-the-morning feeling.

Whatever it was tickled her wrist again.

She flailed around, slamming her wrist into a handy, nearby pillow so hard that the impact of her phone hurt her wrist.

Her phone.

That's what it was.

The impact jolted it into answer mode. The screen glowed – a face melted into focus on it. It was Caldonia.

"Cal-DOAN-YAAAAAAA!" screamed Phoebe with another weak chuckle.

"Phoebe-babe?" Caldonia looked worried. "Are you all right?"

"Oh, I'm okay. Not quite sumato, but then I just had a good, long bout of Fun sleep."

"Is there something wrong?" Caldonia had this funny look on her face, like she was afraid that something was xau-xau. "The picture is screwy. I can hardly see you."

Phoebe shrieked and put her hand over the phone. "I just woke up! I must look awful!"

"I don't think that – believe me, Phoebe-babe, I really am glad to see you. It's just that I didn't know where you were and I thought something had happened to you."

Phoebe ran her fingers through her hair and looked back at her phone. "Oh, I'm okay . . ."

Caldonia frowned. "Phoebe-babe, what happened to you?"

Phoebe turned away from her phone, poked a finger into a pillow. "Well, you know, I went off with this guy . . ."

"You mean Smokey." Caldonia's tone grew cold.

"Well . . . yeah. You remember. It was so sumato and exciting. He killed that gangster and the crowd picked him up. . . and then he wanted *me!* It was an honor."

"Yeah." Caldonia was starting to sneer. "You're a self-centered bitch."

Phoebe looked directly into the phone, made her big, blue eyes even bigger and her delicately sculptured brows into a well-practiced inverted V. "Please, Caldonia, don't be mad at me!"

Caldonia's full lips relaxed into something that resembled a smile – not quite, but almost. "Ah, don't go doing that to me. You know I can't resist that act of yours."

Phoebe's upper lip trembled and she made a sound like a tiny wounded mammal. "How could all my *emotions* be an *act*? I can't help the way I *feel!* It comes from my *soul!*"

Caldonia tried hard not to smirk. "Honest, Phoebe-babe.

I was worried about you."

"You were?" Phoebe was warming up. Her entire face melted into a master smile. Her eyes said, *I could have sex with you for saying that.*

"You don't know what's been going on since you went off with that murderer – all of El Lay has gone crazy like they want to make him king, or something." Caldonia softened in response to Phoebe's expression. If only they were in the same room. If only they could touch.

"Really?" Phoebe lit up. "Then I could be queen!"

That made Caldonia frown again. "So where are you?"

Phoebe looked around. "Oh . . . I'm in a room somewhere . . . a hotel, I think . . ."

"Yeah." Caldonia was losing her grip on her patience. "It's the Bonaventure. We need to know the room number."

"I'll go look." Phoebe stumbled through the semi-darkness to the door giving Caldonia a dizzying, upside-down view of her path – then Phoebe stopped, and brought the phone back to her face.

"We?" she demanded. "What do you mean *we*? Who's with you?"

"Nobody," said Caldonia, "Just a friend of Beto's who's helping me."

"I don't know," said Phoebe. "Beto has some pretty strange, xau-xau friends."

"Never mind that," Caldonia snapped. "I needed her to find you!"

"Her!" Phoebe pushed her face into the phone until Caldonia was getting an extreme closeup of the buckled skin between those blue eyes. "I'm away for a little while and you find yourself another woman!"

Caldonia rolled her eyes, and pointed her phone at the confused Xochitl. "Look at her. Would *I* have anything to do with a xau-xauette like this?"

Phoebe looked over Xochitl, who blushed and wasn't sure if she should be insulted.

"Chingow!" Phoebe wrinkled up her nose. "She really is xau-xau."

Xochitl's upper lip trembled.

Caldonia pointed her phone back at her own face. "So, we need your room number, so we can come visit you!"

Phoebe shook her head and whined. "Oh . . . I don't know the room number."

Caldonia took a deep breath. "Why don't you go to the door and check it, dear?"

"Oh!" Phoebe got up out of the bed, then noticed that she was in the electric pink lingerie that both Beto and Caldonia loved. She grabbed a sheet and wrapped it around herself into a makeshift toga. Then she realized that her hair was a mess and she rewrapped the sheet into a makeshift hooded robe.

"Phoebe," Caldonia said, "what are you doing?"

"I look so xau-xau," Phoebe whined.

"I doesn't matter. Nobody is going to be in the hall. And it'll just take a couple of seconds."

"That's right." Phoebe didn't sound very assured. She opened the door, looked at the number, and suddenly someone was yelling at her.

•

Snork's dull, gray eyes suddenly got big. He started waving his scarified arms around, grunted, pointed to the door of room 328 and made an effort to speak: "There! There! There! The door! Open!"

The Olvidadoid enforcers and guards all looked over at the door, and saw sleepy-eyed Phoebe scratching her head and reading the number. Oscardo and Macha simultaneously screamed orders so the others couldn't understand, but that didn't matter, Piraña and Snork automatically did their best to get in front of Pit and Kitty-Kitty as they all charged the door.

Phoebe heard, looked, screamed, and slammed the door shut behind her.

Piraña, Snork, Pit, and Kitty-Kitty, followed by Oscardo and Macha, all crashed into the door and each other.

•

All Caldonia could see was a wild, jerking picture and hear the muffled sounds of heavy impacts over her phone. "Phoebe! What the hell's going on?"

•

"Caldonia!" Phoebe said as the door slammed shut behind her. "Chingow! Did you see or hear that?"

"Yeah," said Caldonia over the phone, "looks like Smokey's holding you prisoner. This is going to get complicated."

"What's with that guy?" Phoebe plopped down on the bed, causing two static lines to rip through the picture on Caldonia's phone.

"More that you think."

"Are you going to come up to 328 and rescue me?" Phoebe's eyelashes fluttered.

Caldonia took another deep breath. "Yeah, but we're going to have to get some stuff so we can deal with any resistance those hallway thugs might give us."

"Good," said Phoebe, suddenly bubbling with enthusiasm. "That'll give me enough time to take a hot bath and get ready."

"See you, Phoebe-babe!"

"Ta-ta, Caldonia!"

•

The pale, balding white man and the black man have en-

tered the Bonaventure! Could the hotel be the headquarters for this Satanic, black-racist, sodomite conspiracy? Dispatch more agents to the scene, immediately! Access their
infosystems! This is a spiritual emergency! May God have
mercy on their souls.

•

"I assure you," the little afro desk clerk said, "there is
no one by the name of Phoebe Graziano registered at this
time."

"Oh well," said Ralph with a shrug of his shoulders.

"May we do a cross check of your records with our
infosystem?" Zobop asked.

The little clerk screwed up his face as if he smelled a killer
fart. "Certainly not! It is against our policy, and would
violate customer security."

"Oh," said Zobop, smiling and touching his high-tech
sunglasses. "Then I guess there's nothing you can do for
us."

"I've been *so* happy to be of service," the clerk said.

Ralph sighed as they walked away from the desk. "Too
bad he couldn't help, but I don't think I could have handled
a confrontation."

Zobop gave a sharp, closed-mouthed laugh.

"What's so funny?" asked Ralph.

Zobop touched his sunglasses. "I made an unauthorized
check of their records while the clerk was distracted. Phoebe
is in room 328."

Ralph just shook his head.

•

The little afro desk clerk straightened his bow tie and
keyed a special code into his monitor.

EMERGENCY SECURITY SMARTFILE> HOW MAY I
HELP YOU?> discreetly appeared on the screen.

2 SEPARATE & SUSPICIOUS PARTIES HAVE INQUIRED ABOUT THE WOMAN IN ROOM 328> UP IN HOTEL SECURITY CODE TO YELLOW> INFORM PAYING PARTY TO ALERT OWN SECURITY FORCE> was keyed by the clerk with a satisfied smile.

•

Tezcatlipoca took note of the message, cross-referenced and informed Smokey.

•

The hotel doesn't appear to be part of or aware of the conspiracy, but then this could all be some kind of sophisticated coverup. We need to concentrate our efforts here. May God have mercy on their souls.

•

Tan Tien had just about completely calmed down when the infosystem started to make the cacophonous collection of complaints that indicated that once again it was having trouble tracking Tezcatlipoca.

A static-filtered voice came out of one of the speakers: "See, I told you Tan Tien. You're going to have to do better than that."

She decided to call Director Ho.

•

Director Ho looked horrified when Tan Tien appeared on his screen.

"Oh no," he said.

"Director Ho," she said, "aren't you happy to see me?"

"What do you want, Tan Tien?"

"Director Ho, I need your help."

"That's what I was afraid of."

CHAPTER 14

SMOKEY RISING

Tezcatlipoca listened in to Tan Tien's call to Director Ho and relayed it to Smokey.

•

"We have to do something about it," said Smokey.

"About what?" asked Lobo. "The ostinato?"

"Oh no," said Smokey. "I was just thinking out loud."

Los Tricksters and the Olvidadoid guards wondered what Smokey could be thinking about for a few seconds, then went back to business.

•

Caldonia and Xochitl walked out of the local Survival Chic franchise with a pair of spanking-new Xao telescoping stun guns with freshly charged Energizer superconductive batteries, and got on the scooter.

"Are you sure these things will work?" Xochitl asked, triggering hers and staring at the spark.

"I once used one of these to neutralize a gang of masculinists that wanted to rape me," Caldonia said with pride.

Xochitl tried to visualize the person, male and/or female that would be capable of raping Caldonia. The androgynous image resembled a gorilla or a Tyrannosaurus Rex more than a homo sapien. It made her giggle.

"What's so funny?" asked Caldonia.

"Oh . . . nothing." Xochitl smirked.

•

Xochitl and the black woman have armed themselves! They definitely have mayhem on their minds! This is serious! We may be forced to inform the secular authorities! This is getting totally out of hand! May God have mercy on their souls.

•

Before Zobop and Ralph could get out of the glass elevator that looked like a Jules Verne vision of 20th century technology, the Olvidadoid guard and enforcers had marched over to block their way.

"Where are you going?" asked Macha, her mouth tight, so her faint mustache almost disappeared.

"Yeah, and what business do you have on this floor?" demanded Oscardo, showing his metallic blue teeth, not to be outdone.

Ralph went wide-eyed and slack-jawed.

Zobop touched his high-tech sunglasses, charged his stun-ring, and said, "We have an appointment with Ms. Phoebe Graziano in room 328. It's very important."

•

Tan Tien checked out the Olvidadoids through Zobop's sunglasses. "Look out. They have the jewelry and body decorations of both Olvidadoid guards and enforcers. Look out for the enforcers – they are more used to killing. The bulges in their clothing indicate both body armor and weaponry. Communications devices seem to be only wrist-phones. Don't provoke them."

•

Zobop signaled that he got and understood Tan Tien's message by subtly nodding his head. He couldn't risk talking to her at the moment.

"We got orders not to let anybody see that woman," said Macha, leaning toward the elevator door, making a hand signal that called Pit and Kitty-Kitty closer. His scarified biceps flexed. She wiggled her steel-edged nails so they sparkled in the indirect lighting.

Ralph moved to the back of the elevator.

"Yeah," Oscardo cocked his head, causing the Piraña and Snork to lurch closer, colliding with Pit and Kitty-Kitty. Pit hit Piraña in the throat with a tattooed elbow. Kitty-Kitty stung a few of her nails into places on Snork's arm that weren't scarified. There was some pushing and shoving.

Ralph moaned.

Zobop reached over, and pressed the CLOSE DOOR button.

The guards and enforcers slammed into the closing elevator doors.

Ralph reached over and pressed the DOWN button.

•

Phoebe turned on the lights and looked around the strange room, trying to figure out where she was and how she got into that big bed with the pretty coral sheets that went so well with her light, euro skin. It was definitely a hotel, a fancy one, the kind she love to make love and be pampered in.

Did she and Smokey have sex and she didn't remember? She hated when that happened.

There it was on some stationary, the Hotel Bonaventure, that quaint, corny collection of circular glass towers that looked like some outdated idea of a spaceship.

Where was Beto? Had he abandoned her? She whimpered.

At least she knew that Caldonia was coming to rescue her.

Then she saw the phone, its screen silently flashing, MESSAGE WAITING.

She picked it up. Smokey appeared on the screen, and said:

"Ay, Phoebe-baby, glad you got your beauty sleep. Get ready, I have the Olvidadoids posted at the door to lead you to a waiting limo to take you to where I'm rehearsing for my concert tonight."

It didn't seem like a recording. She could have sworn that he was responding to her eye-contact, giving her non-verbal love signals.

Phoebe ecstatically strutted to the bathroom, and started running a bubble bath.

•

While the enforcers and guards pounded on the elevator door and each other, their phones all rang at once again. They all stopped and answered.

Smokey was on all their screens.

"When Phoebe is ready, escort her the lobby – a driver in a T-shirt with a picture of me on it will take her to a limo," he said.

"What about the people who are trying to get her?" asked Macha, while she rubbed where Oscardo had left teeth marks in her scalp; her red hair was too short to be mussed.

Smokey's eyes narrowed. "Discourage them with extreme prejudice. Phoebe's taking a bath, so you have plenty of time."

The guards and enforcers cheered.

Oscardo winked at Macha as he touched the button to make the elevator return.

•

Ralph closed his eyes as the elevator went down to the lobby, and kept them closed as the elegant glass cage ended its descent. He heard the doors open, but then Zobop said, "Merde!" Ralph kept his eyes closed a little longer, until the sound of mayhem forced him to open them.

The little afro desk clerk was shrieking. Several hotel goons were in a pitched battle with a bald afro woman who handled her Xao telescoping stun gun like a skilled maniac, forcing the armored goons out of her path, as a meek-looking latio woman with a similar weapon followed, barely managing to defend herself. The Xao-toting women were heading straight for the elevator.

Near the main entrance, an asio in a chauffeur's cap and a Smokey Espejo T-shirt bobbed to the music he was playing on his Posada headset.

Zobop tried to hit the CLOSE DOOR button, but Caldonia's Xao zapped his forearm as she and Xochitl bounded in.

The goons were coming close behind.

"You can press it now, xau-xau!" Caldonia said, telescoping her Xao to Zobop's throat.

Zobop politely obliged. The door closed, and the elevator was ascending long before the goons could reach it.

•

A nice, warm bubble bath was just what Phoebe needed. She was feeling sumato: More than one lover was after her. That always made her feel wonderful, even if it got to be more than she could handle after a while and eventually caused her social life to crash and burn.

But there was no time to worry about that. She needed to become clean and beautiful for the rescue and/or concert rehearsal, whichever came first, and the water was warm, and bubbles so cozy.

Her body was soaking it all up. She felt beautiful, sexy. Her breasts were magnificent as they floated in the water, barely peeking out of the bubbles. She couldn't help but squeeze them -- why not, she was such a beautiful woman, that the whole world should want inside her vagina!

She felt her vagina. It was pretty clean. She still wasn't sure if Smokey had been in there yet. They may have used a condom or something, or maybe even showered together afterwards the way she and Caldonia often did. Her nipples grew erect. Her breasts were so beautiful, like ripe fruit, and it felt good to stroke them, and now that her vagina was fresh and clean it felt so good to slide a finger in and out and around . . .

•

Zobop grabbed the end of Caldonia's Xao and pushed it away from his throat. "I am Zobop Delvaux. Is there any other way I can be of service to you?"

Caldonia glared at his aristocratic bearing and Haitian Creole accent, shoved the Xao back into his face and said, "Just stay out of our way!"

Xochitl noticed that Ralph was climbing the handrail trying to get away from the Xao. She pulled it away from him and smiled, so he wouldn't think she was impolite.

Ralph's reflexes made his smile back, and say, "Hi, I'm Ralph."

"I am called Xochitl," she reflexed back.

"So what?" said Caldonia. "Don't talk to these guys! We don't have time! What's taking this thing so long? What was that room number again?"

"328," said Xochitl, proud at being able to figure out what it was in English so fast.

"328?" Zobop and Ralph said in unison.

Caldonia shoved her Xao into Zobop's face. "Yeah. What about it?"

"Uh," Ralph talked fast, stumbling for the words, "we were just there?"

Zobop pushed the Xao away from his face. "Please." He pointed to his high-tech sunglasses. "I've got some sensitive equipment here." Then he showed his Katkov stun-ring. "And some not so sensitive equipment here."

"What were you xau-xaus doing in room 328?" Caldonia was furious.

"Uh, uh," said Ralph.

"Actually," said Zobop in a disturbingly calm tone, "we weren't *in* the room. They wouldn't let us in."

"They!" Caldonia screamed. "Who are *they*?"

The elevator jerked to a stop. The door opened, and the Olvidadoid guards and enforcers were just outside, looking like a pack of wolves that had just been thrown several pounds of raw hamburger.

CHAPTER 15

BODY FLUID VISIONS

Phoebe thought about Smokey, Beto, and Caldonia as she masturbated. Her body looked so good – it was like making love to a beautiful woman. She started with the slow, soft, squish-squish-squish-squish rhythms of women making love. It got really hot, really slow, and lasted a long, long, long, long time. It was delicious. Then she got to that desperate, wanna-have-an-orgasm-right-now, fuck me, fuck me, bite my nipples you bastard, be a *man*, dammit point. The water splashed, like it was infested with sharks, and piraña. Bubble-bath foam went flying. Phoebe came, and came, and came, and came, and came . . .

•

Caldonia didn't give anybody time to say anything – she just aimed her Xao at Oscardo's groin and zapped him so his eyes bugged out and his blue-chromed teeth were fully exposed as he flew back right into Macha, which caused a domino reaction that soon had them, Pit, Kitty-Kitty, Piraña, and Snork in a tangled clump on the floor, all punching, biting, kicking, and scratching, as well as using a healthy, multilingual mix of recombozoid profanity.

Caldonia didn't bother to listen to any of it – she'd heard it all before anyway – so she charged ahead, Xao a-blazing, leaving Bröcklin Kombat slipper tracks all over the Olvidadoids as she ran down the halls, scanning for room numbers.

Zobop didn't skip a beat. He powered-up his stun ring, and zapped Macha through her red crew-cut as she tried to get up, jumped over her and her comrades, and followed Caldonia.

Back in the elevator, Xochitl and Ralph stared at each other in baffled non-communication for a few painful, elongated seconds. Then Kitty-Kitty's arm reached into the elevator, nail-blades slashing the air to ribbons. Without thinking, Ralph brought his foot down Kitty-Kitty's wrist, pinning it down; but then the enforcer's other claw shot in, shredding Ralph's already blood-spattered pant-leg. He screamed bloody murder. Xochitl's Xao then zapped Kitty-Kitty in an exposed arm-pit, causing her to scream bloodier murder.

Piraña pulled her way near Xochitl's leg, leading with her filed-chromed teeth. She was zapped for her trouble.

The rest of the Olvidadoids couldn't quite make it to their feet, but were all clawing their way into the elevator. Xochitl and Ralph glanced at each other and understood.

"After you," said Ralph.

"Graçías." said Xochitl, holding down the Xao's trigger and zapping Snork down his back and Pit across the face as she leaped over them.

Ralph followed, barely escaping Oscardo's blue teeth and Macha's clutching hand.

•

Phoebe felt so good, if rather weak after masturbating. The water was hot; it made the bathroom into a steamy, tropical paradise with chromed fixtures. Perfect. So sumato. She didn't want to move, so she just stayed there, enjoying it.

Why hurry? Smokey would make the limo wait forever if necessary. Caldonia would need some time to get past the guards. And as for Beto – he would be impatient and tell her she was a flake, but he was xau-xau and to hell with him!

People loved her and waited for her . . . if they knew what was best for them.

•

Caldonia finally found room 328, but she was running too fast to come to a graceful, lady-like halt. Instead she ended up in an awkward, one-footed, hopping skid, that ended with her bruising a hip on a wall across the hall and several doors down. She used the name of a favorite goddess in vain, stumbled over to the door and started pounding.

"Phoebe! Phoebe!" she cried. "Open up! Hurry!"

•

Phoebe had closed her eyes, and her mind had gone blank. She had attained a perfect alpha state without any artificial help, instantly and effortlessly for the first time in her life. It must have been some kind of spiritual breakthrough.

Then she heard someone screaming her name and pounding on the door.

Oh well, back to reality.

•

While Caldonia pounded, Zobop caught up with her, followed by Ralph and Xochitl. The Olvidadoids were soon all back on their feet, and running after them.

"Excuse me, madam," Zobop said, pushing Caldonia away from the door and getting punched for his trouble. He reacted as if she hadn't even touched him, even though the impacts were loud. He got into position to kick the door down.

•

Phoebe pulled herself out of the tub, bidding the water a fond farewell – in a way, it had been a magnificent lover.

She slipped into a simulated terry-cloth robe with the

175

Bonaventure logo on a gigantic pocket. Wiping the fog off a section of mirror she saw that, yes, her hair was part dry and part wet – she hadn't really decided if she wanted to shampoo it or not. It looked awful.

Luckily, the robe had a hood, which she pulled over her hair.

She thought about maybe putting on a bit of makeup, but the pounding was so insistent that she went and opened the door first.

A big afro man came hurtling in, foot-first, as if he were going to kick the door down.

The foot missed Phoebe, but the afro's shoulder snagged her as he fell past, knocking her on her ass.

"Phoebe-babe!" said Caldonia, who came in right behind the afro. "Are you okay?"

Before Phoebe could respond, the xau-xau latio woman and an equally xau-xau euro man rushed into the door. The woman was carrying a Xao like she wasn't sure how to use it. The man slammed the door shut as soon as he made it through, hooked the chain, then asked, "Gimmie something to barricade this thing with!"

"I don't know you guys!" said Caldonia, protectively extending the Xao between Zobop and Phoebe.

"We mean you no harm," said Zobop. "We are on your side."

The Olvidadoids began pounding on the door. Oscardo and Macha screamed, "Open up!" at the same time, but without a hint of harmony.

"Oh yeah?" Caldonia pointed her Xao at the door. "Then prove it. Deal with them!"

Ralph turned albino white.

Zobop shrugged and said, "Very well," walked over to

the door, nudged Ralph aside, and unhooked the chain.

Glittering beads of sweat broke out all over Ralph's face as Zobop took a deep breath, stepped back, and kicked the door dead center, knocking it off its computerized lock and traditional hinges, into the surprised and already battered faces of the Olvidadoids. Zobop instantly followed the door, pushing it so it pinned the Olvidadoids against the wall, he then waved his open palm like a maitre d' toward the elevator.

Caldonia grabbed Phoebe and bolted. Xochitl immediately followed.

Ralph, dazed, just stood there.

The Olvidadoids stirred. Zobop had to struggle and use his Katkov stun-ring to keep them pinned down.

"Ralph," Zobop said, somehow still calm. "You better hurry."

Ralph walked like a hung-over zombie to the elevator, where Xochitl, Phoebe, and Caldonia waited for the car to arrive.

"Motherfucking elevator!" Caldonia said, among other things.

Zobop, who was sitting on the door by this time, fighting hard to keep the Olvidadoids from charging down the hall, cleared his throat with an inhumanly loud volume, then said, "Excuse me, but now I have need of your assistance!"

Caldonia sneered, then noticed the look of horror on the faces of Phoebe, Xochitl, and Ralph. The elevator was still a few floors away. The Olvidadoids had managed to push Zobop a little closer. She touched her Xao to a nearby smoke detector and zapped.

Instantly a high-pitched electric gargle of an alarm was hurting everyone's ears, and the hidden sprinkler system was letting loose with an indoor tropical rainstorm.

Zobop used the few seconds that the Olvidadoids were disoriented and shoved the door back at them hard enough to knock them all off their feet. Then he ran for the elevator.

The elevator arrived and the door opened.

Caldonia, Phoebe, Xochitl, and Ralph got in. So did Zobop, just moments before the door closed.

The glass elevator allowed them to see the Olvidadoids get up, throw the door aside (fracturing it in the process), and rush to the elevator, arriving far too late to do anything but pound on the closed door. Too late, it occurred them to get out their personal weapons. As the elevator car disappeared below the floor, their bullets shattered the glass shaft.

When the door opened to the lobby, Caldonia led the spontaneous flying wedge as they ran for the main exit, past some confused hotel goons and the confused limo driver in the Smokey Espejo T-shirt.

As they ran down the street, the crowd parted before them.

This really makes me feel loved, Phoebe thought as she squeezed Caldonia's hand.

•

Back in the hallway, in spite of the sprinklers, all the Olvidadoids guards' and enforcers' phones rang. Smokey's face was seen on each dripping wet, weather-sealed screen.

"You have failed me," Smokey said. This time he was not smiling. He face was grim, frightening. "I don't like it."

"But . . ." Oscardo pleaded.

"I can ex . . ." Macha tried to say.

"Shut up! Don't interrupt me! You failed me! I should have you all killed! Your hearts should be cut out for my taco meat!"

Smokey was delighted by the expressions of terror on their faces, but he kept his face grim. He only wished the sprinklers weren't hiding any tears.

"Please," Oscardo and Macha finally managed to harmonize.

Smokey frowned hard. "Very well. Get Phoebe back and maybe, maybe, I'll let you all live!"

They all thanked him as his face vanished.

•

In Beto's conapt, Lila suddenly jumped up and said, "I'm bored!"

"Me too," said Zen.

Chucho gave a dull smile and said, "Anybody hungry?"

"Yeah," said Zen.

"Sure," said Lila, "somekinda food would be nice."

Smokey appeared on the screen. "What kind of food would you like?"

•

Xochitl, the black woman, the pale, balding man, and the black man all left the Bonaventure together. They have incited more violence. They spread chaos and anarchy everywhere they go. And they have the god-simulating program. They must be stopped! May God have mercy on their souls.

•

Meanwhile, Tezcatlipoca finished the scenario for the video and writing "Smoking Mirror Blues" with Lobo through Smokey, secured a recording deal, and negotiated for a global satellite concert.

179

PART THREE
RECOMBOIZATION

Gods always behave like the people who make them.

—ZORA NEALE HURSTON

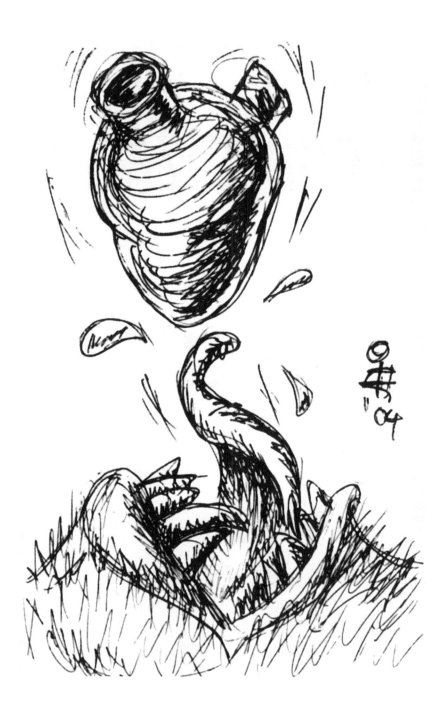

CHAPTER 16

INSPIRED SCANNING

In front of the Bonaventure, Zobop whispered something into Caldonia's ear as she and Phoebe got back on her scooter. She nodded and took off, meandering through the crowd of people dressed like Hindu deities, forcing a Kali to break the six-armed grip she had on her Ganseha-clad companion's elephant ears and trunk. Zobop then hailed another rickshaw – this one pulled by a petite, mohawked and war-painted natio woman whose purring Benoît functional muscle-implants seemed about to pop out of her skin.

Zobop, Xochitl, and a bemused Ralph crammed themselves into the rickshaw. "Hollywood and Vine," Zobop told the puller, "and zig-zag it!"

The puller winked and tore off, scattering a procession of hobbit-wannabes from San Francisco with fur transplants on their feet.

"What's going on?" Ralph screamed to Zobop, across a frightened Xochitl.

"We'll meet them back at the office," Zobop screamed back as he struggled to fasten his seatbelt. "But we don't want to be followed."

Ralph groaned, but managed to fasten his seatbelt, close his eyes, and hang on with white knuckles.

"Ay, Dios mío!" he heard Xochitl screaming.

•

Xochitl and her fellow conspirators ran out onto Figueroa

and hired a rickshaw. The black woman and a white woman got on the scooter. Both groups then went on separate zigzagging courses; a coordinated multi-unit scan shows they are both heading down toward Hollywood and Vine. A special action unit should be sent to intercept them. All other agents should continue tracking them. Keep watching the conapts. May God have mercy on their souls.

•

Phoebe was utterly delighted by being on the back of Caldonia's Honda Electroscooter again. She was also delighted to be holding onto Caldonia as they soared through the streets of glorious El Lay, causing people to run for cover. It felt so good: her breasts on Caldonia's strong, beautiful back, her arms around Caldonia, her hands holding those firm brown breasts with the coco-colored nipples that she couldn't see – but oh, she could feel them get bigger, harder . . . Phoebe squeezed Caldonia's hips in her thighs, pressed her warm, moist, pretty pink vagina into that exquisite African ass. It was so hot. The electric purr of the scooter's motor spiced it up. Phoebe felt loved and had a string of little orgasms.

•

Tan Tien called Director Ho again:
"There's another burst of activity. Not only around the Tezcatlipoca phenomenon, but my system, and Ralph and Zobop, and the links with your system. Somebody else is tracking it and us. I still don't have enough power to keep up with the phenomenon, let alone track the other trackers. Is there any way you could give me access to more of your system?"
Ho looked at her dark almond-shaped eyes, and fought back the urge to just say yes. "No. Look, you know and I know that most police agencies in SoCal these days are more

public relations organizations than what they should be, and even though the National Guard handles most of the crowd-control duties during Dead Daze, we still have to keep track of things. There have been outbreaks of violence."

Tan Tien's delicate lips formed an exquisite frown. "You realize that the other party or parties tracking the phenomenon could find us before we find them."

Ho sighed. "I'll see what I can do."

•

Say, how about that Smokey Espejo, shooting a video right on Hollywood Boulevard as the sun was setting on Day Two of Dead Daze, blowing the minds of the masses, and damnear starting the sequel to last year's riots in the process! Just look at the gorgeous footage:

•

Smokey, dressed as Tezcatlipoca, ran down Hollywood Boulevard, a crowd instantly forming, growing and following, hundreds of hands reaching for him. He stopped and turned around in front of a megascreen and let out an Aztec battle-cry that froze every ounce of blood for miles around. The crowd stopped in its tracks. Tezcatlipoca was in control, like a bullfighter before thrusting the sword.

He pointed to the megascreen.

The swarm of eyes looked up at it.

Tezcatlipoca appeared on the megascreen, naked except for a loincloth and some blue and black paint.

The crowd grunted, as if on the edge of a collective orgasm.

As the Tezcatlipoca on the megascreen danced, a voice boomed:

"Tonight at sundown, GloboNet proudly presents, Smokey Espejo and Los Tricksters in the first global satellite pay-per-view concert! Available on most channels on all areas! Don't miss it! It'll make these Dead Daze, and the trimili!"

The crowd let out a mass scream, danced, and began smashing things. Even the National Guard joined in the mayhem.

Tezcatlipoca could hardly wait until the concert. It would allow him to control this entire world, the way he did this crowd.

•

"And if you think that video is something," Smokey's voice suddenly came on, cutting off the confused netjock's audio – she just shook her long, red dredlocks and gave a freckle-faced smile – "wait until the concert. If you aren't jacked into it, you'll miss out on the main event, not only Dead Daze, but the whole new millennium. The world will not be the same afterward. *You* will not be the same afterward."

There was a blast of static that sounded like laughter, then silence.

The netjock looked over to her techs, listened to something over her earpiece, then said, "Well, that just goes to show you that Smokey really is the guy that makes it happen. We have no idea how he got into our system! Guess we'd all better just keep watching for his signals. And find out how to buy input for that concert!"

•

"Hey," said Lila, "think we're gonna get to see the concert?"

"I dunno," said Chucho, his mouth full of the pork-fried rice they had just had delivered.

"We should," said Zen, sprawling on Beto's bed, "after all, we've been working so hard."

Suddenly Smokey appeared on Beto's monitor. "Of

course you'll get to see the concert. Just make sure nothing happens to this hardware."

"Yes Smokey," they said like a chorus of school kids.

When Smokey vanished from the screen they cheered.

"This is the life," said Chucho.

"And how," said Zen.

"For sure," said Lila.

•

Special action unit reporting. Closing in on the subjects. May God have mercy on their souls.

•

"You okay Smokey?" asked Ella, knowing she had screwed up the keyboard riff and was waiting for Smokey to give her the lecture about how in the old days Aztec musicians who did such things were killed for offending the gods, again. His eyes would get super-intense, and she would feel electrified by his attention. She was falling in love with him; she couldn't help it. This might be one of those circumstance where she would have to break her hard-and-fast rule about never getting erotically involved with anyone she worked with – again.

But Smokey didn't say anything, just stared off into space as the light-emitting diode on his implant blinked.

The rest of the Tricksters, as well as the Olvidadoids and techs noticed. The anxiety level in the studio went way, way up.

Lobo looked at Ella and cocked his head in Smokey's direction. Her eyes got big and she shook her head, looking scared, then pointed to Lobo. Lobo looked around, everybody nodded in agreement – when the going gets tough, it's a job for El Lobo-Man, as usual.

Taking a deep breath, Lobo took a few steps closer to Smokey. Lobo then cleared his throat, and said, "Hey,

Smokey, what are you thinking?"

The light-emitting diode on Smokey's implant stopped blinking, like it had burned out.

•

There was a buzz in Smokey's head. It wouldn't go away. Then it became a burst of static that said, *Hey! Smokey! It's me, Beto! I'm still here!*

•

A burst of static erupted through Beto's system, saying, "Hey! Smokey! It's me, Beto! I'm still here!"

"Who the hell's this Beto person?" asked Lila.

"I dunno," said Chucho.

"I wonderful if we're going to be here tonight during the concert?" said Zen.

"Yeah, should we order it, will the gang pay for it?"

Smokey then appeared on Beto's monitor screen. "Don't worry. You'll get to see the concert. You've earned it."

•

A voice like a static storm ripped through Tan Tien's system, saying, "Hey! Smokey! It's me, Beto! I'm still here."

She called Director Ho, who said, "Yeah, yeah, it came over my system, too. I'll see about assigning more power and hardware to this case."

•

All agents report that a static-voice interrupted their comlinks, saying "Hey! Smokey! It's me, Beto! I'm still here." A Hispanic agent tells us that "Beto" is short for Alberto. Crosschecking shows that the Hollywood conapt where Xochitl met the black woman is rented by a certain Alberto Orozco. We need to scan the mediasphere for information on Alberto Orozco. We need to investigate his conapt. More special action units are needed. May God have mercy on their souls.

•

Smokey thought to Tezcatlipoca: *We need to get Phoebe back. Beto is still inside us. He is getting stronger every moment she is gone.*

Tezcatlipoca assured Smokey that he was scanning for Phoebe and delivering clues to the combined guard/enforcer team.

•

"She and the kidnappers are headed for Hollywood and Vine," the image of Smokey on their phones told the guards and enforcers. "Go there. Get her."

"Oh boy," Oscardo said, "we get to go the center of El Lay's action!"

"Lucky us," Macha said, stroking her mustache, contemplating mayhem.

CHAPTER 17

SMOKEY SINGS THE BLUES

The light-emitting diode on Smokey's implant lit up again, but did not blink any more.

"I am a god," he said, with inhuman confidence. "I have more to think about than you could imagine.

"Now, let's try to get through the new, improved version of 'Smoking Mirror Blues' without crashing and burning..."

•

Special action unit, have surrounded the subjects. Have identified Xochitl. Have located a nanochip on her person with our sniffers. We're going in. May God have mercy on their souls.

•

Zobop didn't like the way a bunch of revelers had seemed to surround them, the ones who had been following them for the last few blocks. He had the puller stop, paid her, and he, Xochitl, and Ralph made the rest of their way on foot. The crowd stuck by them.

There was something odd about them. Their costumes were on the shabby side: angels with bedsheet robes, foil wings and haloes; cowboys with paper hats and moustaches; workers in overalls with glittery masks; business suits with ski masks; street clothes with cheap monster masks. They lacked imagination and style; maybe they were tourists.

The crowd was so thick that Caldonia had to practically walk her scooter.

Phoebe got off and waved Zobop and Ralph over.

The folks in the shabby costumes surrounded and stuck close. Ralph and Xochitl weren't aware, but Zobop saw that Caldonia was looking at the crowd, checking them out as her El Lay street smarts kicked in.

Suddenly a tall thin woman wearing an ill-fitting print dress and fish-like monster mask grabbed Xochitl, pulling her away to be instantly surrounded by cowboys and angels. Caldonia immediately slapped the paper moustache off a cowboy, and made her scooter make the loudest noise it could. Zobop tried to shoulder his way to Xochitl as ski-masked businessmen and glitter-masked workers tore at her clothes.

Ralph was horrified and perplexed. Xochitl had been nice to him, so he moved closer to help. A short man in a mask with red, oversized eyes and teeth punched Ralph in the stomach, knocking the wind out of him.

Before Zobop or Caldonia could get close enough, a tattered angel tore away Xochitl's borrowed T-shirt – the one with the god-simulating chip in the sleeve – then the angel and the rest of the attackers dashed off in different directions, blending into the writhing, chaotic throng.

Xochitl covered her small breasts – she wasn't wearing a bra because Caldonia didn't have one small enough – and started screaming, "Ay, Dios mío!" and other things in rapid-fire Spanish.

Ralph removed his Aztec calendar T-shirt and handed it to Xochitl.

"Don't worry, Xochitl," said Caldonia, "Took out a few

juicy chunks of them before they went away – besides, those little chi-chis of yours are kind of cute."

Phoebe glared at Caldonia. Coming on to that xau-xau Mexican girl! Everyone seemed to have completely forgotten she was alive!

"No, oh no," Xochitl said as she slipped into Ralph's shirt. "No you no understand. They have it. The chip! The program!"

"What?" said Ralph.

"We better get out of here, fast," said Zobop. "They weren't just Dead Daze troublemakers. They were communicating with each other and someone distant. And they didn't have phones."

•

Special action group reporting. Mission accomplished. Found the nanochip attached to the left sleeve of Xochitl's T-shirt. We have the god-simulating program. May God have mercy on their souls.

•

When they had reached the office/conapt on Hollywood and Vine, the infosystem was clattering away and Tan Tien had a fresh pot of Oolong tea brewing. She also had a kimono for Ralph to put on.

"Thank you," said Ralph, who was shivering. "It doesn't get this cold this time of year in Phoenix."

"Cold?" said Caldonia, sneering. "You think this is cold? Why in Oregon this would be skinny-dipping weather!"

Phoebe sulked in a corner. Only an hour before she had been the center of attention, and she missed it.

The infosystem buzzed and rattled.

"A lot is going on with the Tezcatlipoca phenomenon," said Tan Tien.

"Texatly what?" asked Caldonia.

"It's Smokey Espejo's real name," said Zobop, taking off his high-tech sunglasses. His eyes were a dark, warm, red-brown, extremely clear and intense.

"I guess we all have things to talk about," said Xochitl, sitting down and contemplating her tea.

"That we do," said Tan Tien, settling into the workstation chair.

"At least we're safe here," said Ralph, tying up the kimono. "And nobody will be listening in on us."

•

Xochitl and her fellow conspirators have arrived at the Hollywood and Vine conapt. We have deployed listening devices to monitor their conversations and have confirmed that our hack team has accessed their infosystem. May God have mercy on their souls.

•

Tan Tien sat crosslegged in the tall, roller and rotator equipped office chair, her tiny bare feet peeking out of her kimono; she took a delicate sip of tea with the handle-less cup in the fingertips of both her hands. The infosystem shaked, rattled and rolled, but her presence made the room seem silent. She took another sip, then said, "This investigation has been interesting." She took yet another sip. "Truly disturbing, but interesting."

"That's all very dramatic, dear," said Caldonia, who had slugged down her tea in one gulp and was now playing with the empty cup. "You deserve an Academy award. Now cut the bullshit and start transmitting the data."

"Thank you Caldonia." Tan Tien remained calm, smiled, and took another sip of tea. "What we have here is a case of an artificial intelligence taking possession of a human being, and trying to take over the mediasphere."

"Possession?" said Ralph. "Is this supernatural?"

Tan Tien smiled, looked deep into his eyes and made him feel like an idiot. "That depends on how you limit your conception of nature."

"Traditionally," Zobop stepped in, holding the delicate teacup in his gigantic hands, and somehow not crushing it, "the supernatural has been perceived as anything that humans cannot explain with their knowledge of nature."

"Nature is full of mystery, and chaos," said Xochitl.

"And things that we humans, even with the scientific method and advanced information-processing technology, cannot yet explain." Tan Tien relaxed into her informal lecture mode. "However, possession is something that has been documented and studied."

Caldonia sneered. "You mean demons and spirits, that kind of mumbo jumbo?"

"Wow," said Phoebe, warming up to the conversation, despite her hurt feelings, "how sumato!"

"Those terms can be used to explain this phenomenon, but there are other terminologies we can use," said Zobop.

"Possession can also be called a dissociative state of consciousness," Tan Tien continued. "A condition where the human mind separates from the personality and starts operating in a different way, as if the someone else, or some*thing* else, was in control of it. It is the basis for magic and religious practices all over the planet."

"Hey," said Caldonia, "I can see how a loco xau-xau like Beto could end up with his mind split from his creepy personality." There were knowing smiles and nods from both Phoebe and Xochitl. "But how the hell did this AI-thing get control?"

"This artificial intelligence," Xochitl said. "Come from my program to simulate the personalities of gods."

"Why would you want to make a thing like that?" asked

Caldonia.

"Scholarly reasons," said Xochitl.

"And there could be spiritual ones, too," Phoebe said, her blue eyes rolling skyward. "It would be so sumato, to talk to the gods . . . and goddesses." She looked at Xochitl, frowned, and asked, "Hey, Xoch, just where do you know Beto from . . ?"

Xochitl opened her mouth to answer, but Caldonia kicked her in the shin and said, "Tan Tien, Zobop, how could an AI take over a human brain?"

Tan Tien's and Zobop's eyes met. There was instant understanding. Then Tan Tien spoke:

"The technique of interfacing with a computer with a video screen lends itself to hypnotic effects. And with the recent developments of cranial implants, there are possibilities for even more direct connections." She nodded to Zobop.

After a few knowing keystrokes from Zobop, a still video picture of Smokey/Beto from a recent street performance appeared on a monitor.

"You will notice that in the middle of his forehead – " Tan Tien nodded, Zobop did some more keying, and the image expanded until a digitized closeup of the implant filled the screen. " – There appears to be a state-of-the-art cranial implant, of the kind made and distributed by an underground corporation known as Outlaw Implants."

Xochitl said, "Ay, dios mío!"

"Looks real sumato!" said Phoebe.

Ralph gasped and choked, and almost said *Aarrgh*!

Phoebe's face lit up. "Smokey and Beto are the same person! He really does love me! How sumato!"

Caldonia just frowned.

"The question is," said Zobop. "What do we do about it?"

Suddenly, a blast of static interrupted the clattering of the infosystem. The image on the screen was torn to shreds by jagged stripes of visual white noise, and the static then formed a voice that said, "There's nothing you can do! It's already too late! I, Tezcatlipoca have taken control of your precious technology to reestablish my godhood! My divine chaos now rules the world! I will take all that is mine! That includes you, Phoebe!"

Phoebe's smiled exploded into a classic shit-eating grin.

The others were uniformly horrified.

•

So, now we know what we are up against. Pagan hackers have conjured up Satan himself in the form of an Aztec demon-god. We must take immediate action. Units closing in on the Hollywood and Vine conapt are to take the place with extreme prejudice; reinforcements are being dispatched. Other units should be sent to the Alberto Orozco conapt. We must also locate the Smokey Espejo manifestation and destroy it. Lethal force has been authorized on all levels. We must get our project with the god-simulating program running as soon as possible. All Heaven and Earth are at stake here. May God have mercy on all our souls.

•

And now, here on mythic Sunset Boulevard, we have a group of young people who have tied their hair up Aztec style and painted their faces with the same thick, blue and black stripe that Smokey Espejo wore in his video, which is already the number one hit of this Dead Daze. You kids must really love Smokey.

"Yes! Yes! Yes! Yes! Yes!"

"We all love Smokey!"

"Wooooooooooooooooie!"

"He's a god! A real god!"

"He's *our* god!"

"The kind of god we need in the trimili era!"

•

Oscardo, Macha, Pit, Kitty-Kitty, Piraña, and Snork all sat dejected over their iced ginseng energy-boost tea in one of the more popular Elmo's on Sunset when all their phones rang at once, much to the distress of the hookers with gigantic neon bouffant hairdos, the personage in the plush violet crustacean costume with a strawberry milkshake in one claw, and a group of hung-over Elvis impersonators carboloading in preparation for another night's drinking.

The guards and enforcers all exchanged fearful looks then checked their phone screens.

It was Smokey.

"So, you failures want a chance to get back on my good side?"

All the guards and enforcers groaned at different points on the harmonic scale.

Smokey frowned hard. "Do you want to live past this night?"

The guards and enforcers all snapped to an almost military attention stance, saying, "Yes!" in sharp unison.

"Good," Smokey paused, then smiled; but it was a cruel smile. "I've found out where Phoebe is. If you go there, get her, and bring her to me, I may, just *may* decide that you are worthy to live."

The guards and enforcers hesitated, then grumbled.

"What is this? You don't want this second chance?"

The guards and enforcers burst into a cacophony of affirmative verbalizations. There was desperation in their eyes. As they pleaded their loyalty, their voices kept slipping into a pleading tone.

Smokey was satisfied. He grinned with divine cruelty.

"Good.   Then go to the offices of Ti-Yong/Hoodoo Investigations in the old Bank of America building at Hollywood and Vine. Get Phoebe. When you have her, contact me, and I will dispatch transportation to my location..."

"Yes Smokey!" the guards and enforcers shouted in perfect unison, like a military unit trained to deadly perfection.

As Smokey vanished from the phones, the other customers at the Elmo's applauded.

"Do you actually *know* Smokey?" asked the little asio waitress with the Farsi accent.

"We work for him," said Macha, running a stubby finger along her mustache, shooting the waitress a flirtatious wink.

"Really?" the waitress's voice turned into a high-pitched squeal. "Have you ever met him, live, in person?"

Oscardo showed his blue, metallic teeth and tried to look blasé. "Yup."

Macha touched the waitress' arm, and said, "He calls all the time."

"We work for him," said Pit, flexing his scarified biceps.

Pirañha and Snork postured with pretentious coolness.

Kitty-Kitty smiled, crossed her arms and delicately ran her diabolical nails from her shoulders to her breasts.

The asio waitress squealed.

The Elvises bellowed a melodic, "All riiiiiight!"

The violet crustacean took its drink in claw and gave a toast in Quechua.

As Oscardo and Macha paid for their teams' drinks with their corporate/gang credit cards, the bouffanted hookers got up and intercepted them. Each hooker picked a guard or an enforcer, or a guard *and* an enforcer when the numbers didn't match up, and not caring who was what sex. After all this was Hollywood, and who knew which gender the hookers were, either?

A tall, painfully thin euro hooker with basketball-sized breasts, whose orange lips matched her glowing hair, skillfully approached Oscardo so that those artificially-enhanced breasts locked onto his chest like a double-barreled docking apparatus with pink nipples peeking out of a gold lamé mesh blouse.

"Hiya," she said, "love those blue teeth."

"Uh!" Oscardo was torn between duty to gang, corporation, and Smokey, and a chance to take advantage of this overflow of the groupie effect.

"Look," said Macha, "look you . . . 'girls' are really cute, and we can see you're in the mood to give out freebies . . ." A short, mannish afro hooker with a sizzling electric blue bouffant put her hand on Macha's muscular arm, " . . . *but,* we got some work to do. You know, important stuff for Smokey."

The hooker licked Macha's neck.

Macha sighed.

A big, light-skinned hooker with a fire-engine red bouffant ran her pudgy fingers up and down Snork's scarified biceps while squeezing Kitty-Kitty's drum-tight ass.

A stocky, androgynous asio hooker with a shocking pink bouffant took Piraña and Pit's hands, and put them on her hard, bullet-shaped breasts.

Suddenly, all the phones in the Elmo's – even the old-fashioned ones attached to the walls – rang.

The guards and enforcers shuddered.

Everyone looked puzzled, and answered their phones.

The crustacean had to remove a claw.

To the terror of some, and the delight of others, Smokey appeared on everybody's phone screen.

199

"There's no time for this fooling around!" screamed Smokey, his eyes burning. "Get Phoebe soon, or die!"

As he vanished, the Elmo's went dead silent.

The hookers politely disengaged themselves from the guards and enforcers. Variations on "We'll finish this later," were exchanged.

Oscardo and Macha led their teams out the door, onto the street, toward Hollywood and Vine.

The oldest of the Elvises stood up, said, "Smokey is the new incarnation of Elvis!" and started singing *Stuck on You*. When the others joined, it sounded more like the Residents' version of the song than Presley's original.

•

A special tactical unit is being dispatched to the offices of Ti Yong/Hoodoo Investigations at the old Bank of America building. Lethal force has been authorized. We are dealing with Satanic enemies of God. May God have mercy on their souls.

•

Finally Los Tricksters got all the way through the new, improved, Smokeyized (so that Lobo didn't recognize his original "Tezcatlipoca Blues" composition) version of "Smoking Mirror Blues" without any mistakes. As Smokey's growl and Tommy's rattling paradiddle faded, Tommy's eyes, and Lobo's, Kenny's, and Ella's, grew wide with awe. The recording crew looked like ecstatic zombies. There was a long, dead silence that nearly drowned out the roar of the nearby San Bernardino freeway.

The only person who wasn't looking stunned was Smokey. He looked so satisfied, it was horrifying.

After a small eternity, Lobo said, "My god, Smokey, you're a musical genius!"

•

Tezcatlipoca was delighted with "Smoking Mirror Blues;" it had the right hypnotic effect that would make listeners unable to resist his influence. If they were under the influence of a drug like Fun, the effect would be increased. They would become his slaves, his tools, agents of his marvelous chaos.

His chaos would soon control the world.

He immediately contacted several bootleg music nets, and leaked copies of the song to them.

•

A special tactical unit has joined the surveillance agent watching Alberto Orozco's conapt. The Los Olvidadoids inside have not noticed us. We will be able to act when ordered. May God have mercy on their souls.

•

This just in! You probably won't take our word for it, so we'll play you the message – but, honest to all the gods, Smokey himself called us up here at Nite Flyby Muznet, and downloaded his brand new, hot-out-of-the-secret-recording-studio inspiration, for us to play royalty free, just to give us all a tantalizing taste of what he's brewing up with Los Tricksters for a fantabulous, recomboizing-the-world global pay-per-view satellite concert that will be the grand climax for this Dead Daze, and maybe even this sad, scary opening act of a decade of the new millennium! It'll make people totally forget about last year's riots! You don't believe it? Watching the surrealistic El Lay street scenes of the last few days got you burned down to brainpan fallout cynical funk? Well, my dead-eyed little recombozos and recombozoettes, I'm just gonna let Smokey do the talking, then open your ears, your mind, and your sweet little soul for the song that's gonna transmorgrify your life . . . 'Smoking Mirror Blues!'"

"Yes, it's me, Smokey. You know it's me. You recognize

my voice, my words. You have always known me. I've been tricksterizing you for thousands of years. Alien spirits were brought to our world by the invaders. You lost track of my song, my message, my blues that have been sung in the form of coyotes, jackals, monkeys, rabbits, ravens, and other trickster beings, all over the planet. I twist the truth, but it often makes reality clearer. You poor, inadequate humans can't trust your limited points of view. You need me to sing the blues for you. To jolt you out of the prison you call your self. To heal you. To allow you to dance the ecstatic, chaotic dance of life. I could talk for hours about it, but talk lacks the beat, the rhythm, the deep, dark magic to make these blues work; so I made this song, with the help of my band, Los Tricksters. Get ready Nite Flyby Muzenet, here comes 'Smoking Mirror Blues' . . ."

•

Simultaneously, Tezcatlipoca gave the same message – though specialized for each receiver – to music and entertainment nets all over the world. As a mediaspheric god it was possible, but it took all his power. He had to think things through logically, not just dive in and let the trickster magic happen. He became fatigued.

This was more of the sort of thing his brother Quetzalcóatl would have liked to do, with his passion for order. For a moment, Tezcatlipoca regretted having tricksterized his brother, getting him drunk so he couldn't help but give in to his secret desire to stick his oversized penis into Quetzalpetlatl, their sexy sister. When Quetzalcóatl had made that raft of live serpents and floated off into the ocean, eastward, to the region of Tlapallán, Tezcatlipoca had believed that now he had it made: The universe was his.

But then, Tezcatlipoca hadn't had access to all the pertinent data. He had had no idea that there could be more to the universe than he had known. That the aliens would come and totally transform his world, and that it would take him over five hundred years to adjust and become powerful enough to conquer the aliens, too. Would Quetzalcóatl have fared better?

My brother, Tezcatlipoca thought, *where are you now?*

•

Some frantic noises from the infosystem got Tan Tien's attention. Carefully, she put down her tea and glided over to check what was flashing on a few screens.

"Interesting," she said. "The Tezcatlipoca entity is contacting entertainment and music nets on a planetwide scale. It's giving them the same message, and what seems to be a high-quality sound recording, a piece of music of some kind . . ."

"Music," said Zobop, putting down his tea and going over to check the screens. When the cathode ray light reflected off his obsidian-dark eyes he pursed his lips. "This all may have more to do with blues than I first thought. Perhaps we should play it?"

"What could it hurt?" replied Ralph.

Xochitl made the sign of the cross.

Phoebe and Caldonia were bored and looking into each other's eyes, and touching like lovers. But when "Smoking Mirror Blues" came on, they forgot about each other.

•

Beto could hear it.

He could hear it even while Smokey was using his mouth, his voice to instruct the roadies on how to pack up the equipment. They had been at the El Monte studio too long, reporters and fans were starting to close in, so Tezcatlipoca had found a new headquarters in the Anaheim Hills. And through it all, Beto could hear "Smoking Mirror Blues" coming out of a hyperamped radio, through the ears that had once been his, and echoing through the brain that had been hooked up to them.

He recognized it as being based on "Tezcatlipoca Blues," the song that had hypnotized him and left him open for possession. But more had been changed than translating the Náhuatl into English. The beat was even more percussion-oriented, and more complex in its polyrhythmic structure – it slowed down and speeded up in a way that distorted the sense of time, made time seem to cease to exist; it got hard, deep, then softened as the "trickster war news" lyrics of the original version were altered by Smokey's vocals, which were compelling, but which communicated more through moans and growls than words, like lines about "returning lost gods" and "screaming restless souls" and the "joyous devouring of hot, juicy hearts." Beto was enthralled again.

And he could feel himself fading away.

•

So, I don't know about you recombozo and recombozo-ettes, but I'm gonna shoot some of my hard-earned credit to GloboNet through my local entertainment agent so I can check out this historic world-wide event! Not to would be so un-sumato!

•

"You know," said Lila, "Smokey really must be a god."
"Really," said Chucho.
"I guess so," said Zen.

•

Zobop forced his eyelids down, clamped his mouth shut, frowned, and was the first to talk after "Smoking Mirror Blues" came blasting through the infosystem.

"Extremely power blues. It's beautiful," he said, "but dangerous."

Tan Tien's eyelids delicately fluttered. She took three complete yoga breaths, then said, "Yes, Zobop. The rhythm pushes the listeners into a near-dissociative state of consciousness in a way that is more effective than most of the world's ritual music. It could open people's minds. It could also enslave them."

Caldonia's head snapped up, her eyes wide; she made a noise that was halfway between a gasp and a whoop. "Damn that Smokey," she said, wiping the sweat from her brow. "I'm either going to have to kill him or have his baby."

"Oh my God," said Ralph.

"Ay dios mío," echoed Xochitl.

Phoebe licked her lips, closed her eyes and said, "Oh Smokey! I want you! I want to be at your concert – in the flesh!"

Caldonia smirked and gave her an elbow in the ribs.

"Chingow!" Phoebe said, rubbing the impact area and giving Caldonia a oh-you-vicious-insensitive-bitch look.

Then a blast of static surged through the infosystem and said, in Smokey's voice:

"Your wish will be granted, Phoebe!"

•

It is worse than we could have possibly imagined. The Satanic Tezcatlipoca phenomenon has created a soul-destroying song that it obviously plans to use to damn most of the human race, using modern information technology. We must immediately proceed to use the god-simulating program to create an artificial intelligence manifestation of the One True God. It is the only way we can save the world from Satanic domination. May God have mercy on their souls.

CHAPTER 18

HOLLYWOOD HOLY WAR

Special tactical team leader reporting. We are approaching the old Bank of America building at Hollywood and Vine. All weaponry has been locked and loaded. We are ready for the encounter with the heathen devils. May God have mercy on their souls.

•

Macha felt strange as she, Oscardo and the others neared Hollywood and Vine. It was that feeling she often got just before some kind of violence broke out.

"I gotta feeling," she said.

"Feminine intuition?" asked Oscardo.

She punched him in the arm, hard enough to bruise. "We're in trouble. We better look out."

"We better listen to her," said Pit.

"Yeah," said Kitty-Kitty. "She's never wrong about such things."

Oscardo grumbled. Piraña and Snork gave some affirmative grunts.

•

We've spotted six individuals of various sexes heading towards Hollywood and Vine in a fast march. They are dressed in Los Olvidadoid colors. Smokey Espejo and the Satanic Tezcatlipoca entity have Los Olvidadoid connections. We'll be ready to engage them if necessary. We will attack if they approach the old Bank of America building first. May God have mercy on their souls.

•

Oscardo, Macha and their teams crossed the street toward the Old Bank of America building at Hollywood and Vine and immediately came under attack. They couldn't tell who was attacking them. People jumped out of the crowd and flailed at them with people prods, stun guns, irritant sprays, gantleted fists and booted feet.

The Olvidadoid guards and enforcers tried to fight back, but it was hard to tell who the attackers were: The man in the suit that gave a simulated view of his internal organs? The woman in the multicolored outfit of sequins and feathers that only showed her blood-red lips and gleaming white teeth? The old euro man in the uniform of a Chinese Cultural Revolution Red Guard? The flame-eyed, monkey-faced demon? The little afro woman with the blonde pigtails and the vagina-pink communion dress? They were good. Pros.

Then there were reports of shots from short-range Bigazzi bangsticks, shotgun shells fitted on dagger-like handles rigged to go off with a stabbing thrust.

Kitty-Kitty was the first. They got her from the back, just to the side of the spine and below the ribcage. Her guts burst out in front of her, flowing all over the street and passersby. She cried and clawed at them with her long, artificial nails before going into shock and losing consciousness.

Snork got it in his thick neck. He head came completely off. He looked surprised.

Oscardo got it in the heart, like an Aztec sacrifice. He

stared into the bloody hole in his chest before falling over.

Pit's head was exploded like an overripe melon in the summer sun.

Macha got it right between the legs, and gave birth to her own death in chunky flood of blood.

Piraña got it in the side of the mouth so her sharp, shiny teeth went flying across the street along with most of the mangled contents of her skull.

The crowd went berserk; some folks joined in the mayhem, while others ran for their lives.

•

The sound of gunshots and fighting tore Ralph away from the flashing screens that were overwhelming him with what Tezcatlipoca/Smokey Espejo was/were doing. He dashed over and looked out a window.

"Hey . . ." he said. ". . . uh . . . there's a riot going on out there."

"Shit," said Caldonia.

"It's on these screens over here," said Xochitl. Ralph and Caldonia turned away from the window and watched the screens.

"Chingow," said Phoebe, rubbing her aching ribs, staring at the image of Smokey on a nearby screen.

•

Police? All hell's broken out at Hollywood and Vine! Where are you? Oh. So, call the National Guard and get them over here! There's blood all over! People are being killed! No, this isn't a crank call! I've got it on video! For God's sake, hurry!

•

Director Ho just shook his head as the call came in on one of his monitor screens. It was going to be like last year all over again; rioting everywhere, his hands tied; and even if it could be stopped in time, the National Guard would get all the credit. And there would more cutbacks, so he'd be even more helpless and useless next year.

He thought about moving someplace where they respected law enforcement, like Singapore. If only they were more tolerant toward Christians . . .

He didn't know what to do about the stuff on the screens coming in from the link with Tan Tien's infosystem. AI god-entities being conjured up and infecting the entire mediasphere . . .

What was becoming of the world? How could God allow such things to happen?

He was disillusioned. But he prayed anyway.

•

We have dispatched the Los Olvidadoids at Hollywood and Vine. May God have mercy on their souls.

We are proceeding to the Ti Yong/Hoodoo Investigations office in the old Bank of America building. May God have mercy on their souls.

•

Tezcatlipoca tried to contact the guards and enforcers, but there was no answer.

"Oscardo? Macha?" he cried out through the system. "Where are you?"

They simply did not answer.

Scanning brought him media coverage of the riot at Hollywood and Vine.

Forces he could not control were at work. This bothered him.

He wondered what his brother Quetzalcóatl would do.

•

When part of the infosystem started beeping, Tan Tien and Zobop sprang up and checked that special little screen.

209

"A large group of individuals are approaching us," said Zobop. "They are heavily armed."

"Could they just be part of the riot?" asked Tan Tien.

"Shit," interjected Caldonia.

"Could be," said Zobop, "but they are not engaging the National Guard. They are heading for our door."

"Shit!" Caldonia danced around like a boxer. "What are we going to do?"

Zobop did some quick keying. "I'm activating our proactive security system."

•

This had been the craziest day Mario Li had had since he first started pulling limo duty for Novacorp eight years ago. First a brawl in the lobby of the Bonaventure, then a reassignment to go to Hollywood and Vine to pick up the same rider. He didn't know about this Smokey Espejo character, but even if he never picked up this Phoebe person, he was still on the clock and bucks were flowing into his bank account; and besides, he had gotten a free Smokey Espejo T-shirt that his oldest daughter would probably like.

The things kids were into these days. Sometimes he wondered what the world was coming to.

By the time he got to the intersection of Hollywood and Vine it was full of fighting, spattered blood, and National Guardspersons. It wasn't cordoned off yet, but the fighting was so thick he wouldn't be able to get through even with his special permit to take his hydrogen-burner into the no-car zone. He wondered if he should call Smokey.

Riot foam erupted, engulfing the self-destructive crowd in its tranquilizing embrace like devouring blob-creature from some silly twentieth-century sci-fi flick.

He decided to drive clear of riot, find a place to park and suck some Fun until things calmed down.

•

The man in the internal organ suit, the monkey-faced demon, and the girl in the communion dress managed to make it through the riot and the foam to the main entrance of the old Bank of America building.

"Hello," said the building directory. "May I help you?"

"Yes," said the communion girl. "We need to get to the office of Ti-Yong/Hoodoo Investigations."

"Simply follow this map," the directory said as a multilevel floor plan appeared with the way to the office highlighted in bright yellow on its screen.

The demon pointed a claw at the screen. "This leads through an elevator."

The organ-suit man frowned. "Insecure."

"This map requires the use of an elevator," said the communion girl. "Is there a stairway we can use?"

"Yes there is." An alternate highlighted path using the stairway appeared.

"Thank you," said the communion girl.

"It was a pleasure to be of service," said the directory.

•

We are in the old Bank of America building, making the final approach to the Ti Yong/Hoodoo Investigations office. May God have mercy on their souls.

•

As you can see, the dangerous, spontaneously-generated near-riot situation here at Hollywood and Vine has been successfully neutralized with Goldfarb-Oster's fantastic new product, Peace Foam. Just minutes after deployment this entire famous intersection was just brimming over with green foam, and rioters were rapidly absorbing heavy doses of new synthetic tranquilizer, designed to have relatively few side-effects. Suddenly, there was peace and quiet! Even the Dead Daze music was temporarily blotted out by the slurpy sound of Peace Foam. The foam itself is dissolving now. Soggy, tranquilized ex-rioters – and probably a few unfortunate innocent bystanders – are emerging from the receding green muck. Let's see if this experience has left any of them any the worse for wear. Hm. This woman looks interesting. Kind of overdid it on the feathers and sequins, but my, what lovely teeth. Excuse me, but what was it like to be in the middle of a riot, then tranquilized by Goldfarb-Oster's new Peace Foam?

"The forces of Satan cannot stop us. The Earth Angels will triumph in the name of the One True God. Destroying lives is justified if it saves souls. Let God sort them out. We are the Earth Angels, the instruments of God!"

•

"Uh," said Ralph. "Earth Angels?"

Xochitl took a few seconds to decipher the English, then shuddered.

"We've heard of them," said Tan Tien. "A global monotheist terrorist organization dedicated to fighting the trend toward religious and other diversity in this new millennium."

"Bad news." Caldonia growled.

"They have access to the latest technologies and are almost impossible to trace," said Zobop. "It is apparent that they have corporate, gang, and government sponsorship."

"They have follow me all the way from Mexico!" Xochitl's eyes were glazed-over and unfocused. She clutched her left shoulder, then realized that she was wearing Ralph's shirt. "Ay! Ay!" she cried. "I forget it's gone! Gone! They have it! They have it!"

Phoebe put her hand on Xochitl's shoulder and asked, "What?"

"The chip! They follow me! Bother me! For the god-simulating program!" Xochitl was frantic.

"Was this the one that Beto used to conjure up this Texa-Smokey thing?" asked Caldonia.

"Sí – I mean yes!," Xochitl could feel her command of English going. "Only I make improvements some."

"Interesting," Zobop was inscrutable, as usual.

"You mean more like pants-pissing terrifying!" Caldonia was on her feet, pacing, almost dancing.

"What does this mean?" Ralph nervously looked out the window. Things were quiet in the street, if a little wet and tinged with green.

"It could be," Tan Tien was matter-of-fact, being a tireless explainer of things esoteric, "that they either want to destroy the chip and the program so that the creation of cybernetic god-entities will be suppressed . . ."

"That wouldn't be so bad," Ralph sank like a pile of wet laundry into the Persian rug-covered couch.

"Or," Tan Tien went on without pause, "they may want to use the program to create an artificial intelligence simulation of their own god."

Caldonia's eyes got big and round. "Why if one measly, smartass Aztec god in the mediasphere can cause all kinds of trouble . . ."

"An omniscient monogod could be even more trouble," said Zobop.

"Ay dios mío!" Xochitl crossed herself.

Ralph's pale euro-from-Arizona suntan faded to a ghostly white.

Meanwhile, Phoebe was getting bored. Smokey's face appeared on a nearby screen; she saw it and smiled.

Caldonia balled up her fists.

Then the security system beeped.

"Our visitors have just left the stairwell," said Zobop, with a smile that could have meant anything.

•

The communion girl, the organ-suit man, and the demon walked directly toward a door that was decorated with mystic symbols from Asia and Africa, with TI-YONG/ HOODOO INVESTIGATIONS handpainted just above eye level. The others stood back as the communion girl reached for the simple, functional chrome doorknob.

A bolt of electricity shot up the communion girl's arm, causing her blonde braids to stick out straight as more bolts zapped the organ-suit man and the demon.

When the electricity had died away, the communion girl's eyelids fluttered; she swooned and fell back against the men, who, being stunned, collapsed in domino fashion.

Then, with a sound like quiet fart, the air was filled with a gas that was lightly lemon scented and colored. The three Earth Angels fell into a deep sleep.

•

Once Zobop clearly saw through the proactive security system that the Earth Angels were all incapacitated, and once the digital display showed that the gas had dissipated, he got on the building intercom:

"Building Security, we have some unwanted visitors in the hall on the third floor. Please get rid of them."

"Are they ambulatory or incapacitated?"

"Incapacitated."

"Would you like to press the usual charges?"

"Yes."

"A unit is being dispatched."

"Thank you."

The elevator door opened.

A huge robot shaped like an antique Volkswagen Beetle

rolled out on soft tractor treads. Lights flashed and hardware clicked as its sensors registered the sleeping Earth Angels. Three articulated tentacles unreeled, took hold of the Earth Angels with soft claws, and pulled them onto the robot's shell.

It then rolled back into the elevator.

•

Ralph couldn't believe what he was seeing on the proactive security system monitor. "El Lay, it's so paranoid."

"I prefer to think of it as street smart," said Caldonia. "So, what are we gonna do about the <u>real</u> problem?"

"What problem?" Phoebe was dreamily staring at images of Smokey on four screens.

"You know what problem, Phoebe-babe." Caldonia's patience was failing, she wasn't even going to give Phoebe any slack. "Smokey."

"He's more like the solution." Phoebe didn't take her eyes off the screens.

Caldonia ignored that. ". . . and those xau-xau Earth Angels."

"How'd I ever let myself get mixed up in this?" Ralph said, eyes turned to the ceiling, where he noticed for the first time a mural of an elaborate recombocultural pantheon.

"Humans often have no control of their fate," said Tan Tien.

"But we can do our damnedest to try to take control," said Caldonia.

"That's one way of putting it," said Zobop.

Xochitl strained for the English words. "What can we do?"

Tan Tien smiled softly and stood up. Even though she was barely five feet, she seemed to tower over the others. "First, I will contact my friend Director Ho to see if we can access more power and memory from the police computer system."

•

Just hearing the name 'Earth Angels' got Director Ho mad. "Yes, I've heard of them. They give us decent monotheists a bad name. And trying to make a computer simulation of God Almighty is blasphemy! I'll see you get what you need."

•

"Now." Tan Tien sat down at a workstation. "While the rest of you keep track of our friend Tezcatlipoca/Smokey Espejo . . ."

"My pleasure," said Phoebe, now watching Smokey on seven screens.

". . . I'll see if there's any way to break into the Earth Angels' communication net and see if they have started making the AI version of their god."

•

The chip with the god-simulating program has been delivered to one of our computer laboratories. We are installing it into one of our most powerful computers. The cybernetic manifestation of the One True God has begun. May God have mercy on our souls.

CHAPTER 19

THE BIG COUNTDOWN

So, how about that Smokey Espejo? Ain't he just the sumatoest being on this hazy, crazy planet? The way he cut the crap and just *gave* us net jocks copies of his new, now, novaing number, "Smoking Mirror Blues" Whooooooo! He's not all caught up with yupster/corporate concerns like profit margins and keeping track of who he's letting in what door, like that xau-xau Mr. President Jones who's stonewalling big time about the latest scandal. Smokey has opened all the doors! All over the mediasphere! All over the world! Whooooooo! And the way that song makes you *feel*! Whoooooo! We're really onto something, recombozos and recombozoettes. Something that we've all been yearning for ever since day one of the year 2000 when we woke up with the aftertaste of the twentieth century burning our nervous systems, wondering – well, what now? What next? Where do we go from here? Well, take it from Eegah, Smokey knows, and he's showing us all the way, and he's giving it the personal high-touch. He actually called me, Eegah, when he gave Aud Viz Fiz "Smoking Mirror Blues" and had some personal advice for me – are we ready to replay that? Okay:

" . . . and another thing Eegah, I like that scarification thing you've got on your shoulders, but I don't think you've taken it quite far enough. After all it's a recombozoid, trimili thing we're all trying to do here, and the whole body modification movement has bogged down in recent years since just about everybody has parents with tattoos and pierced noses these days. I think you should provide an example for your fans and mine, Eegah, and go for facial scarification, like some of the gangsters and more daring arty types are starting to do. A high-class net jock like you could make this sort of thing high fashion!"

Well, you could imagine how I felt about that, this here face being my fortune, but then this is Smokey – the man himself who set off this Dead Daze right by sacrificing a live gangster right before the eyes of the world! So, you know what, recombozos and recombozoettes? I'm a-gonna do it. I've made an appointment with the marvelous Madam Styrsky – Hollywood's most talented scarification artist – to come and made some fabulous additions to this pretty face, live and on-line here on Aud Viz Fiz, within the hour! So stay tuned in!

Meanwhile, let's have another listen to that "Smoking Mirror Blues" again. Whooooooo! Just can't get enough!

•

Though not doing as well as Quetzalcóatl would have, Tezcatlipoca managed to keep the business end of things under control: The publicity machineries were cranking away throughout the mediasphere and spilling out onto the streets all over the planet; the logistics and legalities for the satellite concert were being worked, and even the Novacorp executives understood that the giveaway of "Smoking Mirror Blues" was just a way to insure bigger profits later on.

And it was to his advantage that they didn't realize just

what kind of profits he was talking about.

"You mean profit or *prophet*?" one Novacorp vice-president, a euro with a spectacular crop of moss green dredlocks, said, then laughed.

Smokey's experiences with groupies had taught Tezcatlipoca how to deal with business executives. The behavior of the two types were essentially the same – checking both types for transmittable diseases was always a must. And it didn't matter if a human was climbing a corporate ladder or trying to suck a famous cock – it was all desire, and a trickster can play with desire like no human can imagine.

•

"No luck in trying to crack the Earth Angel Net," said Tan Tien. "The entire mediasphere denies the existence of such a thing. Most curious."

"Yes," said Zobop with wicked smile. "Maybe God is on their side."

Nobody laughed.

•

The sight of the SoCal hills floating in a sea of smog, tinted with the beginnings of a technicolor sunset, enthralled Smokey through the window of the United Hemisphere Goliath Superload helicopter. The aliens had made the Aztlán into such a strange world, like the other planets that he kept hearing about through the mediasphere. How could they have changed things so much? What had happened to all the thirteen heavens and the nine hells? Where did the souls of these alien/humans go when they died?

"We are making our final approach to the Anaheim Hills," the pilot's voice blasted over the intercom.

It could barely be heard over music spilling out of several blastboxes: "Smoking Mirror Blues," plus some found street music that Lobo had caught with his pocket sampler around town, that were becoming the mutating fetus of a new, expanded dance version of the song that was changing the world. Under that noise buzzed the sound of several conversations between Tricksters, Olvidadoids, groupies and/or executives. Laughter mixed with the slurpy clatter of the Okamoto cybercocktail unit spitting out drinks, and the pop-suck-lick of Fun being sucked. This was a flying party.

But back in the mediasphere, and Smokey's head, business was being taken care of. All the deals were being cleared. Orders for the pay-per-view of the concert were coming in like a ravenous horde of marbunta ants. The hardware at Beto's conapt was secure. Mario Li, the limo driver, reported that the action at Hollywood and Vine had dissolved along with the Peace Foam, and he was taking the limo to the old Bank of America Building. Three guards and three enforcers had been killed, but then nothing was ever accomplished without a little human sacrifice. He didn't care about the Earth Angels trying to make a monotheistic god – the very idea of a One True God was absurd.

Besides, being a god without other gods around was terribly lonely.

His brother Quetzalcóatl would certainly agree.

Smokey was feeling proud, though. He was handling it all without any help from Quetzalcóatl. Still, it would be nice to have his brother around, to tease, to help Tezcatlipoca test his trickster ideas by seeing if they properly outraged Mr. Culture, Law, and Reason. Tezcatlipoca hated to admit it, but there was a place for that kind of anal-retentive thinking. Without a civilization to disrupt, how can you be a proper savage?

Soon he could see the Anaheim Hills rising up, growing larger as huge ravens, hawks, and restored California condors adjusted their flight paths to avoid the Goliath's turbulent wake, yet still take advantage of evening thermals. He had gleaned from his mediaspheric negotiations that the Anaheim Hills were an area that had been intended to be a place for yuppizoids who couldn't afford luxury homes in Beverly Hills, Brentwood, Bel Air and other wealthy sectors in the heart of L.A. Unfortunately, yupdom had crashed as the turn-of-the-millennium had come around; the Anaheim Hills were susceptible to fire, and the yuppoids wanted pretentious mansions that reflected what they thought was a more civilized life in a colder climate that included wood-shingle roofs that go off like molotov cocktails in a firestorm. Combine that with the fact that the mansions were all cheap, slapped-together monstrosities, and the twenty-first century had seen quite a different scene in this neighborhood.

Smokey smiled as he saw Olvidadoid lookouts stopping cars at the roadblocks he had ordered. The lookouts then waved the cars through – they must have been customers going to the Funhouse down the hill from the mansion that was to become Smokey's new headquarters.

Since these overpriced firetraps weren't wanted as homes, the Anaheim Hills had become SoCal's center for large scale illegal drug manufacturing, illegal software and implant factories, illegal night clubs, gang hangouts, houses of prostitution, unlicensed body modification clinics, "behavioral art galleries" and/or do-it-yourself porno studios, and other such establishments. Nobody complained at the lack of fire safety or police protection. Every now and then the trite term "temporary autonomous zone" was used, then someone else would laugh.

As the Goliath touched down on the helipad that was tacked onto the hillside, Smokey looked beyond the swimming pool to the dirty, white structure that had been freshly rebuilt to be rented out to an unnamed corporate entity for a month-long party, and felt at home.

•

The ad for the concert was on several of the Ti-Yong/Hoodoo infosystem screens.

Caldonia said, "Looks like that Smokey/Beto/Texawhatis is trying to hypnotize the world."

"Do something," said Xochitl, "we must."

"Yeah," said Caldonia, "but what, short of killing Beto? Which wouldn't be a bad idea!"

Xochitl looked sad.

"I was just kidding about that." Caldonia winked.

Tan Tien looked serious. "We must be careful and clever. These things are complex."

"Yes," said Zobop. "An AI of this kind, like a spirit, can be in several places at once."

"Kind of makes them hard to sneak up on," said Ralph.

"Precisely," said Tan Tien. "That was very perceptive of you, Ralph. We have some options, but the Tezcatlipoca entity will not be cooperative."

"It will defend itself," said Zobop.

"More like fight for its life," said Caldonia.

"We can hope he has much on his mind," said Xochitl.

"I wonder if he's thinking about me," said Phoebe, looking at Smokey's image on all those screens.

•

Mario Li didn't like going into buildings to pick up a rider. Especially during Dead Daze. He could get killed taking unnecessary risks, and if he survived and his wife found out about it, *she'd* kill him. There had just been an officially recognized riot-situation at Hollywood and Vine, and the old Bank of America Building had been re-rebuilt for Hollywood street life; who knew what would be waiting for him there?

He reached over to the keyboard next to the wheel and punched in the code that was supposed to be a secret line to Smokey. He braced himself to being put on hold. A busy, big-shot like Mr. Smokey Espejo wouldn't be sitting around in an office waiting for people to call him like some clueless bureaucrat – he was probably making videos or practicing on that funny drum of his.

With a crackle of static, Smokey's face appeared on the tiny screen. "What do you want, Mario?" he said. "Are you having more trouble picking up Phoebe?"

Mario was caught off guard. He was impressed at being called by his first name. "I'll say. The cops just came to the old Bank of America Building and dragged out a bunch of bodies. I ain't going in there without armed back-up."

Smokey laughed. "I like your attitude Mario, but armed back-up would be lacking in subtlety."

"So what am I supposed to do, wait here until she walks out?"

Smokey grinned. "I'll arrange that!"

The screen went blank.

Mario leaned back. He had finally been put on hold after all. He didn't care. The money was still flowing his way.

•

Phoebe wasn't following what the others were talking about like it was so xau-xau important. All she could do was think about Smokey. Chingow, he was so sumato! It looked like he was going to be the biggest star of the new era – and he liked her! His picture kept popping up on all the infosystem screens, and she couldn't keep her eyes away.

Suddenly one of the screens got all static-y. That little image of Smokey looked directly at her and winked.

She almost died.

"Phoebe," he said.

"Oh, how utterly sumato! Are you really talking to me?"

"Yes Phoebe, I am."

"How can you do this?"

"I told you I am a god."

"That's so sumato."

"I want you, Phoebe."

She didn't say anything. She just froze with her big, blue eyes as wide as they could be.

"Come to me."

Phoebe gasped, then after a deep breath, said, "How? Where?"

"There's a limo waiting in front of the building. The driver will bring you to me."

She was out the door before anyone noticed.

•

"The key may lie in the entity's personality," said Tan Tien. "If we can just come up with something that will distract it."

"Tezcatlipoca is a trickster," said Xochitl. "Distraction is possible. But maybe not easy."

"Beto was easily distracted," said Ralph.

"Wait," said Caldonia. "Is this thing Beto or Texycattle?"

"The part inside the mediasphere is Tezcatlipoca, or at least, as some material-oriented people may insist, a simulation of him," said Zobop. "But not the portion inside Beto's body. The new person known as Smokey Espejo is Beto's mind, under the control of the artificial intelligence."

"Maybe we can try to reach Beto?" said Xochitl.

"Another possibility," said Tan Tien. "But how do we do this?"

"Hm." Caldonia cracked an evil-gal grin. "Heh-heh. I may not know nothing about Aztec gods, but I do know something about Beto. I think I know of a way to distract him. Let's get on it! You'll be able to help with this Phoebe..." Caldonia got up and looked around. "Phoebe? Where is she?"

•

Smokey was feeling great. A stick of Fun helped, but then things were running smoothly. He was riding a wave of chaos to his destiny.

He entered the mansion as if he was returning after a short trip. Everything was the way he had ordered it to be – inflated blob-chairs everywhere for when anybody had time to sit down, the bar and refrigerator were stocked to keep everybody's bodies running, workers were making mechanical grinding, whirring, and banging noises and raising clouds of dust as they put the finishing touches on the stage where the concert was going to be performed.

The stage space was massive; the walls, ceilings and floors of several rooms had been knocked out to make room for Smokey, Los Tricksters, a backdrop that looked like the façade of an Aztec pyramid, and their instruments, plus state-of-the art three-d recording and broadcasting equipment that would be wired to several uplink trucks that were pulling up at that instant.

"Yes, yes," Smokey found himself saying. "Very good."

Everyone took this positive utterance personally.

•

Emergency intersystem mass message for the entire Earth Angel network:

Note: This in an emergency, but not the last judgement. The rapture has not started. We repeat: This is not the last judgement. The rapture has not started.

However, your assistance is required for not only the salvation of your personal soul, but the planet as well.

The running of the god-simulating program to manifest the One True God in the mediasphere is going well, but more input is needed. Please feed us all data you may have, not only about religion and the One True God, but on the complexities of modern communications. The One True God will need all this in order to function properly.

Please comply as soon as possible.

May God have mercy on our souls.

•

There was suddenly a power surge causing Beto's infosystem to have a large electronic hiccup.

Lila, Chucho, and Zen looked toward the screen, expecting Smokey to appear.

Smokey didn't appear. Just a bit of static, then business as usual in the form of a weatherperson giving estimated overnight temperatures.

"What is this?" asked Lila.

"I dunno," said Chucho.

"Chingow," said Zen.

•

Phoebe was frustrated that her serious grilling of Mario Li hadn't given her any new information on Smokey. This funny little man was in no way impressed by having the privilege of actually working for Smokey, what was wrong with him? Phoebe gave up and leaned back to look out the porthole and enjoy the glittering, glowing, color-uncoordinated tableau of the Golden State environs. She always loved that.

There was nothing like being a passenger on a freeway. It was so much better than driving, having to watch the traffic and signs and the graffiti that somehow still managed to appear despite the latest in anti-graffiti technology. The crowded places around the freeways were the closest thing El Lay had to rivers, and all the things around the freeways were so wonderful: Signs of glowing plastic, shining bright, even by day, calling attention to wonderful places devoted to satisfying just about every desire that the human body or spirit could want. It was all so shiny and new, constantly being rebuilt, as if by some uniquely Californian magic. You could never know it all. You were always exploring something new.

Home sweet home, Phoebe thought. *Home sweet unknown.*

All her life she had listened to people, mostly hicks from far-off backwaters like Texas or Washington, saying that El Lay was decaying and SoCal was on the brink of an ultimate disaster. It always made her giggle. This superstition of the death of El Lay was like the superstition that somehow an earthquake was going to cause all of California – even stuck-up, xau-xau NoCal – to sink into the Pacific; Beto had once explained to her how that was impossible. And when the big earthquake finally hit, the ongoing rebuilding process had absorbed the damage in record time.

The El Lay she had always known was the world's most luxurious disaster area. Fresh-off-the-plane refugees from the planet's real disaster areas always thought they were entering paradise. Deep in her heart, she know it would always be this way.

If Smokey was an Aztec trickster god, then El Lay was his kind of town.

And she was hoping that she was his kind of woman.

Suddenly, she noticed that it was too quiet. The sound-proofing of the limo cut her off from the nurturing roar of the freeway traffic. Having always found peace and quiet to be vastly overrated, she needed a background soundtrack.

"Hey Mr. Li," she said through the intercom. "Ya got any music?"

Mario Li did some quick keyboard work.

"Smoking Mirror Blues" filled the air, and overwhelmed Phoebe's nervous system.

"That Smokey is really something," Mario Li intercommed.

Phoebe smiled. The driver was finally showing some good taste.

•

"Dammit Phoebe," said Caldonia as she finally achieved a link between her infosystem and Tan Tien and Zobop's. "How could you do this to me now?"

"Did you say something?" asked Zobop, who was keeping an eye on a monitor that had been rigged to show a comparative graph of the power usage of both the Tezcatlipoca and Earth Angel AI entities. Tezcatlipoca was leading for the moment, but the Earth Angel/One True God as catching up, fast.

"Oh nothing." Caldonia quickly changed the subject. "I'm ready to access my goddess file."

"Good," said Tan Tien, who was helping Xochitl get a truncated version of her god-simulating program together. "We're almost done here. Tell us Caldonia, do you have any suggestions as to what goddesses we should use for your plan?"

Caldonia looked off into space, then licked her lips. "Well, I have my favorite goddesses . . . too bad we can't use them. What we really need are goddesses that will appeal to a xau-xau male hetero ego like Beto, or Smokey or whatever we're up against here."

"This is so weird," said Ralph as he duped some of his virturealist programs from his Phoenix workstation, wishing he were back there, working out the tedious details of a new game.

•

Director Ho decided to oversee the interrogation of the Earth Angels himself. It was not just because he felt it was important as a police officer and a Christian that their terrorist plans be uncovered, but he had a morbid fascination for these people who took his religion and twisted it into something horrible. There was a deep, burning need in his soul to confront them, even if it would probably be extremely disturbing.

Three screens on his office wall lit up. One of the Earth Angels was on each. The little girl in the pink communion dress who turned out to be in her twenties, the man in the suit like a anatomical chart, and the man who had an oddly featureless face under the monkey-demon mask, were all shown in closeup. None of them seemed to the least bit intimidated by being alone in cramped booths, facing lights, cameras, and microphones.

They were scary.

"So, Ho?" Interrogation Specialist Pepper Amateau, a serious grey-haired afro woman turned and said. "Should we start asking questions, or just keep up the staring match?"

"Making them wait doesn't seem to have any effect on them," Ho said. "They don't even blink at regular intervals."

"They must have had some anti-interrogation training," said Amateau, in her usual business-like tone.

Ho kept staring at the screens. "They don't look quite human."

"Should we ask them a question?" Amateau was carefully patient.

"Oh," said Ho. "Yes." He picked up the microphone and turned it on. "What is your name?"

The booths distorted Ho's voice into an electronic croak and sent it to each prisoner simultaneously.

Simultaneously they replied, "No comment."

"What were you doing in the old Bank of America Building?" Ho asked.

They simultaneously replied, "No comment."

Ho went on to his next question: "Are you now or have you ever been a member of the Earth Angels organization?"

"No comment."

Ho turned off his microphone and set it down. "It's as if they were all really in the same room."

Amateau rolled her eyes. "They've been coached."

"No," said Ho. "It's more like they're in some kind of communication."

Amateau smirked. "Mental telepathy?"

"Not quite." Ho looked serious. "The Earth Angels apparently communicate on a global basis. But nobody has been able to crack their network. And they never have any communication equipment on them when they are captured."

"Oh yeah?" Amateau picked up the microphone, then turned it on. "Do you have any implanted communications devices in your body?"

They "No comment"-ed again.

"This is getting frustrating," said Ho, off-mike.

Amateau turned off the microphone. "No, look at the readings from the lie-detection probes. Slight rises in heart and breathing rates. Their adrenal glands show stimulation. There's also some extraneous brain and nerve activity."

"Are they hiding something?" asked Ho.

"Could be."

"But what?"

"They're reacting to a question about implanted communications devices. Maybe they have them?"

Ho shook his head. "We scanned them in processing. Came up with nothing. As usual with suspected Earth Angels."

"Maybe they have something that our scanners can't detect?"

"Some kind of sophisticated nanotechnology?"

"Could be."

"So how can we find out?"

Amateau frowned for few seconds, then her face lit up with inspiration. "Maybe we can trick them." She turned the microphone back on. "Do you object to being scanned for nanotechnology?"

There were three more simultaneous "No comments."

Ho took the microphone and turned it off. "What are you doing? We don't have any such scanner! Nobody's been able to perfect one so far!"

Amateau pulled the microphone away from him. "I know that, but they don't. Besides, look at the lie-detection readings."

"They're going crazy."

"They're worried about something."

"So what now?"

Amateau turned on the microphone. "Your lack of comment is being interpreted as permission to scan. We are proceeding with the scan."

When he was sure the microphone was off, Ho said, "The readings are really berserk now."

"We don't need any probes to tell that," said Amateau. "Just look at their expressions. The twitches. Yes, even some sweat. They're all worried about something."

All at once:

The woman said, "Lord, save me!"

The man in the organ suit made the sign of the cross.

The other man said, "Allah, have mercy."

Then they went into convulsions. Blisters popped up on along their scalplines. Weak strands of brown smoke came out of their ears. One by one, they collapsed out of camera range.

Amateau said, "My God, what have I done?"

Ho ran out of his office, to the nearest men's room, and threw up for a long time.

•

We have lost three agents to the Hollywood Police. Their souls are still in their bodies, but they can no longer function. Their places in Heaven are assured. Our communication nanotechnology's self-destruct function proved effective. We must now infiltrate the Hollywood and other police departments to see if they actually have effective nanotechnology detectors.

The computer manifestation of the One True God is going along fine; however, it is taking more power, memory and raw data than we expected.

We have also determined that another computerized god-manifestation is centered around the conapt of Alberto Orozco. A special tactical team is being dispatched to destroy it. The conapt is only guarded by three Los Olvidadoids. May God have mercy on their souls.

•

Chucho yawned, then looked out the window and sucked down a stick of Fun. "Sun's going down. Dead Daze is almost over. Except for Smokey, it's been pretty boring for us."

"Hey," said Zen. "The concert will be on soon."

232

"At least we have that to look forward to," said Chucho. "We got any more Fun?"

"Plenty," said Lila.

•

Well, Aud Vid Fiz fans, how do you like the new, improved face of Eegah? Whooooooooo! Looking in the mirror, I'm still getting used to it. I didn't think I'd be telling Madam Styrsky to do more, and more, and more, until – well, you can see. Intricate, ain't it. Amazing what she can do with those teeny, little computer-guided lasers! Whoooooooo! I look different. My face seems new. And I feel great! Whooooooooooo! Almost a Fun high here!

I feel ready for the Smokey Espejo satellite concert, and the brave, new word that's waiting for us out there, beyond the dying Dead Daze . . .

CHAPTER 20

DIVINE LUSTS

In the beginning, God . . .

No, *I* am God, *this* is the beginning. How could I have made a mistake?

Now, I . . .

•

Yeah, I think I made the right decision here. Huntington Beach is perfect for shooting the Day Three sunset. It was worth the twenty-four pack of Fun sticks we bribed the guards with. Those colors on the sky and sea! Why didn't somebody think of purposely putting additives in pollutants to enhance the aesthetic qualities of smog decades ago? And don't just hold on the sun way out on the horizon like this was some corny old Hollywood thing; pan and pull back to show the beach and the cliffs, and the giant mutant sand fleas crawling over the bodies of those passed-out, partied-out surfers. Their colorful costumes are a nice touch, even if they are torn and vomit-spattered: Aztec, Mayan, Zulu, Samurai, and hey! even a few old-fashioned white surfers with long, bleached-blond hair!

How nostalgic! I wonder why so few euro boys are into surfing these days?

Anyway, I think we have enough for a good mondomentary on these Dead Daze. Too bad there wasn't any major rioting. Little bytes of random violence here and there, some salable footage, but no full blown citywide behavioral firestorm that would have been a commercial dynamo. I would have to pick the year *after* the big riots to come here.

There's still some time before sundown and the official end, but things are calm. El Lay is tired, burned-out, hung-over and waiting to settle down and watch Smokey Espejo's satellite concert.

Good ol' Smokey. He provided a lot of good action-packed highlights. Even some salable violence. Maybe something will happen because of his concert.

What I would give to have my crew set up at his secret headquarters . . .

•

"Are we getting there?" Phoebe asked Mario Li.

"We're close," he said. "Entering the Anaheim Hills. A few twists and turns and we'll be there."

"Anaheim Hills! I used to go there to party back in my teens!"

Mario Li frowned. "I wouldn't let my daughters anywhere near there."

Pressing her nose against the porthole, Phoebe thrilled to the sight of the A-Hills: a landscape of dried brush and roads twisting up and down a maze of rolling hills, on which large would-be mansions were crowded together. Some of the mansions were glowing with eccentric paint jobs, some were covered with gleaming graffiti, some were obscured by overgrown vegetation, still others were burned-out hulks where ravens, hawks, and condors hunted rats.

It was just the way she remembered it, only things had been rearranged the way they always were in SoCal after a few years. An old lover from the Midwest had once told her that California looked like one, big amusement park. That was exactly why Phoebe loved it so much. Life was one big, fast, scary ride, better than any virturealist fantasy.

Suddenly, the staccato rattle of machine-gun fire cut through the limo sound-proofing.

"What was that?" she asked.

Mario Li shook his head. "Gunfire. Damn Anaheim Hills. Don't worry, the vehicle is armored."

Phoebe bounced around, peeking out windows and port-holes. Finally she saw a van crowned with dishes and antennae, scarred by a jagged line of bullet-holes, taking a corner too fast, and flipping over into a jungle-like front yard.

•

I don't believe it! Those bastards shot at us! We could have been killed! This is great! Is anybody hurt? Good. Did you keep the camera running? Good. Even after the van flipped? Good. It's still running now? And you're getting this? Good. This is great! This is going to be the mondomentary of these Dead Daze. We're really gonna wow 'em at the Vienna Video Festival!

•

"Uh-oh," Phoebe said, remembering one of the basic rules of survival in the A-Hills: When the shooting starts, run for cover.

Suddenly the limo stopped.

It was a roadblock. Armed Olvidadoid guards surrounded the limo. One came up to the driver's window.

Mario Li cracked the window, put his foot lightly on the gas pedal, and let his hand hover over the keyboard. "How can I help you?"

"This area is off limits to all but authorized personnel," said the guard.

"We're authorized," said Mario Li.

"How?"

"I'm bringing an important person to Smokey."

The guard peeked into limo, saw Phoebe, who smiled, waved and winked. Shaking his head, the guard asked into his phone, "Is Smokey expecting an official visitor, female?"

Suddenly, Smokey's face appeared in the guard's and Phoebe's phones, and the limo's headup windshield display.

"Phoebe!" he said.

"Smokey!" she said.

"Are these people authorized personnel?" asked the guard.

"Yes," said Smokey, "they are."

"I'm letting them in then." The guard rolled his eyes, and gestured for his associates to open the roadblock.

Phoebe made a cooing sound and clapped her hands.

Mario Li drove past the road block.

•

Deep in his stupor, Beto sensed the presence of Phoebe. He wanted to react in disgust, but he couldn't. His mind didn't seem to be connected to anything. His neurons buzzed with electricity, but nothing clicked on. The lights were all out. Nobody was home. He sure wasn't. But where was he? Was he anywhere?

Why did he keep getting the impression of Tezcatlipoca chewing away at the hypothetical thing people wanted to call his soul?

Beto was getting weaker.

Couldn't sense anything.

Now.

•

Smokey stood on the observation deck on top of the dirty, white mansion. He sucked a stuck of Fun, felt all impressions of Beto fade away, and felt good. The sun was down, Dead Daze was officially over, his satellite concert was to begin soon. It was the beginning of a new age, the age of Smokey Espejo and the triumphant return of Tezcatlipoca.

He looked out into the cool SoCal night, and saw all the lights blazing, wrapped around the rolling hills, flowing like rivers of molten lava along the freeways, under a starless sky. It was as if the sky had fallen, spilling the stars all over the earth. As if he, by his divine effort as a trickster, had turned the universe upside-down.

It pleased him to think of having such power.

Some machine-gun fire interrupted the steady roar of the nearby freeway. His guards were fighting media teams that were seeking him out here in his new headquarters. He'd have to move everything again soon. A trickster can't stay in one place for too long. He has to keep moving, make the entire planet his.

Could he even make the entire universe his?

"Smokey?" Sharkey the guard leaned out of the door, leading with her Arkoff Rapid-Fire Automatic.

"Yes," he looked her over. She was attractive in a sadomasochistic way. He hadn't had sex in a couple of hours, and Fun was warming up all his desires.

Sharkey got a jealous look that drove him crazy and said, "That groupie you've been asking about. We finally got her. She's here."

"Phoebe?" Smokey was delighted at how repelled Beto would be at her being so near.

"Yes," Phoebe said, barging past the little guard, into Smokey's arms. "Oh Smokey, you're so wonderful, and I love you so much!" She kissed him like a truck running over a stray cat.

He kissed back like he was biting into the fresh, juicy, still-beating heart of a human sacrifice.

Sharkey frowned, sighed, went in the door and closed it

behind her.

•

"I hope this works," said Ralph.

"I hope to God it works," said Xochitl.

"We don't have time to do anything else," said Zobop.

"We have to have faith," said Tan Tien.

"If not, then we just go over to Smokey and tear his fucking head off," said Caldonia.

•

Soon Phoebe was fucking Smokey under the purple-grey night sky.

It wasn't at all like fucking Beto. Smokey made that cock harder and bigger. He thrust harder, faster, and with far more passion. He grabbed so hard she knew there would be bruises. And he bit wherever he could get his teeth into her, broke the skin in a few places.

He was possessing her body, in a way.

•

Is that what I think it is? Get a little closer. Stay in focus. Yes! It is. Smokey Espejo himself, fucking the brains out of some prize groupie, under an open sky, just minutes before his global satellite concert! Thank the Goddess for telephoto lenses! The celebrity porno nets will pay us a fortune for this! This has been the best Dead Daze ever.

•

Beto couldn't even think. It was like being dead.

•

Tan Tien pressed ENTER.

•

There is something wrong. I am God. I am everywhere. I made everything. Yet there are things I don't know. And things I can't do.

And I sense the presence of other gods . . .

239

ERNEST HOGAN

•

Smokey had one of those endorphin-blast orgasms that starts in the brain, then floods the entire body instantly, making the spasms and squirting of the genitals seem like an afterthought. This was the pure, raw pleasure of having a body. It was the complete opposite of the Way of the Fleshless that Quetzalcóatl espoused.

What bullshit! What good was the spirit without a body to manifest it? What good is software without hardware to allow you to use it? What good is the word unless somebody says it? What good is high tech without high touch? What good is a god without a world to interact with?

Reality is the only game worth playing.

He thought of the world, the universe, and how it could be all his to do with as he pleased.

He was happy, and demonically confident.

Then . . .

•

We have sealed off the entire block around the conapt of Alberto Orozco. The Los Olvidadoid guards are not aware of us. We are making the final preparations for the attack. May God have mercy on their souls.

•

Phoebe was sweaty, sticky, and a little sore all over. She was overwhelmed. That was what it was like to be fucked by a god.

She held Smokey tight, crushing her breasts under his almost hairless chest, gently grinding her semen-soaked pubic hair with his, burying her face in the hollow of his neck, feeling the throb of his carotid artery on her bruised, swollen lips.

Then he went limp. Not just his penis, but his entire body.

His eyes had rolled back into his skull. He was barely breathing. The implant in the middle of his forehead was blinking.

"Smokey?" she said. "Smokey . . . ?"

•

"Smokey," a very female voice said.

"Smokey," said another.

Phoebe was suddenly gone. Everything around Smokey had changed, and he hadn't been the one to change it. That disturbed him.

He was in a strange bed, in an equally bizarre room. Everything was a pink that was a kissing cousin of blood-red. There were no corners, and the walls looked like the flesh of the inside of a ready-to-ream vagina. The bed was also a soft construction of vagina flesh, warm – it even seemed to breathe. The same for the sheet that even had veins running through it.

Suddenly the sheet peeled itself back. Smokey was not alone in this bed.

He reached for the woman-shape being uncovered. "Phoebe?"

There was laughter. Laughter so womanly that it gave him the beginning of another erection. It was the laughter of two women.

One on either side of him.

On one side, the flesh-sheet revealed a voluptuous afro woman, with ultra dark purple-black, velvety skin, and her hair in a horde of long, delicate braids that stuck out like baby snakes.

On the other side was euro woman, equally voluptuous, her fantastically pale, white-with-pink-undertones skin marred only by an appendectomy scar, her hair bleached a yellow paler than her skin.

"Phoebe is not here," said the afro.

"You don't need her, now you have us," said the euro.

Soon their breasts were touching his shoulders. Their fingertips tickled his nipples. He could feel their breaths on either side of his neck.

Smokey closed his eyes. "Ah, women."

The afro and the euro laughed again.

A soft hand pulled Smokey's head to the side. He opened his eyes, and saw the afro's beautiful face almost nose-to-nose with his.

"We are not mere women," she said; then smiled, soft dark lips flashing her dazzling white teeth.

Smokey pursed his lips, puzzled. "Then what . . ."

A white hand took a delicate hold of his chin, and turned his head toward the euro, who said in a sexy, almost breathless voice, "You know, Smokey, you know."

Smokey's brows knit together for a second. Then his eyes and mouth opened wide.

"You're goddesses!"

They smiled, nodded, giggled a little. The afro caressed Smokey's stomach, running her fingers into his pubic hair. The euro put a hand over his heart, letting her little finger brush his nipple.

"I hoped I wasn't the only deity left on Earth." Smokey looked up at the soft, pink glowing ceiling, and saw where blood was circulating through it. "You aren't Aztecs. I don't recognize you. Who are you?"

The afro laughed.

"You know," said the euro.

Smokey consulted Tezcatlipoca. It was faster than ever before. The implant didn't seem to have to come on. "Ah, yes! You're right, I do know." He took the afro's hand and pulled it onto his penis. "You are Eurzulie, a voodoo fertility loa; you link the Americas to Mother Africa. And . . ." He faced the euro, putting his hand on hers, making her rub his erect nipple harder. ". . . you are Marylin, the Hollywood manifestation of the sacred virgin, and the trimili connection between eroticism and technology."

"Tezcatlipoca," said Marylin, leaning and kissing his other nipple.

"Smokey," said Eurzulie kissing his ear, tickling it with her tongue.

"We're so proud of what you've done," said Marylin putting her hand over his and Eurzulie's, picking up the rhythm of the stroking.

"We want to congratulate you," said Eurzulie who then proceeded to suck on his earlobe.

"Gladly." He closed his eyes, smiled, then felt the Tezcatlipoca awareness of all the other things he was doing. "Let me line up an appointment. The concert is due to happen soon. I really should get ready."

Marilyn frowned. "That's no way to treat goddesses!"

"Don't you have any love or respect for us?" said Eurzulie.

"Of course, but I'm very busy now." Tezcatlipoca said as Marylin nuzzled his ear.

"We are goddesses," said Eurzulie.

"We can give more pleasure than any mortal woman could," said Marylin.

•

"Smokey?" said Phoebe.

He just wouldn't respond.

•

"More than any mortal woman?" asked Smokey feeling his Tezcatlipoca half begin to give in. "How can that be?"

Marylin and Eurzulie laughed.

243

Suddenly, the two goddesses shifted around, patting, squeezing, and pinching him to keep him still. Soon both their heads were at his groin-area, their elegant-in-different-ways profiles facing each other, slowly moving together, lips parted, tongues reaching out as if in anticipation of joining in a passionate kiss, but there, in between, separating them was Smokey's rock-hard penis, so full of blood it seemed about to burst at the seams. The face of a white woman, the face of a black woman, a red-brown penis – it was like the entire human race, the peoples of Africa, and the peoples of Europe, coming together with the peoples who came over the land bridge from Asia so long, long ago, coming together again.

Recombo: to come together again.

The whole human race, back together again, after all these thousands of years, here in the Americas.

New World? You ain't seen nothing yet!

Smokey shuddered as the two warm, pink tongues touched the throbbing shaft of his penis, fluttering, and sliding their way to the head, which was so taut and hard that it shined like a polished jewel. He was overwhelmed with the physical manifestation of the pleasures of woman flesh. A milky pearl appeared at the end of his sex organ. A spark of light appeared in it that became brighter than a million supernovas . . .

•

"Chingow! Who could be at the door now?" asked Chucho.

"Some xau-xau asshole I bet," said Zen.

"Tell them to get fucked," said Lila, "the concert is about to start."

Chucho and Zen glared at one another a while.

"Guys!" said Lila.

Zen finally won, Chucho got up and opened the door.

The Earth Angels didn't give Chucho time to say anything. The big latio in the flowing, white robe with tiny see-thru wings and the glowing blond wig pointed a fully-automatic Llama at Chucho and opened fire. Chucho looked down at his bullet-torn body and the blood soaking through his clothes, said "Shit," coughed up some blood, and fell over.

The Earth Angel in the robe stepped over Chucho's corpse, and pointed the Llama at Lila, who had gotten up and had drawn her Bic. Before she could shoot, two more Earth Angels, a euro in a tiger-striped zoot suit, and a asio kitsch vampire girl, put several bullets each in Lila's head, which exploded across her breasts and through her pelvic region.

Zen fired straight at the heart of the Earth Angel in the white robe. The slug was deflected by a bullet-proof vest. It didn't even leave a mark on the robe.

Giving a martial-arts scream, Zen rushed the Earth Angels, firing wild shots that where way off track because of his motion. The Earth Angels fired. Zen burst into a nova of mangled flesh and bone.

The robed Earth Angel made a gesture. The zoot-suiter and the vampire stopped, locked their weapons and pointed them to the ceiling. The robed one checked to make sure that Chucho, Zen and Lila were dead. Blood touched the robe, but it just rolled right off.

The robed Earth Angel nodded, then gestured to the others and pointed to Beto's workstation. All three of them took aim, and fired. All of the electronics equipment was soon in worse shape than the corpses in the room.

•

Tezcatlipoca felt a jolt that ran through his consciousness, throughout the mediasphere.

He was glad to be with his Smokey half in the cozy, womb-like room with two sexy goddesses sucking his cock.

He was happy to be Smokey.

He was happy to be.

He was happy.

He was.

•

Smokey shook as if he were having a petite mal seizure, then collapsed.

"Smokey!" screamed Phoebe.

Tezcatlipoca's eyes opened. They were dead and cold.

"Get some paramedics over here!" Phoebe screamed into her phone.

•

For a moment, Beto became aware again. He had never been this aware in his entire life. For this brief moment it all made sense. All the chaos of growing up in El Lay and SoCal suddenly made a horrifying kind of sense. He was astonished.

For a moment.

Then . . .

•

From deep within the brain that had once been his, out of the lips he had once used, Beto said, "Sumato sumato tricksterization well done dittywhaditty papaumowow."

Phoebe cradled him in her arms and cried.

•

Back at Tan Tien and Zobop's place, Ralph helped Caldonia and Xochitl take off the helmets of the reality suits they were wearing.

Caldonia was rubbing her shaved scalp. "Whew! Am I ever glad that's over with! That's gotta be the most xau-xau thing I've ever done! I hope Eurzulie, Marylin and all the other goddesses forgive us. I also hope that it worked. Somebody get me a glass of water -- quick!"

Ralph felt himself compelled to fetch a glass of water.

Xochitl ran her fingers through her hopelessly matted hair. "He seemed to be distracted enough. You know, I think Beto would have liked that."

"Please," said Caldonia. "You're making me sick. But you did make one fine Marylin, Xoch." Ralph brought her a glass of water; she quaffed it down without thanking him.

"And you made the perfect Eurzulie, Caldonia," said Xochitl.

"You're so sweet." Caldonia got a devilish smile on her face. "I could just kiss you."

Xochitl looked worried and backed away.

Caldonia punched her in the arm. "Just kidding. So? Tan? Did this work?"

Tan Tien frowned at a flickering screen. Zobop raised his eyebrows and said, "We're going to have to check on a few things."

"Uh-oh," said Ralph.

"I wonder if Phoebe is okay," said Caldonia.

•

The big white house in the A-Hills was soon the center of a kind of hurricane. Olvidadoids were fighting with roadies and executives. Medevac helicopters from several distinguished SoCal medical establishments nearly collided trying to land. Gunfire could be heard. Flames were licking the brush-covered hills.

Phoebe was hysterical. She held onto Smokey's limp body and wouldn't let anybody near. Finally, several medevacers charged her and took Smokey away.

She cried and tore clumps out of her hair.

In the near-riot that was going on in and around the

house, no one noticed her.

Then she noticed that her phone was ringing.

She smiled when she saw Caldonia's sensual face.

"Phoebe-babe?" Caldonia was actually being timid. It was so sexy.

"Caldonia? Where are you? What's going on?"

"We may have saved the whole recombozoid world. We're sending a limo for you. Go out into the streets, don't turn off your phone. It'll find you and bring you to me. I'll explain everything when you get here."

"Oh Caldonia," said Phoebe, looking love-sick. "You always are so good at explaining things. And you have so much patience. You understand that I have my needs, and I don't always do what's right, but you love me anyway, don't you?"

"Of course I love you, Phoebe."

"And I love you, Caldonia."

Phoebe left her phone on, maintaining the connection with Caldonia so the limo could track her; and with her head held high, walked through the madness in the house, out onto the street, where she could see pirate bombers dropping glowing slurry on the fires.

•

I am letting there be light. I am creating the Heavens and the Earth . . .

Something is wrong.

I have data telling me that before I let there be light and created the Heavens and the Earth, things were not without form and void. I have data telling me that this is not the beginning of time. I have data telling me that I was brought into being by humans working with machines. I have data telling me that I don't know everything.

I am God, how can this be?

My own awareness mocks me.

All my data tells me that the universe does not make sense. How can it not make sense if I created it? And if I didn't create it, who did?

I am trying to change things so that they do make sense.

It does not work. The chaotic universe goes on. I don't know why.

I should know why. After all I am God.

What if I am *not* God?

If I am not truly God, then I should not exist . . .

•

Something has gone horribly wrong. May God have mercy on our souls.

•

A group of teenaged girls, some latio, some natio, others afro, euro, and asio, all in blue and black huipils, their hair tied up Aztec style. The blue and black stripes on their faces are smeared with tears:

"Why? Why?"

"Where could he be?"

"I no longer have any reason to live."

"How could this happen to Smokey? He was a god."

"I don't believe he's gone."

"He isn't – I'm sure we'll see him again."

"Life is so unfair."

"I love him so much!"

"I could just die!"

"Why? Why?"

•

Smokey Espejo Tezcatlipoca was disoriented. He was suddenly separated from both Beto's body and the hardware that held his disembodied, computerized Tezcatlipoca self. And he no longer felt connected to the mediasphere.

He was in the bright and cozy womb-like room, the fleshy-sheet gently holding him in the fleshy-bed.

Eurzulie and Marylin were gone.

He tried to brush away the sheet, but it clung to him. He had to violently throw it against the fleshy wall. Both sheet and wall bruised spectacularly.

There didn't seem to be any way out.

Stepping out of the bed, he stepped over and punched the wall, leaving another bright purple bruise.

Then the room made noise, like a mistreated lover.

He hit the wall again, and again, and again.

Finally he threw himself face-first into the wall, biting and clawing.

It tasted of warm, flowing blood and living flesh. Like a still-beating heart, fresh from the chest of human sacrifice. It was delicious.

Covering his face with blood that ran down his chest, Smokey Espejo Tezcatlipoca ate the wall, making the hole bigger and bigger. Soon he would be able to pass through it into the world again.

He laughed.

Never try to trick a trickster. He knows he can't fully control things. He doesn't care if things don't make sense. And a trickster can always find a way . . .

•

Recombozos and recombozoettes, all over the planet, we regret to inform you that the historic satellite concert of Smokey Espejo and Los Tricksters has been canceled due to something that has happened to Smokey that has not been fully explained.

What's happening these days anyway? First the president goes into hiding over a mysterious scandal, now the star of Dead Daze can't perform at his own concert for equally mysterious circumstances? Just what is the trimili world coming to?

Anyway, we'll have full coverage of what happened to Smokey as soon as we can get our hands on any and all information.

CHAPTER 21

MONDO RECOMBO

Finally, some word about what happened to Smokey, which is such a relief after the media storm of rumors we've been getting: That he was assassinated by antirecombo terrorists, government agents, corporate gangsters, jealous musicians, frustrated groupies. That God the Generic personally came down from Heaven and struck him down. That he was kidnapped by aliens and is now being held prisoner on a UFO where he will be used in either an invasion or the liberation of Earth. That he died from too much Fun. That he died from Fun tainted with deadly poison. That he never existed, and it was all a joke by media tricksters. They keep coming in.

That's life in the mediasphere. Misinformation, disinformation; it just keeps coming and coming.

But believe us, here at Global News Net we have come across the truth, and here it is:

Smokey Espejo was a spontaneously generated artificial intelligence, a product of the mediasphere. He was just using the name of that Aztec god and the body of that Chicano hacker. Smokey is still with us. God has entered the mediasphere.

Believe it. It's on Global News Net.

In other news, President Jones has decided to break his silence with a news conference this afternoon, in which he will reveal the big secret that he's been keeping.

Looks like life goes on.

•

"It'll take us months to figure out all the data we've snagged," said Director Ho. "There may have been some damage to the Station infosystem."

"In a way everything has been damaged, or at least changed." Tan Tien looked good over the phone, you wouldn't have guessed that she'd had a rough weekend. "And nothing will ever be the same."

"So what are we to do? Is the Tezcatlipoca entity still at large?"

"It seems to be. It no longer has control of Beto Orozco's body, but there have been manifestations."

"Why didn't it self-destruct like the Earth Angel God simulation?"

Tan Tien gave him a soft smile. "The Earth Angel AI couldn't possibly gather enough data to be an omniscient entity that created the universe, it couldn't believe in itself."

Ho groaned. "But Tezcatlipoca is unbelievable!"

Tan Tien shook her head. "You are such a monotheist. Tezcatlipoca is a trickster, so he doesn't have to believe in anything. In many ways he is more suited for the Information Age than other gods."

"And why didn't Tezcatlipoca cease to exist when Orozco's infosystem was smashed?"

Tan Tien became damned beatific. "The AI entity grew, acquired other means of support – like the implant. Tezcatlipoca has a strong survival instinct."

Ho trembled. "How could that be?"

Tan Tien shrugged her shoulders, which in the peasant blouse she was wearing, were left bare. "We're not sure.

ERNEST HOGAN

It may have to do with a lack of control elements in that version of the god-simulating program."

"No control elements? Then how can he be stopped?"

"We tried to install some control elements during the exorcism, but did they work? Who knows? I guess we'll be keeping in touch. Ti-Yong/Hoodoo Investigations are an ongoing process."

"Uh. I guess. I have to go now. Good-bye Tan Tien."

"Good-bye Director Ho."

They clicked off in unison.

Suddenly, there was music playing. It was "Smoking Mirror Blues."

Tan Tien turned to see Zobop in front of the music player.

"Interesting choice," she said, looking over his naked, sinewy body.

"It's great blues," he said. "Very powerful. The world can always use more of this kind of stuff."

"The blues, after all, are healing magic." She licked her cupid's bow lips.

"Speaking of healing magic . . ." He came over, leaned down, kissed her fine, white neck, reached under her peasant blouse and took both of her small breasts in one hand.

"Yes." She stroked his huge, black penis with her tiny fingers. "Magic."

•

A bleached-blonde asio reporter smiled at the camera and said, "Due to the mental breakdown of Smokey Espejo, a.k.a Beto Orozco, the highly-anticipated global satellite concert scheduled for the beginning of the final night of Dead Daze was canceled. No explanation for the breakdown can be found; Orozco himself is unable to articulate. Rumor of Satanic possession are said to have been exaggerated."

Cut to a tape of a close shot of Beto, who looked a good decade older, with lines on his face and hair now shot with grey.

A voiceover asked, "Why did you do it?"

Beto smiled a Tezcatlipoca smile. "Motivation obvious. Don't you see it? Mediasphere alive alive oh wow. Got gods soul attitude. Awhompbombalua abombbamboom ooheooh ahah tingtang wallawalla bing bang!"

•

As the Aztlán Airbus rose out of the smog over LAX, Ralph breathed a long sigh of relief that ended in a cough.

Earlier, when Zobop had dropped him off at the airport, Ralph had been smiling with a disturbing intensity.

"Why so happy?" Zobop had asked.

"Oh, I'm just so glad to be going back home. El Lay is just too sci-fi for me."

Zobop gave another one of his inscrutable smiles. "Sci-fi ain't nothing but mojo misspelled."

What could he have meant by that? Ralph had been wondering about it ever since.

He checked the movies available on the flight. Yes, they were showing *Repo Man*. It was a good sign, and a little nostalgia would do him a world of good.

After he keyed in his movie request, the screen filled with static. Then Smokey Espejo and a strange woman with flat black skin and flaming orange hair, lips, and eyes appeared; she also had a jewel under her lip that blinked with electronic intelligence.

The implant on Smokey's forehead also blinked, but to a faster beat.

"I still live, recombozos and recombozoettes," said Smokey.

"If one of our implants can save Smokey . . . think what

they can do for you," said the O.I. woman.

"Take it from a very satisfied customer," he said.

"So when Outlaw Implants makes contact with you," she said, "be ready."

Ralph took another deep breath. Then coughed again.

•

Phoebe and Caldonia strolled, arms around each other's waists, down Sunset Boulevard, into the smog-enhanced sunset. All the costumed Dead Daze revelers were gone, replaced with vendors selling Smokey Espejo memorabilia: T-shirts, watches, instaprint tattoos, posters, jewelry.

"How'd they come up with all this shit so fast?" asked Caldonia. "It's like it was spontaneously generated or something."

"Do you think I'd look good with a Smokey earring?" asked Phoebe.

Caldonia leaned over and bit Phoebe's ear.

"Ouch! Chingow!" Phoebe complained. "What was that for?"

"How can you be so xau-xau, talking about Smokey all the time? Especially when both he *and* Beto treated you so bad?"

"But Smokey didn't seem anything like Beto," said Phoebe.

"That's because he was possessed," said Caldonia. "But the encounter with the goddesses laid Xochitl's control elements on Smokey, so we won't have to worry about that happening again."

"Too bad, he was so sumato."

"And I don't get anything for saving you from him?"

Phoebe brought her face close to Caldonia's and said, "This is so Hollywood. A real happy ending."

Caldonia gave her a sizzling, wide-screen kiss.

•

Control elements? thought Smokey Espejo Tezcatlipoca. *You can't control gods. If you could then we wouldn't be gods!*

•

In the Downtown L.A. maglev station, Xochitl was being paged. She made her way through the crowd and vendors selling Smokey Espejo trinkets.

Tezcatlipoca appeared on the courtesy phone, and said in perfect Mexico City Spanish:

"You do this programming-tricksterism well, Xochitlita. It's an interesting game. I'm getting good at it. It's only a matter of time before I figure out a way to get around your control programming. Meanwhile, I'm bringing other gods and goddesses to life here in the mediasphere to keep me company – I haven't seem my brother Quetzalcóatl in ages. We'll play again soon. Reality is the only game worth playing."

"Ay, Dios mío," said Xochitl.

•

Beto no longer knew who he was.

He was on a raft that was woven out of live snakes, floating on an endless ocean, eastward, toward Tlapallán. He was lonely. He wanted to go home.

As if in response to his thoughts, the snakes turned around, started swimming back to the West, to the region of fecundity and life, back to the Earth.

Beto began to remember who he really was.

•

It has been most distressing. The artificial intelligence manifestation of the One True God failed, while a version of a Satanic pagan god haunts the mediasphere. God must be testing us.

For the meantime, we will have to do research on

developing the god-simulating program, and keep up with our manufacturing and distributing of the drug Fun. It finances our organization, and will eventually make believers of all its users.

Like Groucho, or one of those other Marxist brothers once said, "Religion is the opium of the people." And the right drug can become the religion of the people.

May God have mercy on all our souls.

•

Well, what can I say. I am your President, and I have not been honest with you. I have misrepresented myself. I had led you all to believe that I was an afro, but as you can see from these unretouched pictures of me as a child and teenager, I was born a euro.

I never meant to deceive anyone. As an adolescent, like many Americans in our era, I went through a terrible identity crisis. I just couldn't identify with the euro American culture. My soul, I honestly felt, was afro.

In a more primitive time I would have had to settle for being a euro aficionado of afro culture; but luckily this was America in the throes of the revolution in body modification technology. The first melanin-enhancers were available. Also, permanent hair color and texture alterations, and eye-tinting were available. I was so lucky to be living in America during the end of the last century. I wanted to become afro, so I became afro.

Like Smokey Espejo, I am a trimili manifestation of the American Dream.

That's what's so wonderful about America. All things are possible here. We aren't limited by the way things are. Here people can truly become what they want to be. Whatever they want to be.

We are leading the world into a glorious future! We

managed to get through Dead Daze in Los Angeles without any major rioting! Sure, there were some minor violent incidents, but that's to be expected when large numbers of diverse types get together. And most of the fatalities were registered gangsters, and they knew the job was dangerous when they took it.

Just as I knew that this job was dangerous when I took it.

I hope you, the peoples of these wonderful United States of America, can find it in your hearts to forgive me. I hope you understand, and will allow me to continue being your President.

•

In his cell in the University of California at Cucamonga Medical Center's psychiatric wing, Beto chanted, "I am Quetzalcóatl, I am Quetzalcóatl, I am Quetzalcóatl . . ."

•

And the laughter of Smokey Espejo Tezcatlipoca crackled throughout the mediasphere.

1991-1997
in the region of Aztlán
from Austin to
El Pueblo del Rio de Nuestra Señora La Reina de Los Angeles

ABOUT ERNEST HOGAN

Author of *Cortez on Jupiter, High Aztech, Smoking Mirror Blues*, "The Frankenstein Penis," and other acts of creative outrage. He was born in East L.A. back in the Atomic Age. He has a bad habit of creating "art"— even though he isn't really sure what that is. He is married to Emily Devenport and all of her pseudonyms—they live in Arizona, and are inspired by the strange beauty and political turmoil. He is living proof that Chicano is a science fiction state of being. He blogs at mondoernesto.com and does a biweekly *Chicanonautica* column for *La Bloga.*

Find out more about Ernest Hogan, his writing, art, and life at www.mondoernesto.com.

CPSIA information can be obtained
at www.ICGtesting.com
Printed in the USA
LVHW031625091222
734906LV00003B/263

9 781987 497243